Her Pretty Words

Amber Evergreen

Other Title(s) by
Amber Evergreen

The Moment Promised

To those who lift their face to the stars,
searching the constellations for the ones who are never truly lost.

Her Pretty Words

By Amber Evergreen

© 2024 Amber Evergreen

This book is a work of fiction. Any references to real people, or real places are used fictitiously. Names, characters, businesses, organizations, places, events, and incidents are the product of the author's imagination or are used fictitiously. Any resemblance to actual events or places or persons living, or dead is entirely coincidental.

No part of this book may be reproduced in any form or by any electronic or mechanical means, including information storage and retrieval systems, without written permission from the author, except for the use of brief quotations in a book review.

Cover art by Silver Grace at bittersagedesigns.com

Editor: Amy Briggs, Briggs Consulting, LLC www.editsbyamy.com

Paperback book publication, copyright © 2024 Amber Evergreen

ISBN: 979-8-9889690-3-7

ISBN: 979-8-9889690-4-4

All Rights Reserved.

Chapter 1
Macy

I nearly killed a man earlier. Perhaps that's on the melodramatic side, yet my palms bear crescent marks from squeezing my fists together to restrain myself from punching my fiancé in his beautifully cruel face.

The words "I do" pound against my skull like someone's beating me over the head with a baseball bat again and again and agai—

"Do you need some help, miss?"

I blink a couple of times, realizing I'm crumpling the magazine I mindlessly picked up. I meet eyes with an older woman stationed behind a gift shop desk with a concerned, borderline frightened, expression.

I clear my throat. "Sorry! I'll take this," I say, a bit high pitched for my liking. I put the magazine I have no intention of reading and a pack of gum on the counter. She's quick to swipe my card, eyeing the plastic bag she places my items in as though extending them to me would put herself in danger like petting an alligator. I grab my purchase and stuff it into my suitcase. "Thank you," I say with a smile.

Thousands of voices infiltrate my ears when I step out of

the store and into the organized chaos. I'm lost among the crowd of travelers in the JFK airport, far ways away from Walter, my fiancé.

By now, I've triple checked I'm at the right terminal for my layover. The white boarding pass in my hand says so, but for safe measure, I make my way to the screen that displays today's flights. A tight crowd gathers in front of it, and I have to force my way between people to read the words, during which I smack into a wall of muscle.

A huff of air escapes my lips. "Excuse me," I say with a smile in my voice. When the owner of such a hard chest doesn't move, I crane my neck and nearly blush at the striking man towering above me. "Excuse me," I repeat, assuming he didn't hear me the first time.

His gaze seems to make its way slowly up my body, pinning on the boarding pass I'm holding for a moment, and finally settling on my face with not so much as a blink. Lips parted, he doesn't step aside. I clear my throat, causing him to blink several times at me, as though he's coming out of a trance.

"Your flight is canceled," he says, voice deep and masculine.

I reel back, raising an eyebrow at the stranger in front of me. He doesn't know what flight I'm on. I step aside, finally able to view the screen. My eyes travel over the different flights. Once I spot mine, I drag my gaze across the row to the flight time. The word canceled is in bright red. *That can't be right.* I check again, dragging my finger horizontally in the air, and still reaching the same conclusion.

My expression falls and I can feel my heart begin to speed.

"Told you," a deep voice says from directly behind me.

I slowly turn to him, getting lost for a moment in light

blue eyes, the shade of glaciers. But then, as if the grin spreading across his face is an anecdote to the spell I'm under, I immediately sober. The stranger's cocky grin is a feather rested on top of the crushing weight I've carried today, suppressing me whole.

"Excuse me?" I squeeze my hands into fists in an attempt to contain my emotions, worsening the marks from earlier.

His eyes crinkle at the sides, as if the ruination of my day is amusing. I can't help but notice how undeserving he is of the luscious eyelashes framing the glaciers. Before I can stop him, he pulls my boarding pass out of my hand.

I swallow down the annoyance brewing beneath my skin. Hanging on to the last thread of my patience, I say as kind as one can through gritted teeth, "Give that back." I inhale a deep breath. "Please."

"All flights to the west coast of Florida are canceled," he says calmly, holding up my boarding pass.

Before I can respond, a muffled voice comes through the intercom. "Flight 547 to Fort Myers, Florida has been canceled due to weather."

The guy's eyebrows raise in the most infuriating *told you so* face I've ever seen.

My sweaty palms grip the handle of my suitcase. I bite back the words I have for him, and weave in and out of the mass of bodies.

"Excuse me, coming through," I say countless times. Once I'm finally spit out of the crowd, I need to find my way to a ticket counter. Several minutes go by, and when I find it, my entire body feels as if it's frowning. There are already dozens of people forming a line.

As though he can sense my presence, the guy turns right as my eyes lock on his. They wrinkle in the corner when he sees the displeasure on my face. He's second in line. I'm sure the crowd naturally parted for all six foot four of him—if I had to guess his height.

My legs carry me right up to him before my mind can stop them. Countless voices complain, protesting about me skipping the line. I *need* to be on the next flight to Fort Myers, so I muster up my sweetest smile and wrap a hand around the guy's arm—which feels like steel beneath his hoodie. *Of course it does.* I turn to the people behind me and give them a polite smile. "I'm with him."

The guy peeks down at me with a raised brow. I widen my eyes, silently pleading with him to go along with this. The corner of his lips tick up in amusement. We both step forward when the person in front of us leaves the line. I smile wide at the ticket agent, who looks no older than eighteen.

"Hi. I need to book another flight," I say, putting my boarding pass on the wooden counter and sliding it in his direction.

His eyes go everywhere but my face as he mumbles, "There aren't any flights to Fort Myers until further notice." I can hardly hear past the lisp caused by his bright blue braces.

"Sir…" I glance at his nametag. "Erick. I live on the other side of the country. This is my layover." I look at him with pleading eyebrows. "What am I supposed to do?"

"Sorry for the inconvenience." He cracks his knuckles. "I can put you guys on standby for tomorrow's flights. I'll need your boarding pass too, sir."

"Oh, we're not togeth—"

"Here," the guy interrupts me, handing him the slip of paper. I shoot him a questioning look. "I was on the same flight as you," he says, so only I can hear.

"I put you both in the system. I can't guarantee you'll be

on the same plane, but we'll notify you when there's a seat available."

"All right, thanks, man," the guy says. He tries to pull away, but I tighten my grip.

"Are you *sure* there's nothing for today? I have nowhere to sta—" I start to ask but am quickly interrupted.

"There's no flight, Macy. They can't fly into a storm just so *you're* not inconvenienced."

I scoff. *How does he know my name?*

"You coming?" He gestures with a flick of his head to follow him, but I stay put. I'm not going anywhere with him.

Someone behind me clears their throat. I shoot them a glance, realizing the line has grown even longer and several people are directing their frustrated looks at me. I feel my face get hot and quickly step out of line.

The guy stands tall with only a backpack, waiting for me like I belong with him. "Thanks for your help," I say as I walk past him, wondering why every good looking man possesses the same arrogant personality as the next. I nearly trip when my luggage gets caught on something behind me.

I turn around, realizing the guy has a firm grip on my suitcase.

"Let. Go," I say through my teeth, hoping I come off at least slightly intimidating.

"Macy—" he says calmly.

"How do you know my name?" I ask in an accusatory tone.

"Macy Brookes." His lips curl over my name. "It's printed right there." His gaze lands on the hand holding my boarding pass. *That's curiously intrusive of a mere stranger.*

I'm exhausted from plastering smiles on my face to placate assholes who make me uncomfortable. Each encounter with these copy and paste individuals has slowly unraveled me by pulling loose a thread. It's in this very moment that I come undone. "Are you going to hold me hostage by my luggage all night?" I glare at the hand on my suitcase.

He watches me for a moment, then releases his hold on my luggage. I only make it two paces away before I nearly trip on my shoelace.

He laughs huskily from behind me.

I slowly turn to him, hoping my glare is scathing. Deep shadows peek out from his cheeks. It's strange to see something as boyish as dimples on a face that's all-sharp edges and contours.

"Good save," he says. "If you'd fallen on your face, it surely would've ruined my afternoon. Blood freaks me out."

I stare at him, my mouth nearly agape at his audacity.

"You need me to tie your shoe, Macy?" The moment he says my name, he grins.

"Stop…saying my name." I grind my teeth.

"What would you prefer I call you?" His eyes sweep over my face, landing on my worn-out University of Idaho hoodie. He looks up with a smirk. "Idaho. Interesting."

"Why's that?" I narrow my eyes.

"I just didn't know anyone actually lived there, let alone attended the state college." He pinches his chin in a considering manner. My eyes home in on the strand of dark brown hair hanging over his forehead while the rest is a tousled mess. He has sharp cheek bones, a slightly crooked nose, and a hardly noticeable scar on his upper lip. He's handsome in a different way than my fiancé. Walter has ash blond hair and a face symmetrical enough for magazines. I've grown to dislike perfection.

"Potato." He snaps his fingers. "No wait…" His eyes

sweep over me once more before he says, "Tato. Short for potato."

I blink several times. "What?"

"You said to stop saying your name, so instead I'll call you Tato." He crosses his arms and shrugs.

"Don't call me anything," I say, my eyes hopefully burning holes into his skin. This is a ridiculous waste of my time. I slip my phone out of the front pocket of my hoodie. Not a single missed call or text from Walter. I don't even think he realizes I've left the house, let alone the state. I booked the first flight I could get, grabbing everything out of my dryer, and with the addition of the warmer clothes tucked away in my closet, I threw it all into a suitcase. I figured if I wore it in the last week, then it'll do.

I open the airline's app, fumbling with the screen, trying to get another flight. If I have to fly to a different airport in Florida, I'll rent a car and make the long drive.

I just need some fresh, salty air. Maybe then I'll remember how to love the man I agreed to marry. I'll unlearn all his mannerisms that double as my biggest pet peeves. Like the way he clips his toenails on our dining room table and doesn't bother cleaning it up. Or how the spare bedroom in our house automatically became his video game room, when I'm the one who works from home and needs an office.

"You look like you're going to murder that phone of yours," a voice I've grown unfortunately familiar with says.

Oh, you're still here, is what I want to say. "I appreciate you helping me back there in the line," I say as a way of farewell.

I pocket my phone, accepting there isn't a single flight to Florida I can book this late into the day. It's already almost eight p.m.

A woman to my left catches my attention. She looks to be

in her mid-twenties, slightly older than I am at twenty-three. I catch the tail end of her frantic phone call. "I can't keep these kids entertained the entire night in an airport." She sounds on the verge of tears.

My eyes travel down to a toddler yanking on her mother's pant leg. Another kid with the same bright blond hair jumps along the chairs in the terminal.

I sigh and go back into the gift shop I'd just left before my plan for redemption fell apart. I buy coloring books and crayons and then find the blond mother and her children again. She doesn't notice me as she makes phone calls. I bend down, eye to eye with the little girl. She can't be much older than two or three. "Do you like to color?" I ask.

She looks at me with two big eyes and nods her head.

"Here." I hand her a coloring book with a box of crayons. Her face lights up when she sees the princesses on the cover. "Is that your brother?" I ask, pointing to the blond boy who stands on a chair, jumping up and down as if it were his personal trampoline.

She nods.

"This one's for him." I place it on the nearest chair.

I stand and grab my luggage. When I turn around, I find the guy right where I left him, except now he gazes at me with the most confused look on his face. As though he's trying to solve a puzzle.

I need to get a hotel for the night or else I'll have to sleep on the airport floor like several people already are, so I walk past him. My stomach squeezes, releasing a noise that gets drowned out by the thousands of people. I haven't eaten since breakfast, other than the few complimentary crackers from my first flight. I'm hangry and stranded in New York, billions of miles from my fridge. Okay, maybe not billions, but it might as well be.

It takes nearly half an hour to get out of the airport. *And I thought it was hectic inside.* Horns beep, and cabs zip in and out of the lanes to pick people up. Bodies knock into me as if I'm not even standing here.

This is no Idaho. I try to book an Uber on my phone, since that's what I'm used to, but every time it looks like I have a driver, it gets canceled right before I can confirm. I clutch my phone, about to sink onto the dirty concrete so everyone can step on me.

"Macy!" a deep voice calls, distracting me enough that I drop my phone. The moment it touches the ground, an alert flashes across the screen. *"Crash detected. Enter passcode to disarm or a notification will be sent to your emergency contacts."* I hastily input the numbers so my parents don't get a concerning notification.

The only person looking my way is the guy, who holds the door to a cab open with a raised brow. He gestures with his head for me to join him. My stomach growls again, and it feels like I might pass out if I don't eat soon.

I don't give the guy a single glance as I attempt to steal his cab.

"Where to?" the driver asks as I buckle my seatbelt.

I've never even been to New York. "Uh—" I start but am cut off when the car is filled with the scent of something woodsy, like sandalwood.

"Just start driving and we'll let you know from there," the guy says, making himself cozy in the cab. *Lovely.* In the dim space, I notice that his eyes are more silver like the full moon, and then I want to kick myself for even noticing.

You see, I was blind to anything but the color of Walter's

green eyes, so even the red flags he wore like a uniform appeared green to me, so much so that I agreed to marry him, and can't seem to find my way out of that one. He has a beautiful face, but a hideous personality, and I refuse to be blindsided again by a pretty man.

I nearly glare at the guy just thinking about it. He merely glances at me before looking out the window. If he wanted to murder me, I've given him the perfect opportunity to do so, since I'm stuck in this cab. Him and the driver can split the profit on my kidneys.

"I need to get to a hotel. Do you know if there's one nearby?" I ask, assuming he lives here based on how easily he hailed the cab.

He doesn't respond.

"Hello?" I push his shoulder.

He turns and his eyes scan my hand with an unreadable expression.

"When someone talks to you, the polite thing to do is answer." *God, where did* that *come from?*

He stares at me for an uncomfortable amount of time before answering. "And you're well versed in manners?"

"You don't know me," I sneer.

He scoffs, then shakes his head, like he thought better of whatever he was going to say. My raised brow answers him, daring him to speak whatever is on his mind.

"You're Macy Brookes, a brunette with olive skin and an attitude the size of Mount Everest. You probably live in Idaho since you're wearing the college hoodie and your flight to Fort Myers was canceled, leaving you stranded in New York with a handsome stranger you are quick to dislike."

"You *are* going to kill me," I say more to myself. "You've kidnapped me, and now you want to kill me."

He laughs without humor. "If someone were to hypothetically kidnap you, they would return you after five minutes." He looks up like he's considering something. "Make it two."

"Excuse me? Can you take me to the nearest hotel please?" I speak up to the driver.

"Stop at a diner first. The Mrs. gets catty when she's hungry," the guy says, handing the driver money.

"Just the hotel is fine," I say, but he ignores me as he pockets the extra cash. *Humanity at its finest.*

We stop for the hundredth time. I don't think we've made it more than half a mile from the airport. I've heard that a five-minute drive anywhere else could turn into an hour in New York City.

"Tell him to take me to a hotel!" I whisper-scream at my cab mate.

"No."

"No?" I gape at him.

"It's a word used in speech that indicates something is not entirely tru—"

I interrupt him with a groan. "You…"

"Me?" he asks with raised brows and a smirk.

"I don't like you," I say, matter of factly, ignoring the honking and constant stopping. I think I'm going to be sick.

"You don't even know me." He throws my statement back at me.

"You are…" the guy probably has a name, but since I have no interest in learning it, I let that part of my sentence trail off. "You're a very rude man, who probably doesn't have any friends because you're ridiculously obsessed with yourself. Oh, and I'll bet you have a cat who hisses and claws at everyone and it's no coincidence that it only takes a liking to you."

He seems amused by this, fighting a grin by pressing two

fingers to his lips. His features reflect the traffic surrounding us. He glows red like the devil. "Would a rude man offer a stranded woman his cab?"

A serial killer would. "I wasn't stranded." I roll my eyes. "Can you just be a decent human being and tell him to take me to a hotel, since he refuses to listen to the woman who's clearly in an uncomfortable situation, thanks to the help of your bribery."

He sighs. "I'm Grayson." *Of course, he'd have a sexy name like Grayson.* "I was supposed to go home today from a business trip in the city, but my flight was canceled."

I try to ignore him by looking out the window.

"Let me buy you apology food. Do you like chicken tenders? There's this diner by my hotel with the best you'll ever eat."

I mumble, "I'm not hungry." My stomach betrays me, choosing this moment to let out the loudest growl. I lift my chin even higher.

A smirk plays on his features when I glance at him. "Fine, you aren't hungry. But *I* am, and you're riding in *my* cab."

This guy's got to be a narcissist or something. I once read the best way to win an argument with one is to ignore them, so that's what I do. I watch the city surrounding me. The people who walk the sidewalks, the names on the buildings, the benches with ads on them.

After forty-five minutes of being confined in a car with Grayson, I can finally stretch my legs. We stand in front of a diner.

"You coming, Tato?" He flicks his head toward the restaurant.

"No," I say, walking in the direction of a hotel I spot only a block away. A breeze goes right through my sweatshirt, rattling my teeth and carrying the scent of cigarette smoke.

"You can't go walking these streets all by yourself. It's dark," Grayson says, walking into step with me.

"What do you care?" I wrap my arms around myself, the autumn chill is nothing compared to Idaho's, but I'm always cold, even when it's seventy degrees. Like I was meant to live someplace warm.

"Just come eat with me. That, or I'm walking you to the hotel," he says like he's fine with either option. He's like a cockroach you can't get rid of.

"Why?" I stop walking. The city around us is full of life, and people are passing us on the sidewalk while traffic congests the street.

He is expressionless, but his eyes lure me in. Despite their cold color that should deter me, they feel oddly familiar. Like the nostalgic scent of sunscreen on a summer day. "Because you're in a huge city that's crime rate is quadruple whatever yours is in Idaho. Are we eating or going to the hotel?"

I blink at him once. Twice. Three times before sighing. "I'm a little hungry."

Chapter 2
Macy

Minutes tick by before either of us says a word, almost like it's a challenge of who will break and start a conversation first. I fiddle with my thumbs, fine with sitting in silence. The light above our booth flickers, giving me a headache.

"Where are you from?" Grayson eventually asks, losing our silent battle by default.

"Idaho."

His earlier assessment was accurate. He grins. "Do you like it?"

No one has ever asked me that before. "No," I admit.

"Are you moving to Florida?"

"No." I bite my tongue before I spill my entire life story to him. Twenty-year-old me would be beaming if she were in my current scenario, since it's something out of the countless romance novels I consume like water. Either my frontal lobe has developed significantly since then, or the naïve trust I had in the world slowly died the more I've gotten to know my fiancé.

A waiter sets down two glasses of water. I grab mine and

take a long sip through the straw. Grayson orders the chicken tender appetizer, which according to the waiter is big enough to share.

"So, if you don't like Idaho, and you're not moving to Florida, what *are* you doing?"

I sit up straighter. I can only hope he sees fire sweltering in my eyes. "None of your business." Direct and to the point, nothing like that twenty-year-old girl. I nearly nod in approval at my newfound boldness. Some would call me a bitch, hell, a younger version of me probably would, but I don't owe this stranger who's told me nothing of himself aside from his name details about my life.

He stares at me for several seconds, and I shift in discomfort. When he doesn't peel his gaze from me, I ask, "Are you enjoying yourself?" I cross my arms.

It's as if he's looking directly through me, and then he frowns. He clears his throat, like he's pushed aside whatever thought he had. "Yes. I am, actually."

The waiter brings our food and a basket of fries. I'm suddenly too hungry to care about Grayson or the prospect of him potentially stealing my kidney after this. I grab a chicken tender, dip it into ketchup, and take a huge bite. Thankfully, he's silent as we eat. Once I'm finished, I suck the grease off my fingers and let out a sigh of relief.

"You eat like an animal," he says.

"Was I not enough of a lady for you?" I roll my eyes.

"You were perfectly lovely," he says with what I assume is sarcasm. *Asshole.* "What do you do for a living?" he asks.

"Why should I tell you?"

"Because I'm buying you dinner, depending on the answer."

My lips part. The audacity of this unfiltered man is bewildering. "While you've been interrogating *me*, you haven't shared a single detail about yourself. How do I know you're not a serial killer?"

"You don't think I would've been caught by now?"

"People tend to overlook red flags if someone's good looking enough."

He grins. "You think I'm good looking."

Oops. "No."

"You can't take it back." He places his palm over his chest. "I'll store your compliment right here."

I search the restaurant for our waiter, hoping we get the check.

"I work in finance," he says. "You're turn."

For some reason that I can't explain, I answer before I can bite my tongue. "I'm an author."

His eyes seem to light up before he steals his expression. "What do you write?"

"Romance."

"No," he says, disagreeing with me.

I reel back, squinting my eyes. "Yes."

"Nope. I don't buy it."

"Buy it or don't buy it." I shrug, indifferent to his opinion.

"I've never heard of an author named Macy Brookes."

"Of course, you haven't. I write as Minerva Day." My eyes widen at my slip-up. "If you tell *anyone* my real name, I'll offer you up for a blood sacrifice."

He laughs, yet the sound seems foreign coming from him, like an old book that's been tucked away, coated in a layer of dust. "Did my little Tato just make her first joke?" He touches his chest. Before I can chastise him for using the word "my" as though I'm his possession, he pulls his phone out of his pocket and types something.

"What are you doing?" I whisper. He turns his phone around, showing me the three Minerva Day books he put in his Amazon cart. Something strange happens to my chest. Not because I'm embarrassed for him to read my writing, but because no one in my life has ever shown interest in my work.

I wrote my first book when I was seventeen. When I closed my laptop after writing *The End,* I ran downstairs to tell my parents. They're reaction was underwhelming, despite the pride I felt and the stammering of my heart that told me this was just the beginning.

When I was twenty, and finally learned how to self-publish my book, I felt like I could conquer the world. Walter was the first person I called, and all he said was, "That's cool."

When he got home that night, he didn't bring it up. No one did, for that matter. The parade of joy happening within never touched my external world. No one cared. Strangers read my books and wrote reviews, but no one in my life read a single page.

I celebrated my achievements alone.

And now, Grayson, who I met not even two hours ago, put three of my books in his cart the second he found out I wrote them. "Wow," he whispers more to himself. "This one has eleven thousand reviews!"

I look away from him before he can see the confusing emotions I try to bury.

"Here's the check, whenever you're ready." The waiter sets the bill down. I quickly unzip the small pocket to my suitcase, reach my hand inside, and try to feel for my credit card. Grayson stills my wrists beneath the table.

"I'm sure you could buy like five hundred chicken tender

platters, but I have the sudden urge to be a gentleman, so put your wallet away."

"I'm not putting out because you paid for a greasy meal, if that's what you're thinking."

He flinches and his eyebrows drop, forming a crease between them. "That's not even close to what I was thinking."

With reasons unbeknownst to me, I believe him.

He's quiet when he signs the bill and slides out of the booth, and like the gentleman he claims he has the urge to be, he grabs my suitcase and rolls it behind him so I don't have to.

"Oh, you don't have to do that," I say, to which he ignores me. I clear my throat. "Thanks." He simply nods.

Stepping outside, I wrap my arms around myself as the nighttime chill goes through my clothes. The city is even more alive this late into the night, with girls dressed in sequined miniskirts, gathering in a bar right across from the diner. Waitresses and waiters stumble along the sidewalk, like they are finally done with their shifts, walking back to their apartments. A woman smoking a cigarette walks past with her little white dog. There's life on every corner, chaos, and even a little shouting here and there.

I start walking toward the ginormous hotel. Grayson lengthens his strides to catch up to me. "You don't have to follow me," I say, looking forward. "You can give me my luggage and I'll be on my way."

A man tucked away in the alley shoots me a hungry look. His eyes seem to travel down my body, leaving me feeling filthy. I pull my shoulders back and pickup my pace.

"I'm not leaving you alone. Besides, I need a hotel room for the night too."

I wouldn't admit it to him, but I hoped he wouldn't. Men

don't infringe in other men's space, and I know if I'm within Grayson's, I'll be safe from their advances.

I tuck my hands into the pocket of my hoodie and fumble with my thumbs. We step through automatic doors and into the grand lobby of the hotel and walk up to the front desk.

"I need to book a room for a night or two," I say.

"I'm sorry, miss. We are booked for tonight," the man behind the counter says.

"How can you be booked? There are hundreds of rooms in this place."

"We book several weeks in advance."

I glance at the lobby, noticing women in dresses sitting with men who wear suits, sipping cocktails. A server who holds a silver tray hands a lady a drink, then takes the empty glass she holds. I'll admit this place is fancy, but acquiring a *waitlist*? Is the toilet paper made of gold or something?

"I checked out about four hours ago. Is my room still available?" Grayson speaks up, handing him his driver's license. The clerk types away at the computer.

My pulse slams into my ears. I am about to leave to find another hotel, but Grayson grabs ahold of my elbow, stilling me.

"Your room won't be filled until tomorrow afternoon. If you don't mind the beds being unkept, I can extend your stay."

"Perfect," Grayson says, accepting a plastic card the clerk hands to him.

I pull my arm away.

"You can have the room," Grayson says.

I look at him hesitantly and then shake my head to decline his offer.

"It wasn't up for choice, here." He hands me the card key.

A large part of me realizes how much I need this room, considering how late it's getting. I don't want to explore the streets by myself, but the smaller, more prideful part doesn't want to accept his help. It's a strenuous effort not to leave, and I hope my silence is an answer in itself.

"All right then, it's settled. I'll walk you to your room," he says, already making his way toward the elevators. I catch up to him.

"That's really unnecessary," I say, when he follows me into the elevator.

There is no hint of that sarcastic grin. He looks genuine when he says, "I'll stay at the other end of the hallway if it makes you feel better. I just need to see you make it to your room safely. Peace of mind and all." He whispers the last part, his gaze faraway as if something sparked his memory. I don't know what compels me to grant him peace of mind, but I nod.

I shift up and down on my toes, unable to sit still. "Is there a bar here?" I ask before thinking.

Grayson's left eyebrow raises. "Probably."

I slowly nod my head. The elevator opens with a ding. He gestures with his arm for me to exit first, following directly after. The narrow hallways smells of essential oils, as though the hotel spa is on this floor too.

"You want to go to the hotel bar?" he asks.

"No."

"I can tell you do." He grins.

"I don't." I kind of do. There's one bar where I live, and Walter threw a fit the first and only time I went there with some girls I went to college with.

I search for my room, going in the wrong direction when

Grayson calls, "This way." I follow him down the rows of doors, until we get to room 9500.

I don't move to grab the key card from my pocket. Something deep down urges me to follow that call, the one shouting at me to live. Not just survive the day, but really, truly *live*. I'm in New York City for the first time in my life. I want to see it. Experience something new.

I observe Grayson standing before me. There's a hint of stubble on his face, like he hasn't shaved in a couple of days. His dark brown hair lays in a way that looks like he just rolled out of bed, but he doesn't look sloppy. He looks good. It's infuriating, to be quite honest.

As irritating as he is, he seems trustworthy. At least to accompany me to the bar. Plus, he's freakishly tall, meaning no one is going to mess with me as long as I'm seen standing near him. The only downside is the ego boost he'd get if I asked.

He leans against the wall, crossing his arms with a hint of a grin playing on his lips. His eyes drop to my throat the second I swallow. My body tenses as he slowly leans into me, gaze never straying from mine.

He carefully brings his hand into the front pocket of my sweatshirt and grabs my key card. He steps out of my proximity and opens the door, holding it for me to enter. There's a tingle in the air as I pass him, taking my suitcase back as I do so. I set it on one of the beds, eyes glued to the view out the window. The city glitters with a million flecks of light coming from the tall buildings. Cars line the streets and tiny ants of people parade around like it isn't almost eleven p.m.

"It's no Idaho, I'm sure," he says from the door, his voice husky and deep.

I turn around.

"I've never seen a city so alive," he says, voice soft with something akin to awe. "Have you?" He steps into the room. I should tell him to leave, but instead I shake my head.

I haven't seen even one percent of the world outside of Idaho and a small island in Florida. I haven't done much of anything, despite the books I write where my characters fall in love somewhere beautiful in my imagination. Everything I've never had lives within the pages of a story for people to read.

"Let's go somewhere." His lips spread into a wolfish grin. My heart stammers from the sight, which is completely not okay with me.

It's a tempting idea. "No."

He shakes his head, like he can see through me. "Get ready. I'll change in the closet," he says, removing his backpack and bringing it with him into the surprisingly large space. *I guess fancy hotels with waitlists come with walk-in closets.* He doesn't give me room to object.

I unzip my bag and pull an army green dress out of my suitcase. I only packed flip flops, tennis shoes, and a pair of black high-top Converse, no heels to go with it.

I hide away in the bathroom to change and brush my teeth. I comb mascara through my eyelashes and pinch my cheeks to mimic blush.

Grayson is already done changing by the time I come out. He's wearing dark gray suit pants and a button-down with the cuffs rolled up, showing off his forearms. "The airline still has my checked bag. I put my business clothes in my backpack, so I'd remember to take it to the dry cleaner when I get home." He shrugs when he sees me eyeing his outfit. I don't say anything as I bring my hair over my shoulder and work out the tangles with my fingers.

"Do you have a jacket?" he asks, while unzipping his

backpack and pulling out a folded blazer that matches his pants.

"No," I say right as he hands it to me.

"You might get cold." His eyes rake over my dress. "Wow," he whispers.

I blink at him. I wore this dress last week to change things up when Walter and I went to the restaurant we eat at every Wednesday night. I wasn't surprised when he didn't compliment my appearance, but I was foolishly disappointed.

Instinctively, I reach for my left hand, feeling the need to twist the engagement ring that always digs into my finger, except I only feel my bare skin. I glance down, about to rummage through my bag to find it, but I already know where it is. The counter in the airport bathroom, where I left it to wash my hands. It's probably stolen by now. I should be more upset than I am, but it feels more like fate is slapping me across the face.

Chapter 3
Grayson

I'm afraid one wrong move will send Macy running to her room and locking me out. She's so reserved, I find myself grasping onto the smallest details she reveals about herself. I etch each one to memory. I wasn't surprised by her career choice.

The elevator opens, and by some miracle, she follows me in.

"Do you come to New York a lot?" she asks, looking at the numbers that drop at the top of the elevator.

"This is my first time. My boss sent me for a financial convention, and since I'm the newest and youngest employee, I couldn't exactly say no. Plus, it's good experience," I say. She doesn't answer, but I keep talking. "He doesn't like flying."

"And you like *finance*?" she asks, like the idea of anyone enjoying my career is insane.

I walk out, hoping she'll continue to follow, and when she does, I suppress a smile. "I'm good with numbers, and it pays the bills."

"I failed algebra twice in high school," she says.

"Creative people tend to be bad at math," I say. "I once read that writers and artists use the right side of their brain more than the left." She doesn't answer, and I realize what a weird thing it was to say. I find myself elaborating. "The left side is more analytical, like me. The right is more imaginative, like you."

"You don't know anything about me," she points out.

Right. "You're an author. I'd assume you are both creative and imaginative." I shrug.

Smooth jazz is playing when we enter the dimly lit hotel bar. There are six people here, all of whom appear to be in their sixties or older.

Macy clears her throat. "This wasn't exactly what I had in mind," she whispers. "I saw a bar across the street that seemed a bit more…lively."

I chuckle and place my palm on her lower back, leading her away from the dull room. "Should we go?"

She tucks her bottom lip in like she's considering it.

"Say yes," I encourage.

She blows out a steady breath. "Okay fine."

As soon as the automatic glass doors open to the outside, cold air hits us, and Macy puts on my gray blazer. She practically drowns in the fabric. It's longer than the dress she has on, showing off her thighs.

"I've never been to a bar like this," she says when we near it.

I like the idea of experiencing a first with her, even if it's as simple as taking her to a crowded bar. The door is already open and music floods outside.

Macy enters first, tensing at the environment. The smell of alcohol is strong, and the music makes it hard to hear anything else. She picks up her voice. "Should we go sit?"

I lean down so I don't have to shout. "Sure," I say against the shell of her ear.

I follow her through the crowds of people, noticing a few dancing. *Maybe I'll see Macy dance tonight.*

We find two bar stools next to each other. I pull one out for her and she gives me a strange look.

"What can I get you?" a female bartender asks Macy.

She tucks her brown hair behind her ears. It makes her look younger. "What do you normally get?" she asks me.

Normally? This is beyond normal for me. I quickly skim the drink menu. "Listen, Tato, I'm going to reveal something about myself, but you need to promise you won't tease me about it."

Her eyes squint and then she nods.

"I know all these guys are drinking beer or whiskey, but honestly, I hate both. I was going to order a strawberry daiquiri."

Her head tilts and she slowly smiles. "I like that," she whispers. "Own it."

I peel my gaze away from her, my stomach somersaulting. Maybe she's starting to warm up to me. I press my palm flat on the bar top and say proudly, "I'll take a strawberry daiquiri."

"I'll do one too," Macy says. Then turns to me with a mischievous grin, "And we'll take two tequila shots."

I lean my head on my hand, widening my eyes at her.

"Is there anything else I can get for you, sir?" The bartender eyes me seductively, playing with her hair.

"Nope, all good here."

After a minute, the bartender sets two small glasses in front of me. I grab both, handing one to Macy. She tilts her head back, slowly gulping the liquor and then slams the glass down. She scrunches her nose. I eye the salt on the corner of her lips and fight the urge to wipe it away. I take my shot and put my lime in my mouth like I've seen in movies.

Her big eyes look up at me as she sucks on the lime, scrunching her nose and shaking her head. "I'm going to vomit."

The bartender sets down our strawberry daiquiris, but her eyes don't stray from me. "Are you sure there's nothing else I can get you?"

"Yup."

She props her head on the heels of her hands, leaning forward to show off her chest. Jesus, lady, take the hint. I steal a glance at Macy, who mindlessly sips the drink.

"Can I get a beer," someone calls, thankfully getting the bartender's attention off me.

Every song that plays sounds the same as the previous, but when a new one begins, Macys eyes widen, and she stumbles out of her stool. "I love this song," she says with a lazy smile and then grabs my hand. I let her lead me into the crowd of sweaty bodies.

Someone knocks into Macy, causing her to trip and fall against my chest. My hands instinctively grab her hips to keep my balance, so we don't go tumbling backward into the people behind me like falling dominos.

She looks at me wide-eyed and before she can create space between us, I grab one of her hands and twirl her. Brown hair floats around her from the swift movement, and when she stills, a lock of it falls into her face, so I gently tuck it behind her ear.

Her eyes slowly fall shut as she lifts her face to the ceiling. She begins to sway in such an effortless way, as if the music itself is stringing her along.

I'm a tense body among countless dancing ones but I don't mind how stiff I probably look. I watch Macy like she's the first glimpse of land after spending months at sea.

When a new song starts, her eyes meet mine, glistening like morning dew. She steps closer, drowning out the smell of sweaty people with her vanilla scent. Her hands are soft when she wraps them around my neck, and as though it's what the music needs, she tilts her head to the side.

I'm under her spell when I begin to sway. It's not much of an effort, I just let her rhythm guide me. I take advantage of her shut eyes to notice everything about her. The faint freckles on her face remind me of constellations and there's a shadow tucked beneath her full lips.

Her eyes open and meet mine when the beat picks up. My hands find her hips. She doesn't tell me to remove them. Her gaze moves over my face like she's taking a good look at me. I hold my breath.

"How'd you get that scar?" Her thumb brushes over my top lip. "This one," she whispers. My eyes fall shut of their own accord from her touch.

"I caught a frisbee with my face when I was younger."

"Ouch." She winces.

She lifts her arms in the air and jumps up and down. I watch her in complete awe, the image is something akin to a memory. This time, when she looks up, her eyes catch on my lips.

I stop thinking and wrap my hands into her hair and breathe in the strawberry on her breath. My eyes fall closed, and my lips hover an inch above hers.

An alarm drowns out the music. It's raining. *Inside.*

My eyes shoot open. People start running toward the small exit, slamming into me, and making me fumble backward. It's complete disarray, and Macy is nowhere in sight. I push through bodies.

"Macy!" I shout, but it gets drowned out by the alarm and panic.

I go in the opposite direction of everyone else, but every step I make forward I get pushed three paces back. There's a girl on the floor that I quickly pull up from beneath her arms, so she doesn't get trampled.

There's not even smoke. I bet some drunken idiot pulled the alarm.

"Macy!" My scream leaves my throat raw, as if I've swallowed a razor blade. Damp people clash against me, but none of them are her.

I reach the bar. Water pools and drips from the top. I pull myself onto the wet surface, standing tall above the crowd, searching for a specific brunette in a crowd of them.

I could never live with myself if something happened to her, but right as the horrific thought forms, I spot her. With hair cascading down her back like a waterfall, Macy helps people off the floor. She pushes them in the direction of the exit instead of getting herself out. *Of course, she does.*

"Macy!" This time when I call her name, her eyes find mine.

I jump down, pushing through to get to her, and once I do, I grab her hand and lead her to the exit. Once we make it outside and past the crowd that gathers around the bar, I finally look at her. I examine her body from head to toe, ensuring she isn't injured. Her chattering lips are pale and her wet hair drips along her goose fleshed skin. Black makeup runs down her cheeks. I rub her arms, trying to warm her with friction since my blazer isn't doing much good getting stepped on in the bar right now.

"I'm f-fine," she chatters. "Let's go back to the hotel."

We make it there shortly; I follow Macy to the elevators. Once we are shut inside the confined space, her gaze is on nothing in particular when she rings out her hair and begins to laugh. Her entire body seems to shake with the wonderful sound.

I can't take my eyes off her. My heart picks up and I *burn*.

I stared like an awestruck idiot when she ran into me at the airport before remembering how to speak. And when I locked eyes with her before getting in the cab, it was like fate stepped in right before I could leave her.

I thought bribing the driver to take us to the diner was harmless. All I truly wanted was to have more time with her. Looking back, no wonder her assumption of why I was buying her meal was so crass. I just wanted to *be* with her. I wanted to make her laugh but instead, I managed to make her dislike me within minutes.

But now, her laugh echoes off the elevator walls, making my heart skip a beat. When the door opens, her cheeks are pink and her laughter quiets into just a smile. "That was crazy," she whispers more to herself than to me. "Was there even a fire?" she asks, stepping out of the elevator.

I shrug to appear unaffected by the laugh I earned from her. "Someone probably pulled the alarm."

She doesn't say anything else, and when we reach the room, she doesn't make a move to open the door. She slowly turns to me, meeting my eyes. "You might as well change your clothes in here since you need to grab your bag," she says, gesturing to my soaked outfit.

I tuck myself into the closet and struggle to pull my wet pants down my legs. I put the outfit I wore earlier back on and when I step out, I hear the water running in the bathroom, so I take this time to hang my soaked clothes to dry.

Shortly after I hear the shower turn off, Macy comes out in her pajamas. She eyes my attire. "You don't have anything else to wear?" she asks with a frown.

"It's all in my checked bag." *Still at the airport.*

She rummages through her suitcase and pulls out a T-shirt that's too big for her and some sweatpants. "You can wear this."

I glance at the men's clothes, wanting to ask why she has them, but her phone rings. I glance at it since it rests on the bed right where she layed the clothes for me.

The name Walter flashes across the screen.

Chapter 4
Macy

"When will you be home? I'm starving." Walter's voice comes through the receiver as soon as I answer his call.

My eyes clash with Grayson's.

"I'm…in New York."

The line goes silent. The only sound is my breath that begins to feel heavy.

"What?"

I amble to the other end of the small room to gain some privacy. "I just needed a break." I sigh.

"Hold on, bro," he says to someone. "Macy, what the fuck are you talking about?" I hear familiar gunshots in the background. He's playing video games as we speak. It's already ten p.m. in Idaho, and he's just now asking where I am? No, he's asking when I'll be back to feed him. I clutch the phone, my knuckles no doubt paperwhite. I'm seconds from chucking the expensive device it into the wall, if only so I have an excuse not to speak to him.

"Order a pizza. I don't know when I'll be back." I hit the

red button, ending the call, before I can do anything irrational. Like call off my wedding.

Grayson looks at the clothes I gave him on the bed, slowly picking up the T-shirt and inspecting it. I'm not surprised Walter's clothes made it into the dryer with mine, considering he rarely does his own laundry. "You have a boyfriend."

"*Fiancé*," I correct him.

His eyes drop to my left hand, searching for a diamond that isn't there.

"I lost it. My ring," I whisper.

His eyebrows come together while he nods carefully, and then long legs carry him to me. "You're engaged?" His eyes search mine like he's trying to understand. "Why are you here, Macy?" he asks.

"I—" I think back to the beginning of my day.

I woke up to the bed empty, like I do nearly every morning now. I found Walter asleep in the spare room on his gaming chair. His headset was still on, and his controller rested on his lap. I stared at him for far too long.

You should look at your partner and feel…*something*. A warmth in your belly or a flutter in your chest. At least that's how my characters feel when they're in love. It felt as though the wind was knocked straight out of my lungs.

It was wrong, so *incredibly* wrong. In the process of writing romance, I couldn't help but dream of my own great love story. And the scene before me certainly wasn't it.

His tired red eyes shot open, startling me. "Did you wake me up with breakfasts or are you just here to nag me about something?"

He only seeks me out when he needs something. And when I need the bare minimum from him, he calls it nagging.

Love isn't finding your significant other valuable when it benefits you.

A million thoughts swirled through my mind, but the one I clung to like an anchor was *I don't deserve this.* So, I left, and I have no idea when I'm going back.

I've decided to let the beating thing in my chest lead me from here on out, rather than my brain. My head is the one who got me into an engagement I feel trapped in, so heart it is. But even now, I still can't seem to end things with him, no matter how unhappy he makes me feel.

But I'm certainly not sharing any of this with Grayson, so I say, "Because my flight got canceled."

"No." He shakes his head. "Why did you leave?"

"That's none of your busine—"

"Macy, we just spent the night together and you didn't mention once that you were engaged."

I reel back, warmth spreads throughout my face. "What's your point, Grayson? I don't owe you the details of my life just like you don't owe me yours. We're strangers." I laugh without humor. "You act as if we didn't just meet a couple of hours ago," I say, before grabbing my toothbrush and locking myself in the bathroom.

I expect him to be long gone when I come out, but as soon as I open the door, he's right in front of me, like he was standing there about to knock. He clears his throat. "It's almost one in the morning and I'm exhausted."

My teeth ache as I grind them. "Fine. Take the room." I try to walk around him, but he steps to the side, blocking me from passing.

"No, I don't want—" He sighs, pinching the bridge of his nose. "I was just asking if I can share the room with you."

I'm about to say no, but he continues.

"And we aren't strangers. You're Macy and I'm Grayson. We might not be friends, but I hope you've realized by now that I have no ill intentions when it comes to you," he says. He gives me a once over before adding, "I'm sorry for prying just now. I won't say another word if that's what you prefer. I just need someplace to sleep tonight."

What can I even say? It was his room to begin with, and there's no way I can walk around looking for a hotel this late into the night. With no real choice, I just nod.

Chapter 5
Grayson

acy walks around the hotel room like I'm not even here. She grabs one of the complimentary water bottles and chugs the entire thing. She's wearing soft pink shorts and a T-shirt that says *Reading is sexy.* She plugs her phone cord into an outlet and climbs into bed, tucking her body beneath the comforter. The only sound is fabric rustling as she tries to get into a comfortable position.

Being in the same room as someone while they unwind from the day feels much more intimate than I'd imagine.

I don't wear her fiancé's clothes. I folded them and put them back in her suitcase. I lay in the second bed on my side.

She stares at her phone, eyes drifting horizontally along the screen like she's reading something. Maybe an e-book.

I break the silence. "What are you going to do in Florida?" I ask for the second time.

She looks up at me through dark lashes, setting her phone on the mattress beside her. "I thought you weren't going to talk."

Right. I did say that. But clearly her presence ruffles me enough to forget my basic social skills, leaving the impression that I'm a prick. I'm such a moron when I blurt out, "I *did* buy you a hotel room." Deep down, I think I like saying things just to see her eyes roll. *Maybe I am a prick.*

"I'm going to my grandparents' house in Sanibel," she whispers. "I used to visit them every summer, but the year before they died, my fiancé convinced me to stay in Idaho, since he didn't want to come with me." She clears her throat and whispers, "I never saw them again."

I squeeze my eyes shut. "I'm sorry," I say. "It sounds like you and your grandparents were close."

"We were."

"Are you going there to sell the house?"

She immediately shakes her head, like the idea is insane. "No, of course not. I love that house." She smiles, and I truly don't deserve to witness something so beautiful. "I've always dreamed of living there as a little girl."

"Why don't you?" I'm quick to ask.

She looks at me like no one's ever suggested it before. Like the idea is impossible. "Because I live in Idaho."

"Well, that *is* the purpose of moving," I say. "You leave one place to live in another."

"Walter won't leave Idaho," she whispers.

"I don't like Walter." It's an easy opinion to come to.

She rolls onto her back, staring at the ceiling like she's in deep thought. "Goodnight, Grayson." She rolls over, pulling the string to the lamp beside her, flooding the room with darkness.

I hear the static of the sheets as she tosses and turns.

"Macy?" I call into the dark.

Her soft voice does strange things to my chest. "Yeah?"

I speak before I lose the nerve. "You're too good for him."

Silence stretches.

"I know," she whispers so quietly, I might've imagined it.

A clicking sound forces my eyes open. I blink several times, allowing my vision to adjust to the dark. I sit up, and slowly, the events of last night return to my memory. I face her.

Macy sits against the headboard, the comforter loosely wrapped around her and falling from her shoulders as she types away on her laptop, oblivious to the world around her. She wears big black framed glasses that reflect the white screen. The hair that was smooth and laying perfect yesterday sticks up and out in every direction like she slept through a storm.

Before I can filter it, gentle laughter passes through my lips and her face snaps toward me. It's slightly terrifying, her face glowing from the screen. Everything else is cloaked in darkness, like she's holding a flashlight beneath her chin around a campfire, telling scary stories.

"What time is it?" I ask, my voice choppy from sleep.

"Six."

"In the morning?" I rub my eyes.

"Obviously." She turns back to her computer and continues typing, as if my presence is easy to disregard.

I don't know what compels me to, but I climb out of my bed and into hers. I read aloud. "Fighting for his love was like trying to reach the shore in a riptide." She tries to close the laptop, but I pry it from her hands. "The harder you try—"

"You are infuriating!"

I hold it out of reach. "The faster the air leaves your lungs until you're nothing but the water that destroyed you."

She stands on the bed and finally pries the technology from my hands.

I face her. "Is that for one of your books?"

She nods.

"Was it about the love interest? Because I don't know much about romance novels, but it doesn't sound like she likes that dude."

She tilts her head back and laughs. My stomach heats. *I caused that.* "No. It's about her husband. The love interest comes later in the story."

"Scandalous. I like it." I cross my ankles on the bed.

"Want to know how she meets him? The love interest, I mean." She lights up, so I'm quick to nod. "He's her husband's dad," she says slowly.

I let that sink in. "No!" I gasp.

She laughs. "Kidding."

I sit up a little more. "Well? How do they meet?"

She shrugs with a little smile. "I guess you'll have to read it to find out."

"You're leaving me on a serious cliff hanger here, Minerva." I grin. "When does it come out?"

"Probably a few months. I'm editing it now."

"So, it's already written?" I ask.

"The first draft."

"Let me read it."

She pauses for a moment, eyes on mine and a tilt to her head. "You can't. The first draft is a complete mess."

"That's fine. I'll read it now and when it's published, that way I can appreciate it even more."

"You'd read it twice?" she whispers.

"If the whole thing is as good as what I just read, I'd read it ten times."

She only blinks.

"Well?"

"I'll think about it," she says quietly, and I almost swear she blushed. Her eyes are bright and shining like maple syrup. I'm about to offer to take her downstairs for breakfast, but the annoying ring of her phone pierces the air. I glance down and see the name of her fiancé. I hand it to her.

She rolls her eyes and answers the phone saying, "Walter," as a way of greeting. Something about her sitting here with me and aiming that attitude of hers toward him makes me want to grin.

I can hear him through the phone's tiny speakers. "The fridge is making that weird beeping sound again."

Her whole body winces in what looks like annoyance. She speaks through her teeth. "It's not closed all the way," she bites out.

I hear the faint sound of him closing the fridge. "Oh," he says slowly. "My bad." *What an idiot.*

She straightens. "Is that all?"

"Yeah."

"You don't have anything you want to say to me? Anything to ask?"

"Um." It's silent. "No?" he says it like it's a question.

Her shoulders tense and I swear there's a flicker of hurt on her face. It passes all too quickly. Like she shoved it into a drawer and slammed it shut.

"You know what, Walter?" She throws the comforter off her body like she's suddenly burning hot. "Don't call me again unless your eyeballs are falling out or the house is on fire. Even then, I want you to count to one hundred, and when your done with that, I want you to ask yourself 'Is it really worth giving my fiancé an ulcer over, or am I a big boy who can figure it out myself?'" Before he can reply, she hangs up, and then lets out a frustrated groan. With her eyes aimed at the ceiling, they begin to glass over. And then she cries.

My chest is on fire. "Macy," I whisper, hesitantly placing my hand on her shoulder. She leans her head on the appendage. Her warm tears are dripping onto my skin and some buried instinct within me kicks in. I grab her and hold her in my arms until the sobs leave her body.

I don't know how much time goes by until she pulls her head away from my chest, but when she does, her nose is a hair away from mine. Feelings I've never felt in my life over-whelm my senses. I'm losing my grip on reality, staring at her mouth, and wondering what it feels like.

She stops breathing for a moment, as though she's wondering the same thing as me. Our lips are so close, and the longer I stay not kissing her, the more a ball of fire ignites in my chest.

Macy Brookes is turning me to ash without lifting a finger.

She's suddenly off the bed, rubbing at her arms as if she's trying to wipe away invisible grime.

My mouth is agape at what a mess this has all become. Maybe she has the right idea of trying to wipe off my touch like it's a stain. "I'm sorr—"

"Thank you for the room, and for not murdering me. But I don't know you." She grabs her suitcase, not bothering to change out of her pajamas. She steps into her sneakers and throws open the door to leave.

I'm up in an instant, needing to rectify this before she goes. I grab her suitcase like I did yesterday, so she can't leave. "Macy," I say like I'm trying to calm down a wild animal before it darts away. "I know you're engaged, and I shouldn't have…" I shake my head. "There are no excuses for my actions." I don't know anything about the relationship she has with her fiancé other than the fact that he made her cry only moments ago, and that certainly won't do. "I don't think you should marry him, Macy."

She looks like she's about to skin my balls and feed them to me.

"I know. We aren't friends." I hold up my hands. "I just know you deserve better."

"Go ahead. Keep telling me about *my* engagement," she says painfully calm. She releases her hold on her suitcase to cross her arms over her chest.

"Look, I'm well aware that it's none of my business but—"

"Damn right it's not!"

"But…" *I care about you.* "You aren't happy with him."

"You don't know what you're talking about. I lo—" She winces. "I *love* Walter." She picks up the handle of her suit-case. "Let. Go," she growls. "Now."

I don't remove my hands. "Why are you marrying him?"

"Excuse me?"

"Why doesn't he seem to mind that his girlfriend left the state without telling him? He didn't even ask if you were safe. Why would you marry a guy like that?"

Her nostrils flare. "I'm not his girlfriend, you imbecile. I'm his *fiancé.*"

"You didn't answer my question."

"I don't have to explain myself to you. I don't even know you!" she cries out.

I want to grab her by the shoulders and shake her awake, but instead I let go of her suitcase, and she leaves.

Chapter 6
Macy

If I go the rest of my life never seeing those blue glaciers, I'll consider myself lucky. To hell with him and his annoyingly accurate assumptions about my relationship. I despise his extrospection. *Am I really that open of a book?*

I haul my suitcase into the elevator, glancing down and realizing I'm still wearing my pajamas.

I'm mortified when I'm spit out into the lobby and four sets of rich eyes pin on me. I didn't even have the chance to glance in the mirror today. I tuck myself away in the public bathroom to comb through my hair and brush my teeth.

I step into a pair of jeans and leave on the T-shirt I'm wearing. I zip a jacket over myself since it's going to be chilly outside, and I have no idea how to hail a cab. I might be standing out there for a while.

I roll my shoulders and walk out of the bathroom, passing the other people in the lobby who I give a curt nod to.

I'm finally on a flight to freedom.

The attendants go over their safety demonstration while I put my phone on airplane mode. As I click the little airplane icon, I picture the next three hours of peace, with no way of Walter contacting me.

I put headphones on and rest my temple against the glass window. The plane begins to roll forward and my heart picks up with the anticipation of taking off. I shut my eyes as the world seems to speed up. I'm pulled into the seat, feeling heavy for a split second when we lift off the ground. My eyes open at the sensation, and the world shrinks all too quickly until the view of New York City looks fake. The autumn trees are beautiful from above. The music amplifies this moment, fueling that fire in the pit of my stomach that makes my heart say *type, type, type.*

I open my laptop once we reach a safe distance in the sky to do so. I let words flow through my fingertips, not even bothering to check my spelling. It's rare that passion ignites like this. I never know what I'm going to write when it happens, I just know that when I open a blank word document, the possibilities of what will go on the page are endless.

I forget about my own life as I become someone else entirely. I embody a man with a lifetime of love that came and went all too quickly. I squeeze my wife's fragile hand that has no strength left. The hand I pressed my lips to on our first date, when we had our entire future ahead of us.

Now, her fingers are so thin it's as if there were only paper covering bone. So tiny that her wedding ring would clatter to the ground if I tried to put it on her. The story of us, that was constantly unfolding, has reached its end. Just like that. There's nothing left after this. I know it all from beginning to end.

I bring my lips to the pale skin above her brow, my tears wetting her sleeping face. I cling to her hand like I can will life back into her. Like I can keep her here with me a little longer if only I could hold on tighter. The steady beeping of a machine goes completely flat, with one solid line that never seems to end.

"Are you okay, dear?" A hand touches my shoulder. I wipe away the tears I hadn't realized were rolling down my face.

I turn to the woman sitting beside me, coming back into reality. "Yes. Just writing something sad." I want to smile at that. At the beauty and the pain. At the endless possibilies only twenty-six letters can bring. I can evoke a rainbow of emotions from my readers with those letters. It's brilliant, and I wish someone in my life could see it as that. I wish I could tell my fiancé the things that drown me in passion. I wish I could see pride lighting up those dull eyes for once.

I wish my mom would read a chapter of my book and call me immediately before beginning the next one, just so she can tell me how much she loved a quote or how a certain line made her want to toss the book across the room.

I wish my dad would think of my career and life's purpose as more than a hobby. I wish he could see the layers that make up the stories I write, but most importantly, see me.

I wish the town I grew up in referred to me as more than "Mr. and Mrs. Brookes' daughter" or "Walter's fiancé."

No one in my real life bothers to know me. But Grayson, a man I'll never see again, strangely seemed to care.

Chapter 7
Macy

I stand in the short driveway of my grandparent's home and lock my rental car. The air smells of salt, and the waves sing their calming song against the beach behind the house, but everything feels different. It's almost as if I'm looking through dirty glasses. The once bright home is now faded, like I turned down the saturation of a picture.

I've never visited Sanibel in the fall. I always came for summer vacation. The shiny silver Volvo that I rented shouldn't be parked in the spot my grandfather's truck belongs.

Unlocking the front door with tears in my eyes, the hinges squeak as I prepare myself for what's on the other side. I shut my eyes, but humidity slams into my face like a rough day at sea. It smells musty, like the air hasn't circulated the house in years. If I focus, I can smell the lingering hint of my grandma's flowery perfume. I can almost hear her contagious laugh echoing off these walls.

I slowly open my eyes but try not to look around as I remove my shoes and leave them by the door. The cold terrazzo floors feel nostalgic under my bare feet. I crank open the dozens of small jalousie windows. They squeak and groan like they have since I was a little girl.

My grandparents never bothered to grease them, even when my mom complained about the muscle strain it caused to open them. The worn-out silver trim is covered in a layer of dust.

The outside breeze blows through the narrow house, creating a sound you can only hear when you bring a seashell up to your ear. The home was built so you wouldn't need an air conditioning unit, at least that's what my grandparents always said. I go outback, sliding the glass door open so more wind can cool the house.

The ocean sparkles and shines, not a single cloud in the sky, contrasting my cold and cloudy days in Idaho. The sun rays tingle my skin.

I tuck my legs into myself on the porch swing, closing my eyes to listen to the waves. The wind chime I helped my grandma make is what sends the dominos flying to my emotions, and I lose it. I cry for the little girl who misses her grandparents, who never got to say goodbye. For the twenty-three-year-old, trapped in a life she's wanted to escape since she can remember. For lost dreams.

I breathe the salty air and let myself pretend, just this once, that this is where I live. That my grandma is just inside, cooking some fresh sea food that my grandpa caught. I drift off into a peaceful sleep and wake sometime later face to face with a pelican. It's standing only three feet away on the porch railing. "Shoo," I tell him, using my hands to scare the crea-ture off, but he stares at me, waiting for a treat like I'm another tourist to feed him.

I lift my eyebrows. "I'm not feeding you."

It cocks its head, as though calling my bluff.

I cross my arms over my chest and go inside. The pelican stares at me through the glass door like it has a much higher IQ than I do. I scoff at the bird and click the lock into place.

The living room, dining room, and kitchen are all visible from where I stand. They aren't sectioned off by walls. A breeze drifts in as though I were still outside, blowing delicate strands of my hair. Without a single light on, the walls glow orange from the setting sun.

There are dozens of dead bugs on the floor. I don't know how I didn't notice right away. I dig around the utility closet for a vacuum, but my grandparents—bless their old-fashioned hearts—never owned one. Instead, I find a small handheld broom and dustpan.

The cool floors are hard beneath my hands and knees as I get to work, sweeping up small spiders, moths, even a few palmetto bugs shriveled up on their backs.

With no air conditioning or circulation for years, the heat created the perfect home for these insects. After only a few minutes of cleaning, my shirt is soaked through and the flyaway hairs that always get in my face are slicked back by my own sweat. Once the floors are bug free, my stomach twists and lets out an angry sound.

I don't know why I bother checking, but the fridge is empty, save for an old bottle of ketchup and a loaf of bread; I nearly gag while carrying to the trash can on the side of the house. I should've stopped by a grocery store on my way in from the airport.

I drag my suitcase into my bedroom. My grandma took me to a furniture store when I was fifteen, old enough that my taste was somewhat mature, so I wouldn't grow tired of what I picked out.

Her logic still proves true. My heart sings at the sight of

my bamboo bed. My nightstand and dresser are made of the same color wood as my bedframe. Pastel orange flowers swirl along the accent wall.

I chose the wallpaper because I wanted a permanent sunset in my bedroom. I believed it to be the most magical time of day, because each night a different painting lights up the sky. Sometimes it looks like the clouds caught fire, and other times it's a gentle pink that fades into purple. But no matter what happens in life, the sun is always promised to set.

It's one of the few things you can ever truly count on.

I open the closet to find my light blue bedding in a vacuum sealed bag. There are a few shriveled up bugs on the mattress, giving me the heebie-jeebies. Thankfully, there is a roll of toilet paper in the bathroom, which I use to pick up the insects.

After cleaning the mattress, I spread the sheets onto the twin bed, putting covers on the pillows and finally fluffing out the comforter.

I unpack my suitcase, neatly folding my clothes into the drawers. I pull on a pair of denim shorts and a T-shirt that says *I look better bent over a book*, laughing to myself as I do so. I bring my hair into a half up half down ponytail, letting a few strands in the front loose.

I step into my white tennis shoes and go out the back door. The tires of my teal bike are flat, so I pump air into them and then put my keys and phone in the basket. I ride half of a mile to The BARnacle.

The bar hidden at the dead end of the street is packed with locals. There aren't pretty surfboards lining the walls or conch shells by the door. Nothing to attract vacationers.

It's dark inside, with wood floors and cozy booths. I spent my summers eating shrimp tacos and laughing with my family here. The cushiony booths have whisked me into slumber a dozen times. My grandfather always insisted on carrying me to the car instead of waking me up to walk myself. But as soon as his hands wrapped around me, I secretly woke up. My grandmother once caught me peeking open an eye as her husband held me in his arms. She pressed her lips into a thin line and never said a word. Those little moments that I thought would fill the rest of my days are long gone.

"Little Miss Brookes, is that you?" a woman in her seventies with bright rosy cheeks calls from the bar. She makes her way to me and then squeezes me into a hug that is borderline suffocating. She smells like salt water and cigarettes. "Tammy!" I beam, squeezing her back.

The old woman worked with my grandma for over twenty years at the library. I would spend hours a day sitting on the floor, my back against the shelves, living in the pages of a story. She always picked out books for me to read, and the two of us would spend hours discussing them.

"I was just thinking about you last night, isn't that funny?" I nod and she pinches my cheek. Her eyes skim over the words on my shirt and she lets out the loudest laugh. No one looks our way, like they are accustomed to Tammy's nightly laughter. "What brings you to town?"

Other than needing to escape my fiancé, I say, "I missed it." Not a lie.

She links our arms and brings me to the bar to sit beside her. "Minerva Day." She giggles. "I changed your diaper once and now you wear shirts with dirty jokes on them. You're making me old." She sips on her iced tea. The bartender comes over, and I recognize his dirty blond hair immediately.

"Elliot!" I stand on my knees, the stool wobbles as I lean

over the bar to hug Tammy's grandson, catching him by surprise.

"Um, hi…strange woman hugging me from behind the bar," he says. I pull back so he can see me. It takes him two seconds before he pulls me back into our hug.

He was never into reading or hanging out with me at the library, but Tammy had us over her house once a week for dinner in the summers. Elliot and I would play with the other kids on his block when we finished eating.

I sit back down, smiling wide at my old friend.

He grabs a wet glass from the dishwasher and dries it off before filling it with tap beer, sliding it in front of me. "It's on the house," he says.

"Thank you." I glimpse a simple black band around his ring finger and smile. "You're married."

"You remember Sarah, don't you?"

How could I not? She lived on his street, and we would play after dinner until the sun fell. He's had a crush on her since we were eight. "So, after all these years she finally started liking you back."

"It only took her eleven years and two boyfriends. But yeah, she likes me. I hope."

Tammy grins at me. "Are you still seeing that boy? The one you brought here a few summers back?"

I want to say no. It would be much easier than explaining, but I was never good at lying. Especially to Tammy. "Yeah, we're still together," I mumble.

"Is he here?" Elliot asks.

When Walter was here that one summer, he insisted we stay home while my family went to Tammy's house for dinner. It was the only time we were truly alone, and he wanted to make the most of it. It's hard to remember us like that, touching every chance we got. It lasted less than a year before it felt like a chore—like it was only for his pleasure.

"It's a solo trip." When I say it, I see a hint of realization flicker across Elliot's face.

"Let me guess. You want a grilled chicken sandwich and fries?"

I'm grateful for the change in subject. I grin. "And a side of ranch, please."

"Coming right up," he says.

I spend the rest of the evening chatting with Tammy about books, even the ones I've written. Elliot tells me how he proposed to Sarah on the beach where they had their first date.

I'm laughing so hard that tears trickle out the corners of my eyes as he re-enacts how she tackled him to the ground. He dropped the ring, and they spent thirty minutes digging in the sand for it.

I tiredly ride my bike home. Mosquitoes feed on my exposed arms and legs, and by the time I set my bike against the back porch, I'm itchy and cursing every bug that lands on me.

I soak in the bathtub; the water is cold by the time I'm done reading on my phone for the night. I towel off and wear only my underwear and a T-shirt. It's pitch black outside my bedroom window, except for the dim yellow light coming from my neighbor's window.

My family and I never got to know who moved into the house after my best friend moved out of it when I was five or six. But whoever it is, I can't help but decide I don't like them. Not when they replaced that sweet boy whose name I can't remember.

It's on the tip of my tongue, but before I can form the

name, I drift off to sleep, dreaming of an annoying man I met once at the airport.

It's one p.m. when I wake up and since I haven't gone shopping, I have no food. I find coffee pods tucked in the back of the pantry. Once my mug is full of the nearly black liquid, I throw away the empty pod.

I take the trashbag to the garbage can on the side of the house, even though it's hardly full. The bugs at the bottom of the bag freak me out. A delicate gust of wind blows against my damp skin, sending a chill down my spine. The side of my face tingles, like something to the right is begging for my attention. When I finally acknowledge the sensation, I see a man.

Christ, he's tall. With his back toward me, I watch him. He drags a sponge covered in white suds across the car in my neighbor's driveway. He's wearing a hat with dark wispy pieces of hair sticking out from the sides. As much as I enjoy the view of his backside, I'm dying for him to turn around.

I bite my cheeks as he walks around to the other side of the car. Once I see his sharp, angular face, all logical thoughts die, and I duck behind the garbage can.

That couldn't have been...*no*. There's no way I just saw Grayson washing my neighbor's car.

I yelp, slapping away a wasp that stings my arm, leaving behind searing hot pain that spreads through my muscle. I let out a colorful string of curse words, inventing a few new ones.

Tears sting my eyes as I hear the crunch of gravel beneath someone's shoes, getting closer and closer. Suddenly it's no longer shady, and when I open my eyes, I realize the garbage can was dragged away. My gaze slowly moves up his body, landing on a face I'm all too familiar with.

I use my hand to shield away the sun and his gaze. "No." I don't know what I'm disagreeing to. All I know is I'm completely *not* okay with this scenario. I gape up at him, my jaw permanently unhinged.

Grayson stares down at me with an amused grin I despise. "Maybe you can school me on what a 'motherfucking cock-bucket' is after you tell me why you're ransacking my neighbor's garbage can."

"What?" I shake my head. "*Your* neighbor?" Still on the ground, I say, "You live here?"

His pompous smile hasn't wavered for a second. "Yes."

I hoist myself up and I dig a finger into his chest. "Are you *stalking* me?" *What the hell is happening right now?*

A dark eyebrow shoots up. "Funny, I was going to ask you the same thing, seeing as I caught you watching me from behind a trash can."

I laugh without humor and pull out my phone. "Okay, I'm callin—"

He snatches the device with graceful strength and puts it in his front pocket tucking his hands away as well, making my skin flame with annoyance. I'm not sure who I was even going to call and what I was going to say. "As much as I love being a part of the scenes you cause, I'm a little busy." He gestures to the car. Soapy water drips onto the white pebbles that make up the driveway. "Oh, and Macy?"

"What?" I growl.

"You've got some dirt—" He steps into my personal space, bringing his soapy thumb over my cheek. "Right there."

I jolt backward and lose my balance. His beautifully crafted hands still me. *I'd rather him let me fall.*

He smells woodsy but being this close to him I catch a hint of something else. It's almost like…strawberries? I meet his eyes and bring my hand into the front pocket of his shorts to retrieve my phone. I pay no mind to the goosebumps that erupt over my body.

He's watching me expressionless, but I swear there's a flicker of something behind his eyes that disappears too quickly. His hand shoots out, grabbing my forearm and inspecting the angry red welt as though he's just now realizing why I was cursing to begin with. "Are you allergic?" His eyes flit to mine.

"I don't think so."

"Well, I'd assume your throat would be swollen shut by now if you were. Since you haven't stopped reprimanding me for the past two minutes, I think it's safe to say you're fine." He runs the pad of his finger over the raised skin. "Does it hurt?"

"Yes."

"You don't look like you're in pain."

"How astute of you," I say dryly. "I have a high pain threshold."

"Well, I think you'll live." He smirks. "I'll be at The BARnacle tonight around seven. I'd assume to see you there since, well, you're stalking me." He turns and walks off, hosing the suds off his car.

I scramble away, tripping over my own two feet toward the front door. I hear husky laughter coming from his driveway. I lock my door, cursing fate that Grayson, of all eight billion people, is my new neighbor.

I don't care how hot this house can get, I don't need him watching me. He peaks up when he hears the loud squeak of me shutting the first window. I don't bother waiting for his reaction as I move onto the next one, until the house is only lit by the sun coming through the sliding glass door.

I drink the warm black coffee. I can already feel a bead of sweat dripping down my forehead, so I take an ice-cold shower once I finish the mug.

Still hungry, I make a quick trip to the gas station's convenient store and get a few snacks to hold me over until I get groceries. Thankfully, Grayson is nowhere in sight.

Licking the powdered sugar off my fingers, I toss the wrapper to the mini donuts away and then prop my laptop open and begin working away at the dinner table. I edit until my stomach growls again, and when I check the time, it's a quarter after seven.

I can either go to The BARnacle and feed into Grayson's delusions, or I can eat another packaged snack. The latter makes me queasy, so I set my pride aside and throw on a sundress with tiny shorts underneath so I can ride my bike without giving the whole island something to stare at.

I don't let my eyes wander when I enter The BARnacle. I head straight for Elliot, taking an empty seat at the end of the bar.

"Twice in two days, how did I get so lucky?" He smiles.

"Don't get too excited. I'm ordering to go." I give Elliot my order for shrimp tacos and shrink into the bar stool.

Two petite hands cover my eyes, and a sweet voice says, "Guess who?" My lips curve upward, and I turn around to find a girl with short brown hair. Sarah, Elliot's wife, and my lifelong friend.

She steps to my right, letting her arm rest over my shoulders like we see each other every day. No hug, no formalities, just two people picking up where they left off. She smells like coconuts. "And hello, Mr. bartender." She smirks at Elliot.

I could almost swear he blushed, but he plays it cool like he has since we were children and gives her a nonchalant wink before ambling off to take more drink orders.

I grin. "That man is so in love with you."

She shrugs. "I know." She takes a seat on the barstool beside me. "How long are you in town for?"

"I haven't decided. I'm hoping at least a month."

Her husband hands me a paper to go bag.

"You're leaving me already?" Sarah frowns.

I bring my voice to a whisper; Elliot is already on the other end of the bar making a drink. "I'm hiding."

Her eyes narrow. "From?"

I glance around but don't see him, maybe he already left. "Grayson."

"Who?"

I shrug. "Tall, really dark hair, pale blue eyes—"

"Dracula?"

I laugh. "What?"

"The guy brooding over there at the other end of the bar." She leans back so I can see what I missed before. Grayson leans on his elbows, taking a large bite of a burger.

I nod. "That's him."

She scrunches up her nose. "Yeah, I refer to him as Dracula because…well, look at him." She shakes her head. "He gets takeout every day. This is the first time I've seen him actually sit down to eat. I don't think anyone on this island knows him." She lifts a shoulder, then calls out to her husband. "Beer, please!"

"I better go." I grab my bag and hand Sarah a twenty-dollar bill. "Give that to Elliot for me."

"Fine, but I expect a phone call soon. I want to know all about why you're hiding from Dracula and where that engagement ring of yours went…" She glances at my hand. I try not to wince at the reminder.

Backing up so I can escape without gaining anyone's attention, I whisper, "I'll call you." And then I book it to the door and sigh with relief the second I'm outside.

I put my bag of food in the basket of my bike and peddle off. The breeze against my face makes my lips curve up. I cruise for a while, enjoying the peace and quiet.

"Cute dress. It really masks what a ferocious woman you are."

I give Grayson, who is now walking right next to me, my middle finger. "Stop following me."

"I'm just going home." He shrugs, feigning innocence.

"Yeah, about that, you didn't want to tell me you *lived* in Sanibel? It could've saved me the trouble of an ulcer or two."

He chuckles. "That, Tato, would eliminate all the fun." I dare a glance at him and nearly roll my eyes at his outfit choice. His pale skin is like porcelain against the sheer darkness of his clothes. No wonder he earned Dracula as a nickname.

I scoff. "Of all the people who could be my neighbor, you would be my last choice."

"Pleased to hear I make the ranking at all," he says through a cocky grin. "And I'm not your neighbor. You don't live here."

I lift my chin, keeping my expression neutral despite the nerve he struck. I hate that I'm an outsider to the island I call home.

He doesn't seem to mind the silence. I wouldn't care if he did. The sun has fully set by now, everything shines cobalt from the moon. I listen to the roaring sea and the wind ruffling through palm trees, and not the sound of Graysons footsteps so close beside me. I should go faster so I can get away from him, but for reasons I can't place, I don't.

I turn right on my street. So does he. I don't say goodbye or give him the curtesy of a glance. I walk my bike through the sand to my back porch.

"Sweet dreams, neighbor." There's a grin in his voice. I hear him entering his house, so I peek over my shoulder. The dim yellow glows through the windows, as if he's flicking on each light as he walks farther in.

It's probably eighty degrees when I step inside my house. I have no choice other than to boil all night or open the windows. I choose the latter.

Once I've let Sanibel's delicate breeze whisper through the house, I take another cold shower and throw on my usual bedtime attire in the bathroom. I climb under my plush crisp comforter and open an e-book on my phone. I read one sentence when an Airdrop notification blocks the words. It's a selfie of Grayson, holding up a peace sign.

I ignore it, getting back to my book when another picture pops up of my house through his window, and captioned on the photo is "My grouchy neighbor." If I zoom in, I can see right into my bedroom.

I storm to my window, lifting the shades for him to see my two middle fingers, then slam them shut.

Chapter 8
Grayson

A smile is plastered to my face when I wake up the next morning. I will my lips into a frown, as though I'm tying weights to the corners, but it's useless.

I pull on black shorts, deciding against wearing a shirt in the morning heat. My black running sneakers are perfectly lined up beside my everyday sneakers. I step into the ones for running, the soles are chalky white from the bleached pebbles of my driveway.

The sun is usually still rising when I do my daily run. I never set an alarm, my body always wakes me up before the sun has even peaked above the horizon, but today I was surprised to see it was nine thirty when I first opened my eyes.

There are children building sandcastles and splashing around the beach. Adults are wearing floppy hats that shade them from the relentless sun. I ignore the static prickling the side of my face that's begging to glance at her house, to see if she's dancing behind those tiny windows.

I run so fast that sweat burns my eyes and my muscles strain to hold me upright, and then I push myself even farther, until all I can think about is pulling oxygen into my lungs and not the woman living next to me. The one I've mistakenly given a hundred reasons to dislike me.

Once I'm back on my street, I slow to a walking pace, with my chest heaving and sweat gleaming. There's an Amazon package at my front door, and I already know what it contains when I bring it inside. Three novels that Macy wrote. I flip through the pages. There are thousands of words all thought of by her.

I go out onto my back porch, not even bothering to clean myself up as I sit on the white wooden chair, perch my leg onto the other and read the dedication page.

To those who prefer a fictional man to a real one.

I laugh and flip to page one. By the time I'm thirty pages in and fully invested in the characters, a sound catches my attention.

Macy is shooing away a pelican that stands on her porch railing, only a foot from where she's sitting on a swinging bench, laptop resting on her thighs.

I clear my throat, knowing she'll hear it from the twenty feet that separates us. Her eyes flit to mine, then down to the book in my hand. I grin at her, then go back to reading. I feel her gaze on me, but I will my eyes to focus on the page, hardly able to focus with her staring.

In the span of four hours, I sneak a few glances at her focused expression. Her lips are moving like she's mouthing the words she types. Every so often she goes inside only to return a minute later with a mug of what I can only assume is coffee. I think she's on her third cup by the time I get two hundred pages in. My stomach is empty, no doubt hers is too. I call a delivery service on the island to pick up some food from The BARnacle.

I read twenty-six more pages by the time the delivery person is ringing my doorbell. I walk through the house, hand her some cash and retrieve the three heavy bags. Macy is concerningly unaware of her surroundings while she works. "You look hungry," I say.

She jolts and when her eyes set on me, an expression of pure disdain is my only greeting. I ignore the incredulous look she's giving me as I set the takeout bags on her little wooden table and start grabbing boxes out of them. I thought the airdrop thing would make her laugh, but now I'm starting to think I pissed her off even more than I already have. "I didn't know what you liked, so I got a little of everything."

She blinks up at me. "Why?"

"Because you've been out here for hours, and I haven't seen you eat once. And I'm starving too."

She sets her laptop aside and peeks in each box, settling on the order of shrimp tacos. "All this food is going to go to waste." She takes a bite, and a piece of grilled shrimp falls out of the taco.

A second later, the same pelican perches itself on her railing. I reach into Macy's box. "Don't," she says fiercely, pointing a finger at me. I toss the shrimp to the bird, who gobbles it down without chewing.

I feel myself smile as I take a seat on the chair across from her. "You don't like our friendly neighborhood pelican?"

"He stares at me as if *I'm* the one with the pea sized brain."

I want to laugh at that, but her expression is so serious that I think better of it. "Are you afraid he's right?"

She rolls her eyes and finishes her taco, moving onto the next one.

"How do you do it?" I ask, digging into my french fries.

"Come up with an entire world with characters that seem so real." I shake my head. "Judith is my favorite, by the way."

She laughs. I would teach myself to be the best comedian if only I could hear it daily.

"Everyone else thinks she's bitchy."

I give her a long once over. "I think she's misunderstood. I like her fire."

Her eyes soften and she nods in agreement. She holds up her last taco. "Thank you."

I know she's referring to the food I bought, but I need to stretch that kernel of niceness she's given me, so I ask, "For?"

She shoots me a pointed look.

I grin.

"I feel like I should try to eat the seven remaining boxes, so it doesn't go to waste."

"You can," I say. "Tonight, for dinner."

She glances at the ensemble of food and then I clarify. "With me. At my house."

She shakes her head immediately.

I carefully place all the boxes of food back into the bags and step down her porch, calling over my shoulder. "See you at seven, Tato. Or else I'll have to throw away all this perfectly good food." I won't let the food go to waste, but I don't tell her that.

Chapter 9
Macy

I'm not going. It was out of the question as soon as Grayson invited me over for dinner at his house, which I'm currently standing in front of. I don't even know how I ended up here to be honest, but before I can decide to turn and go back home, the door swings open and his woodsy scent wafts around me.

"I was just coming to retrieve you." He smirks.

I roll my eyes and think better of walking away like a coward. I brush past him and pad into his house, the one I spent an entire summer playing in as a kid, but it looks completely different. The walls are a crisp white that nearly strains my eyes, contrasting his dark brown couch and minimal furniture. As I walk further in, I see a plug-in airfreshner, which explains the sweet scent I caught before that must linger on his clothes. "Is that strawberry scented?" I gesture to it.

Grayson stands a few feet behind, probably observing me as I take in his house. It doesn't feel like a home. It's pristine and clean but not cozy and warm. There isn't even a dinner table.

"It became my favorite scent ever since losing a bet," he says. I think back on the strawberry daiquiri he ordered in New York.

I notice a book laying open on the countertop. I flip it over, seeing that it's one I wrote. It's open to page three hundred and one. He's almost finished reading it.

"You're a phenomenal writer." He picks it up and inspects it closely.

"I-um, thank you."

He doesn't say much more, he just opens the fridge, and pulls out the to-go boxes. He microwaves them on plates.

I wrap my arms around myself and glance around, not sure what to do with myself.

Grayson pours two glasses of red wine, and hands one to me. "The furniture isn't for show. You can sit."

I roll my eyes and pull out a barstool, it squeaks against the hard wood floors. The air is crisper in his house than mine next door, and I realize that he has an air conditioning unit beneath his window. Where my grandparent's house is old, Grayson's is completely modernized.

I chug my wine, setting the glass down on the counter when Grayson hands me a plate. He eyes my empty glass with amusement. "Would you like some more?"

I take a bite of a fry and nod.

He sits on the stool beside me after filling my glass. We eat in silence. By the time I'm finished, I realize what a horrible guest I am for not making decent conversation, but then again, when did I start to care?

"Thought for thought?" He sits with his body facing mine, so when I turn to him, our knees brush together.

I'm not sure if it's the wine that makes me compliant, but I shrug and say, "You first."

"I didn't expect you to show up at my doorstep, but I'm glad you did. It's been…a while since I've had company."

Something about his vulnerability has me deciding to follow the rules of the game, sharing one of my thoughts. "I'm thinking…" I give him a once over. "It's sad someone like you isn't used to having company."

His gaze is on my face for so long I nearly squirm. "Someone like me?" He finally breaks the silence.

"I…I just mean you don't deserve isolation." I take a sip of wine. I remember what Sarah told me. How no one in town knows him.

He leans in a fraction, and if I wasn't watching, I wouldn't have noticed him any closer. "And you don't deserve to marry someone you're unhappy with," he says softly, in a low voice.

I grind my teeth. "I *am* happy."

"Then why come here?"

"I—"

"Don't answer. Just think on it." He stands and takes our plates to the sink. "Put on your shoes," he says, rinsing the dishes with water.

Is he kicking me out?

"The BARnacle has great food but horrible dessert, and the ice cream shop is too busy with sticky fingered children. The gas station has decent ice cream." He says all while putting our plates in the dishwasher. "Assuming you like ice cream."

"I'm not a total monster."

~

"What's your favorite flavor?" Grayson asks once we make it

to the tiny convenient store. He opens the freezer of wrapped ice cream sandwiches and cones.

"Brown."

He swivels his head to raise an eyebrow at me.

"That's what I called chocolate when I was younger." I smile, remembering the way my grandma continued to call it that even after I learned the flavor's proper name.

"Chocolate ice cream…" He wrinkles his nose. "That one is a little questionable." He reaches into the case and pulls out a prepackaged cone. He turns it around so I can read the label, and I'm not surprised to see that it's strawberry.

"What's the point of getting a healthy flavor like straw-berry? You might as well go eat the fruit instead."

"Once you have a taste, you will understand the appeal."

I huff out a laugh, biting my tongue so I don't make a *that's what she said joke.* "Doubtful." I grab a chocolate ice cream cone and make my way to the cashier, but before I can pay for it, Grayson steals it and sets it on the counter with his. He swipes his card and hands the dessert back to me.

"You didn't have to do that," I say.

He grabs the door before I can, using his backside to hold it open for me to pass. "I'm happy to."

"Thank you."

He breezes past me on long legs, and I trail behind him. "Where are we going now?"

He spins around with a raised brow. "We?" he asks, feigning confusion. He faces forward again. "*I* am going to the beach."

He is insufferable. This is why I don't like hi—

"Care to join?"

"Nope."

I can hear the smirk in his voice. "Still playing that game, are we?"

I scoff at his backside. "What *game?*"

I follow him between our yards, onto the sand of the beach. I kick some behind me as I walk, and the tiny particles get into my flip flops. It's dark now, the only light is offered by the moon. He walks backward to face me. "The one where you pretend not to like me," he says, voice smug.

"Don't flatter yourself." I roll my eyes and open my ice cream. I'm about to put the wrapper in my pocket so I can throw it out later, but Grayson reaches out and steals it from me. He tucks it into the pocket of his pants instead.

"Don't worry, Tato. We can play a little longer." He winks.

I roll my eyes and hold up my middle finger.

He stops walking once we are about ten feet from the shoreline. He sits in the sand with his legs bent, taking the first lick of his cone.

I watch him, unsure if I am going to sit with him or go back home.

His calloused hand engulfs my ankle and yanks in a way that makes me lose balance and fall on my butt. I give him a scathing look, picturing flames in my eyes.

"I was making the decision easy for you, since I know how stubborn you can be." Before I get the chance to answer, he changes the subject. "I never sit on the beach."

Curiosity gets the best of me. "Why?"

"It's never fit into my schedule." He lifts a shoulder.

I laugh, arranging my body like his so my knees are tucked against my chest. "This is literally your backyard. Do you have time to go to the bathroom with that tight schedule of yours?"

"I guess I never thought about coming back here, honestly."

"Well, *I* used to sit out here all the time. My grandparents and I would lay on our backs and look for shooting stars."

Grayson turns to me. I can't explain what's happening to my body, but I instantly run ten degrees warmer. "Try it," he says, putting the dessert close enough that if I dart my tongue out, I would taste it. So, I do just that. It tastes exactly as he smells up close.

"Good?"

I take another lick, savoring the taste. "Fine," I growl. "Yes, it's good."

He smiles, showing off two dimples. "Let me taste that brown ice cream of yours then." He gestures to the cone in my hand. I hand it to him.

His eyes light up when he takes a bite. Not a lick, but a bite. How does that not hurt his teeth? "Let's trade. Yours is way better than mine."

I find myself laughing. "Have you never had chocolate ice cream before?"

"Obviously I have. But it really hits the spot."

I grab the strawberry from his hand and let him keep mine. I finish it off, licking the remains from my fingers from where it melted.

Grayson sighs as he leans all the way back so he is flat against the sand.

He turns his head; his eyes are glittering from the moon-light. "Search for shooting stars with me, Mace." The nick-name rolls off his tongue as though he's said it a million times, yet I've never been called anything other than Macy before. Despite the cold ice cream I devoured, my stomach warms.

Our shoulders are feathering one another when I lay down. I should scoot over so no part of us touches, but that one connection point electrifies every inch of my body in a way I've never experienced before now.

There are millions, if not billions, of specks in the sky. Blue and yellow and white. Some seem to twinkle, and others are so faint you have to squint to see them. A flash of light shoots across the sky so fast that if I had blinked any sooner, I would've missed it. I shoot up in excitement. "Did you see that?"

His glittering eyes are glued to the sky as if he didn't hear me. *Rude.*

I slowly press my back against the ground, admiring the beauty above.

He clears his throat after a few moments. "I've never seen a shooting star before."

I turn my head to look at him, waiting for him to continue.

"That felt—" His mouth opens and closes, like he's decided against finishing his sentence. He shakes his head with a humorless laugh.

"Felt like what?" I press.

His gaze meets mine, and something about the softness in his expression feels wholly intimate. Just the look on his face is the most vulnerable I've ever seen him, as though he's let his mask slip for a moment. "Like I'm looking up at heaven and it's looking right back, waving hello."

I take in the sparkling sky, thinking of my grandparents. Another shooting star winks at me. I laugh through a tear that escapes, turning to him once more. "That's such a beautiful perspective." I feel my face stretching into a genuine smile and his eyes seem to widen. In this brief moment everything between us fades away. Like the stars falling over us have stolen a paragraph from the rest of the story and placed it into the pages of a more beautiful one.

There's a calmness in his gaze. Something resembling peace, and I find myself wondering who waved hello to him from heaven, and how long he's been waiting for it.

We aim our gaze back toward the sky. The soft sand beneath me and the sound of waves rolling over shore whisks me to sleep until I wake up sometime later, cuddled up to Grayson's chest with his heavy arm draped over my middle.

"Grayson," I say, moving his arm and sitting up.

His eyes blink open. They are red from sleep, making his irises appear bluer. He sits up and takes in our surroundings. "We fell asleep?"

"I have to go." I stand, wiping the sand off my body as I back away, toward my house.

My eyes glaze over as I stare at my fiancés face on my laptop. "Are you frozen or just choosing to ignore me?" Those cruel, uncaring lips say.

I blink back into reality, remembering the way a conversation works. "Sorry, bad connection here," I lie.

"I still don't get why you're there. You hate Sanibel."

"*You* hate Sanibel." I'm about to bite my tongue but think better of it. I deserve to speak freely to the man I'm marrying without fearing he'll shoot down my hopes and dreams. "I wanted to live here as a little girl. I still do."

He laughs in an unamused way. "Like you'd ever leave your hometown."

"I'm here, aren't I?"

"Which I still don't get." He shakes his head. "You always do this."

"Do *what*?"

"This." He gestures toward the device he's using to video chat. "I look away from you for two seconds and suddenly you're across the country. If you want my attention so bad, then go…" he waves his hand around. "Get a boob job or something."

An incredulous laugh fills the room and there's no color in the world except my red-hot rage. "You think I'm here because I want your *attention*? If I had stayed in that house with you for another second, you'd be fishing your engagement ring out of the toile—"

"See? This is what I'm talking about. You're self-destructive." He shakes his head like he pities me. "Right when things get too good, you ruin them for yourself."

"*Good?*"

"Yes, Macy. Good. You're engaged to me." He pauses like that sentence is supposed to drive home his point. "We have a nice house, and you get to plan a girly wedding and buy a fancy dress. You stay home all day while I go out and work. Maybe you should go to therapy."

My anger goes from candy apple red to crimson. "Is that what you think I do? Just sit around at home all day waiting for you?"

He smiles, like that's exactly what he thinks.

I say slowly, so each word hits its mark, "While you're 'out working' I've mastered the art of creating a perfect fictional man. Every detestable trait you possess gets written down solely so I can ensure the men in my books are nothing like you. Every love interest I've ever created is so carefully opposite to you that they don't even share the same eye color." I slam my laptop shut and pull out my phone.

I hesitate, my thumb hovering over my mom in my contact list. I want to tell her I'm calling off the wedding, but for some reason I can't. Maybe Walter is right. Maybe I do self-sabotage. Just not in the way he thinks.

I hate myself for staying with him, but what will I do if I leave? Both of our names are on the house I paid for. I've put all the deposits down on the wedding and sent invitations to everyone in town. Worst of all, my parents think he's perfect.

I clench my fists in and out and decide I can't sit still in this anger. I'm afraid I'll explode, so I do something I've never done recreationally. I put on a pair of sneakers and run.

The sun has barely made it over the horizon, meaning it's around three in the morning in Idaho. Walter decided to video call me—for the first time since I've left—at three in the fucking morning. As if I was the afterthought that finally caught up to him before going to bed.

I don't focus on anything as I take off into a full-blown sprint in the middle of the street. I'll run all the way to the other end of Florida if that's what it takes to feel slightly better about my life's circumstances. But I'm winded by the time I make it to the stop sign at the end of my street. I clutch at my knees to keep myself from falling over.

"*Now* it's a good morning," a husky male's voice says from behind me.

I glare over my shoulder at a chipper Grayson, who's sporting loose black joggers and sneakers. No shirt. His hair looks like he just ran his fingers through it, except for one strand that falls onto his forehead.

"If you're this breathless now, I can only imagine what

would happen if I ever got my hands on you." He smirks. "Perhaps I'll buy you an inhaler for such an occasion."

I have no words.

He bends at the waist and easily touches his toes for several seconds. He does a range of stretches, never saying another word to me. I just watch, trying to catch my breath and think of a clever comeback to put him in his place, but words don't come to me at this moment.

"Kidding. That would be a very unneighborly thing to say." He grins. "And you're gasping for air because you didn't pace yourself. Running isn't always about speed, and if you start off going as fast as you can, well—" He gestures to me and the state I'm in. I straighten self-consciously.

"I always start off slow. At first, it feels like I'm doing nothing, and I want to increase my speed. But after a few minutes I'm dripping in sweat." He continues to stretch by going up and down on the tips of his toes.

The picture he paints is unwelcomely vivid in my mind, with sweat gleaming on his skin, highlighting every unfair inch of his impressive body.

"Want to run with me?"

"No."

"Let me rephrase that. I would like it if you ran with me." He gives me a look I can only describe as puppy dog eyes. "Please?"

"*No.*"

"Why? You were going to run anyway."

"You're going to point out everything I'm doing wrong."

He stares at me for a moment, his typical grin is absent, like my honesty caught him by surprise. "I'll let you know if your posture is going to cause shin splints or if you're about to trip from a pothole in our poorly paved road, but I would never judge you or be a know-it-all prick." He smirks. "If you want me to get down on my knees and beg, it's not above me."

I give him a pointed look, to which he slowly kneels down so his knees are on the asphalt. "Macy Brookes, will you make me the happiest man in the world…" He grins, and I fight back my own at how ridiculous this is. "And run with me on this lovely morning?"

Instead of responding to that, I touch my toes like he did. After about ten seconds I straighten to go into the next stretch I saw him do. There's a smile etched on his face.

We don't say anything else to one another. He's starting into a slow jog that matches the speed of a brisk walk. I match his pace beside him. It's only a short amount of time before sweat starts beading on my forehead and my lungs beg me to catch my breath.

"Once you push through the initial desire to stop it'll get easier. Stay with me, Mace." There he goes again with the nickname that seems to roll off his tongue with ease.

I find a glimpse of will power and push myself to keep running, even though every instinct is telling me to stop. I mark a palm tree in the near distance and decide that I'll finish once I reach it, but before I even come close, that willpower slips, and I stop. The muscles in my legs are on fire and all my huffing and puffing could blow down that Little Pig's brick house.

"You made it way farther than I did my first time running," Grayson says easily, not even slightly winded.

I don't have the lung capacity to answer.

"You can walk to keep your heartrate up. It'll help with your stamina." He ambles back to our houses. I continue beside him, trying to pull enough air into my lungs. "Not that you don't look *great* in those pjs, but I think next time athletic clothes would suffice."

I look down at myself. In my elegant fit of rage, I didn't change out of what I slept in. I'm wearing cotton shorts, which is nothing short of a miracle given that I never sleep in anything besides underwear and a T-shirt.

Since I don't have the breath to express it vocally, I shoot him my middle finger. He playfully tosses it away with his hand, but I don't miss the surge of electricity shooting through my body from the brief contact.

If you're this breathless now, I can only imagine what would happen if I ever got my hands on you.

My cheeks heat.

Coming into view of our houses, he says, "Come inside, I'll make you breakfast."

"That's okay." I turn toward him. "I normally just have coffee."

His right eyebrow shoots up. "Yeah, that's not going to work. You'll pass out in that house all by yourself, and I'd feel sort of guilty I hadn't insisted you ate after running."

"Fine. But only because your house is closer to me, and my legs are about to give out."

He chuckles. "I'll take it."

Once we're inside, I toe off my shoes since everything is so pristine. He gestures for me to make myself at home on his couch but I'm sweaty and gross, so I sit on the barstool.

Grayson moves with a certain type of grace, bouncing back and forth between scrambling eggs, cooking bacon on another pan, and toasting two bagels.

He pulls a matte black mug from the cabinet and places it beneath his coffee maker, which is far from simple. He has one of those expensive espresso machines you'd find in a café.

I have no idea how it works, but he's moving swiftly, like he uses the appliance every morning. His ability to mindlessly multitask is an elegance in itself.

He's careful with the steaming mug, holding the handle and securing the bottom with his other hand. It's filled to the brim, and when he places it on the counter before me, brown liquid spills over the top. I lean over and sip it with a loud slurp, nearly burning my tongue in the process. A delightful flavor coats my tastebuds. This is the best coffee I've had, and that's saying a lot, considering I've been to every café within the vicinity of my house to write.

"This is delicious," I say with foam on my top lip. I swear his eyes drop as I lick it away.

"Careful, Mace, I think you accidentally complimented me."

"I was merely noting the excellent taste your fancy machine created." I stick my nose higher in the air.

He vibrates with a soft chuckle, plating the meal he prepared. After setting the dish before me, he grabs another from the cabinet, and I note it's the only other plate he owns. When it's filled with food, he sets it beside me. The ceramic is chipped on his plate, but mine is perfectly whole, and I realize he gave me the better one.

He ambles around the counter. The stool's legs squeak against the floor and his body heat is touching the entirety of my left once he's seated.

I can hear Walter's hateful words ricocheting inside my head as I eat. My heart is pumping faster, and frustrated tears prick my eyes. I can't let them fall in front of the man beside me. Knowing him, he will ask me what's wrong and somehow figure it out without me saying a word. But my emotions are running wild in this place of comfortability. And not this house. I mean Grayson sitting beside me. Despite how irritating he is, he makes me feel *safe*.

I urge the shine from my eyes and once I'm successful I clear my throat. "You cook?" I ask. I take the last bite and set my fork on the empty plate, causing it to clatter.

He watches me through thick eyelashes. "Only breakfast items and peanut butter and jelly."

"Is that why you order takeout so often?"

He raises a brow. "Only a stalker would know something like that, Mace."

I bite my cheeks. The only reason I know is because Sarah told me, but if I tell him that, he'd learn I was talking about him. I don't say anything. Instead, I reach for his empty dish to take to the sink. He grips my forearm, his touch surprisingly gentle. "I'll take care of that," he says.

Like once before, this page seems to get ripped from our story and folded into a different one. One where he's not removing his hand and I'm not asking him to. His thumb gently swipes across my skin, making me shiver with goosebumps. Our gazes catch for a moment, then my eyes drop to his adams apple that bobs as if he's just swallowed.

Instinctively, I tuck in my bottom lip to wet it. His eyes track the movement, and when they flit to mine, they seem to have darkened.

"Stop looking at me like that, Mace, because I'm two seconds away from forgetting you're engaged to another man and hauling you on top of this counter."

I should react to his words as if they were a threat, but instead my breath catches. Everything else falls away. It's only Grayson, his hand on my arm, and my imagination running wild.

"You're self-destructive." Walter's voice chastises me from the comfort of my own mind.

I blink my intrusive thoughts away, and then pull my arm from him, his fingertips brushing the length of it. "Looking at you how?" I ask as though I'm clueless. Like whatever fell over us was something innocent.

Before he can bring his guard of steel back up, something that looks like disappointment flickers across his features. His smile isn't touching his eyes when he carries our plates to the sink.

"I'll see you later," he says without looking up from soaping a sponge.

I squeeze my eyes shut for a moment then nod. I walk myself out, and as soon as I'm inside my grandparent's house, my emotions catch up to me, regardless of how fast I ran.

I don't want to marry a man who pushes my dreams to the side like they're something worthless. A person whose heinous words attempt to belittle me. Nobody deserves to be treated the way I've allowed him to.

A picture on the wall snags my attention. My grandpa looks at his wife like she's the most special sight he's ever beheld. The small, individual memories I have of them this way could be compiled into several movies. Their love was endless, and it was real. The moment lives on forever in the photo.

If my grandma was here, she would see right through the façade Walter and I put on. One look and she'd tell me to call it off. I can almost hear her voice. *"Forget about the deposit and what everyone thinks. The memories you make are all that matter in the end. Don't waste your life on someone who doesn't deserve to share it with you."*

I can't help but feel like a coward, knowing that if my

heroine were in my predicament, she would love herself enough to go out and get the happiness she deserves.

I slide down the wall, and my knees touch my chest as sobs break free. With shaky hands I reach for my phone that somehow ended up on the floor beside me. Before I lose the nerve, I send a text to Walter.

Chapter 10
Grayson

I put on my wireless headphones and do my daily stretches the next morning. Dawn is my favorite time of day, it's when the world feels entirely my own. There aren't any people outside yet, and sometimes I glimpse dolphins along the horizon as they feed.

I touch my toes, the music blaring in my ears wakes me up. I slowly stand, startled to find Macy in front of me.

I quickly tug off my headphones, putting them around my neck.

She stands on one foot, holding the other behind her to stretch her thigh muscles.

"Well, this is a pleasant surprise," I say.

"I can run alone."

"Don't be ridiculous." I copy the stretch she does and then move into another motion. She does the same.

"How did you sleep?" I ask.

"Great," she mumbles and then yawns.

"I take it we're not a morning person, are we?"

"The only reason I didn't turn off my alarm and go back to sleep is because I promised myself I'd take a nap later."

My shoulders shake with soft laughter. I roll out my ankles to get them warmed up. We stretch in silence for five or so minutes before starting our jog.

Running has always cleared my mind, but with her next to me, she's at the forefront of it. I can tell she's worn out by the second block, but she doesn't stop. She runs a little farther than yesterday before she slows to a brisk walk. I jog backward so I can face her.

Her cheeks are pink and glistening. This woman is easily the most beautiful sight I've ever set my eyes on.

"Show off," she says with a huff.

"You're doing great," I say easily.

Her glare heats my skin in sync with the grin starting in my eyes and moving down my face. "God, don't look at me like that."

Her head tilts and I know if she wasn't so out of breath, she would ask me why.

"When you look like you want to kill me, it makes me want to kiss you."

She halts, stares at me expressionless for eight heartbeats —yes, I counted—then bursts out into laughter. There's not a song that comes close to the wonderful sound. So. Fucking. Pretty.

She wipes the corner of her eyes. After a deep inhalation she says, "I'm ready."

My eyes widen and my heart speeds. "For?"

"To keep running."

My eyebrows shoot up. For a second, I thought she meant she was ready to kiss me. *Only in a fool's dream.* She darts past me into a sprint, and I chase after her like muscle memory. Once I'm running into step beside her, she speeds up. "First one to the stop sign!" she calls out.

I add to her sentence. "Earns a favor from the loser."

"Fine," she calls over her shoulder. "Nothing dirty."

"Can't make any promises." I grin. She's about a foot in front of me. I kick it into high gear and shoot past her, winning by a couple of inches.

She grips her knees, and damn, I'm winded too. We take a few moments to breathe normally.

"You're good," I tell her honestly. "Like if a grizzly bear was chasing you in Idaho, I think you'd have a pretty good chance."

She laughs and my heart stammers. "I've never encountered one, but I'm relieved to know that if I ever do, I might *not* get mauled to death." Her shoulders sag slightly. "I have a feeling a grizzly bear is faster than you. And I just lost our race."

"If we keep running together, you'll beat me. Easily."

She bites her bottom lip, I don't think she realizes she's doing it. "That's a tempting thought."

"Same time tomorrow." I head in the direction we came.

"Maybe you'll see me. Maybe you won't." She grins, and as though my vision goes straight to my heart, it skips a beat.

"Trying to keep me on my toes, Mace?"

She shrugs.

"I'll save the favor you owe me for a rainy day." I wink and she shoots me a glare.

She's right on time the next morning. We run side by side and she makes it farther without stopping than she has the last two days. Once we make it to the space where our yards connect, she turns to me with a grin and then shoots off toward the ocean.

I have to push myself to reach her, and once I do, I grab her around the waist and spin us in swift circles.

She claws at my arms when I drag us both into the biting water. I laugh into her vanilla scented hair and release her once we are shoulder deep in the ocean.

She faces me, her jaw unhinged like she's shocked by my audacity. Or maybe it's the cold. I tilt my head back and laugh, swallowing a mouthful of salt water when she splashes me in the face.

She dunks her head beneath the surface, and when she comes up, her hair is down from the ponytail she wore, like she took the blue band out underwater. The strands drip down her shoulders like silky fabric, reminding me how she looked after the sprinklers went off in the bar.

"Thought for thought?" I ask.

Her gaze is searching and I'm afraid she'll deny me but instead she nods.

"I like running early in the morning because I enjoy the quiet, but I never realized how lonely I was until three days ago, when you started running with me."

She pushes away a patch of seaweed that drifted to her before she gives me her thought. "I broke off my engagement."

It would be wildly inappropriate to smile right now. "Oh?" I say like it's a question.

"I did it over text," she admits.

"A *text*?"

"And then I blocked him before he could answer." *This just keeps getting better and better.*

"Wow." I blow out a breath, mostly to suppress my grin.

Not at her expense, but because the asshole didn't deserve her and I'm proud that she left him. I know it wasn't an easy situation to walk away from, seeing that they were engaged and living together. "Are you okay?"

She lifts a wet shoulder above the surface and then drops it, the water rippling in circles where it disappeared. "I had my whole life planned out."

"Did you like it? The plan, I mean."

"No," she whispers, then looks away. Her face is glowing gold from the rising sun. I've never truly cared for honey, but seeing the color of her eyes in the light makes me crave some.

"I don't know why I told you all of that." She looks at me with the slightest frown.

"You can tell me anything." A wave rolls in. I steady myself and accidentally brush her hand beneath the water.

She all but throws herself at me, catching me by surprise. I suck in a quick breath when she wraps her arms around my neck.

I-I can't remember the last time I was hugged. My eyes feel heavy with emotions I don't attempt to place. After too many seconds of not returning the embrace, I slowly twist my arms around her. We hold on to one another in the span of nine waves rolling past us.

She reels back with wide eyes, as though she suddenly realized it's me who she was hugging. "I'm sorry."

I don't know what to say, so I don't say anything at all. I only watch her step out of the water, and her golden, sunkissed skin makes it seem like she commands the sun. Like it shines just for her.

Chapter 11
Macy

I gasp for air. Dreams of my grandparents chase me awake. The familiar ones where we spend the day together, and every detail is so vivid that I never once question the reality of it, until moments before I wake up, and I realize how out of place they truly are. How they don't belong in this world anymore.

The image of my grandmother's smile is still so clear in my mind's eye. My grandfather reading me a bedtime story echoes as if he's only just left the room. Sobs are breaking through the silence of the night. It feels as though there is no air left to feed my lungs. The wall caging my heart has been blown to bits, leaving the organ exposed to the world.

I think of the deep blue sea. How some days, the water is so still it becomes glass, and others it rages with whitecaps so powerful, the salty water could easily replace the air of the strongest lungs. It deceives as a calm sea until a storm strikes, so similar to grief.

I slip out of bed, cold terrazzo beneath my bare feet. My chest is heavy, and tears stream endlessly down my face as I walk throughout a home that belonged to the people I mourn. I run my fingertips over the familiar texture of the hand-knit blanket my grandma made that rests over the back of the couch. She'd drape it over me when I'd fall asleep watching movies together.

A loud sob breaks free, and I barrel over in pain. My head is pounding, and I can't see anything past my tears. The walls seem to cave in on me.

I manage to open the back door with my unsteady hands. A breeze blows against my face, cooling the wet skin beneath my eyes. I grab onto the wind chime before it's sound touches my ears. I unhang it and set it down, so I don't hear the reminder of what once was. What will never be again.

I curl into fetal position on the porch swing, letting it gently rock me back and forth. I try to forget the pain, block out the truth just for a little while. I close my eyes and make up scenarios in my head like I did when I was a kid.

I used to imagine people and places and conflicts to keep me entertained during the long flights every summer. Sometimes I would continue the scenarios in my head before bed as if it were a TV series.

When I open my eyes again, I see that damn pelican. We stare at each other, and right when it cocks its head, a star draws a line across the sky in my peripheral.

I gasp, my eyes focusing on the spot the flash disappeared. Something magical fills the air. My eyes slowly drag back to the bird. "Hello," I whisper.

It's flapping it's wings as if answering me. My chest squeezes and I almost believe the bird to be a sign from my grandparents. I sigh after a few moments, realizing how ridiculous it sounds, but before the thought can fully form, I look to the left and a bright flash of light blinks into the darkness. My hand flies to my mouth and awestruck laughter falls from my lips. I smile and lift my face toward the sky.

The pelican flies toward the ocean, its silhouette is proud above the horizon, diving into the water and coming up with a tail flopping from its mouth. I laugh.

The ocean has its rough days, but it always returns to its peaceful state. Maybe I need to learn to surf the waves long enough to stay above water.

I finally have a fridge stocked with real food. The gas station snacks weren't going to cut it anymore. Once I unload my last bag of groceries, I give myself a nod of approval.

The handheld dustpan just wasn't going to work, so I bought some modern-day cleaning supplies. I play music on my phone and get to work, throwing my hair into a bun at the nape of my neck. My entire playlist runs until I'm done wiping every surface. There's not a speck of dust in sight.

I pick up my phone and find Sarah in my contacts. She answers on the first ring and is cheery when I invite her and Elliot over for dinner tonight. When we hang up, a bead of sweat drips down my temple.

I desperately need a shower, but the ocean is right outside, sparkling under the sun. I change into a bikini and grab a sheet from the closet. I bring my laptop with me so I can write.

My skin warms beneath the bright star in the sky, and I kick sand behind me with every step I make. Once I've found the perfect spot near the water, far enough so a wave can't wet my sheet, I spread it over the sand, using my flip flops to hold the corners.

Hundreds of washed up shells are digging into my bare feet as I amble toward the waves. The water moves up my legs, and once I'm waist deep, I dive in. The chill makes me breathless, but it feels refreshing after all the cleaning I did. I wade out until I feel something round and hard in place of soft sand. I dive down and grab it, and once I break the surface, I smile at the white sand dollar taking up the palm of my hand.

I swim back to shore. I place the fragile sand dollar on my sheet and lay flat on my stomach. The sun beams onto my exposed back. I open my laptop and edit fifty pages by the time I need to get ready for dinner.

Once I'm out of the shower, I throw on denim shorts and a black baby T-shirt. I let my hair air dry into its natural waves and drag a wand of mascara through my eyelashes. The freckles dusting my nose and cheeks are darker, and I have a slight tan for the first time in years.

I'm about to throw the burgers on the grill out back when Sarah and Elliot pull up on their bikes. "Back here, guys!" I call.

Sarah rests her bike against the porch. She pulls a bottle of vodka and cranberry juice out of the basket. Elliot's following on his wife's heals as she climbs the steps. He wraps an arm around her waist and places a kiss on the crown of her head before getting cozy on my porch swing.

Sarah's eyes always seem to smile, but now it's spreading to her lips. She gives me a hug accompanied by the smell of coconuts. "Long time no see. Oh, and I saw Dracula leave shortly after you at The BARnacle the other day," she says while raising her brows. "Did he catch up to you?"

"Unfortunately," I say, leaving out the part about how

we've been running together for the past three mornings, and how I'm starting to enjoy his company.

She ambles toward her husband, joining him on the swinging bench. "You just let me know if he's bothering you."

Elliot chuckles. "And what will you do?"

She flexes her bicep, and Elliot's eyebrows raise. I should get her workout routine, but we're just lucky I've stayed consistent with running. I'm not one who enjoys lifting weights.

I chortle. "He's not bothering me. Well, he irritates me sometimes, but not in the way that requires your Super Woman strength." I turn the dial on the grill, but nothing happens. I twist it several times before sighing. "I think the grill is dead."

"Where's the propane?" Elliot asks.

I frown. "You need propane?"

"Probably," Sarah says. "Or that thing is older than us and probably doesn't work."

"I guess I can make the burgers on the stove," I say. I wanted to have a barbecue, though.

The side of my face prickles. I glance over and see Grayson on his porch with my book in his hand. He grins and waves at me. I ignore him, or maybe I'm trying to ignore what the dimples accompanying his smirk does to me.

"You know that guy?" Elliot asks.

"That guy has a name," I say, a touch defensive. "And yes, I know Grayson," I say, forgoing the nickname Sarah assigned to him. I mess with the barbecue, trying to get it to work.

"Dracula is your *neighbor*?" Sarah says a touch too loud.

My cheeks warm. "Shh!" I peek at Grayson, who's oblivious to our conversation.

"Now I really need to know why you were avoiding him

the other night, since you say he's not bothering you." She grins, her eyes squinted on me like she's working out an equation.

"I told you. He's irritating."

She glances at her husband, still smiling knowingly. "No, you said he irritates you, not that he's irritating."

"That's the same thing," I deadpan.

She elbows her husband for backup, to which he shrugs.

"Well, he has a grill," Sarah notes. I give her a questioning look. She shrugs. "Yours is broken, and your *neighbor* doesn't look like he's got anything going on. Let's ask if we can use his."

"I'm sure he's busy—"

"He's always by himself; I'm sure he'd like the company. Besides, he's only reading." She stands and waves before I can protest. "Grayson! Mind if we come over there and make you some burgers?"

He glances at us, solemn momentarily. His head tilts to the side and then he gestures for us to come with the wave of his hand.

I quietly groan and shoot Sarah a look. She shrugs with a smile and grabs the alcohol. I squeeze my fists at my sides before I grab the stuff to make the burgers, taking my time as I do so.

"How long have you lived here?" Sarah asks Grayson as I climb his porch steps. But before he can answer, I step on the back of my flipflop and nearly trip, but Grayson is quick to grab me beneath my arms. *Why is this man always catching me? And why am I always falling around him?*

I glance up at him and for a moment it's just him and I and unwelcome feelings brewing beneath my skin.

"Hey man, thanks for letting us intrude," Elliot says.

Grayson releases me to shake Elliot's hand, then claps him on the shoulder. "I'm Elliot, and the woman asking you a million and one questions is my wife, Sarah."

She shrugs. "I want to get to know the new guy in town. Sue me."

I let them talk while I start on the burgers. Grayson's grill is shiny and new. I wonder if it's ever been used before now. I feel a hand on the small of my back. Grayson's breath touches the shell of my ear. "I'll grab you some tongs."

I quickly notice that even with Sarah and Elliot sharing a seat, there's only one chair left.

Back with a pair of tongs, Grayson carefully hands them to me. The tips of my fingers brush his and he quickly clears his throat. "I'll just be inside," he says wryly. He turns to walk away but I quickly reach out.

Before I realize what I'm doing, his hand is in mine. "Stay. Meet my friends," I say so only he can hear.

He stares like he's trying to read me. "If that's what you want."

"It is."

He nods, then backs up and sits on a chair across from Sarah and Elliot.

"Do you drink vodka and cranberry?" Sarah asks him.

"Sure," he says.

"You want any?" Elliot asks me.

I nod. I feel like I'm going to need a drink or two tonight.

I turn on the grill and start cooking the patties. Elliot starts pouring our drinks. He places two on the patio table and Grayson grabs one. I feel the heat of his stare as he's walking over to me. He puts the cup in my hand.

I take one large swig. "Is there even any cranberry juice in this?" I laugh, scrunching my face in disgust.

Grayson lifts an eyebrow, takes my cup out of my hand, and slowly brings it to his lips without breaking eye contact. "I think he's trying to get you drunk," he says.

"No offense, Macy, but you seem like you can use some… loosening up." Elliot calls from his chair.

Sarah laughs.

I scoff at them. "I am plenty loose—"

Grayson's teeth skim his bottom lip to hide his amusement. I shoot everyone a look. "Whatever. You can expect your burgers to have spit in them."

I pad by Grayson to the empty chair and collapse onto it while the burgers cook. The smell of burning charcoal fills the air. I swish the vodka around in my mouth, having a hard time swallowing it. I place my cup on the table.

Grayson still stands by the grill, as if he's unsure of what to do with himself. Where he fits. I clear my throat to get his attention and scoot over so there is space on the chair.

His expression doesn't shift, but I see his chest slowly rising as if he's taking a deep breath. He saunters over and places his palm over my knee to lower himself. I stiffen once he's beside me, so much of our bodies touching one another. He drapes his arm over the back of the seat, and then he turns to me and says so only I can hear, "I'm not going to bite you, Mace."

I don't want him to know how much his proximity unnerves me. I glare at him and slowly relax my body. The base of my neck rests against his arm.

I hear a photo being taken. I swivel my head forward to see Sarah lowering her phone. I shoot her a pointed look.

"What? You guys are funny with his smug expression and your evil glare."

Elliot chuckles.

"I'll send it to you later," she whispers with a wink.

I feel myself blanch.

"So…" Elliot changes the subject. "Where are you from?" he shoots that question toward Grayson since he already knows us.

I feel his arm flex for a moment before it relaxes. "Fort Meyers."

"Oh, so not far from here." Sarah says.

"Where are you guys from?" Grayson says, as if he's trying to get the attention off himself.

"We're all from here. Well, except Macy. Technically she's from Idaho but she's just as much from here as we are. She lived here during the summers. We grew up together, actually," Sarah says. "Oh, and you have such a nice house by the way. Most of the ones here aren't modern like yours. What do you do for a living?" Sarah's conversation style gives me whiplash with every direction it goes.

Grayson talks a little bit about his job, and once he's finished, Sarah says, "Macy is an author."

He slowly turns to me with a grin. "No kidding."

"Yup," I say, since he clearly knows this already, and I'm not fond of Sarah trying to play wing woman. She means well though. "I'm going to flip the burgers," I say, about to stand.

"I've got it." Grayson gets to his feet by using his ginormous hand to hoist himself up on my knee.

Sarah and Elliot start talking among themselves, so I take the opportunity to watch Grayson flip the burgers. He's wearing all dark colors, making him look like a storm cloud. Wispy pieces of hair are sticking out from his hat, and his toned arms flex as he works the burgers. He's all rigid and sharp lines, making everything about him masculine. He closes the grill, forcing my gaze on his hands. I can feel his phantom touch against my torso, his palm taking up most of the space.

His eyes immediately shoot to mine, as if he could hear my thoughts. Something about the way he's watching me feels intimate, as if he's running those hands across my skin and memorizing the dips and curves of my body.

Fire creeps into my cheeks and I look away, realizing Sarah is watching. Suddenly she's standing up grabbing my hand. "Let us know when the burgers are ready," she says.

I'm unable to protest when she tugs me down the porch steps and toward the shore. Once we are far enough that the boys can't hear, she says, "No judgment here…but are you cheating on your fiancé with Dracula?"

"No!" I say defensively.

Sarah holds her hands in the air. I sigh, sitting down in the sand and bringing my knees to my chest. Sarah does the same. "I'm not engaged anymore. I broke it off." I tell her about the text I sent to Walter and the conversation we had over video chat, and then I find myself spilling everything he's ever done wrong.

"Screw that man. Wait no…" She looks around, considering her words for a moment. "*Boy*," she corrects. "I think this vacation is exactly what you need." She turns around and I follow her line of sight to Grayson, who's sitting across from Elliot. His hands move while he talks, and it brings a sense of pride to see him break out of his shell.

Sarah grins at me. "Maybe you need a steamy fling with Dracula."

I laugh. "Never."

"Can I give you some advice?"

I nod.

"I wouldn't be too quick to shoot down whatever is

happening between you and Grayson. That brooding vampire looks at you like he's *obsessed*." She stands and says, "I think you could use some of that right now." She winks, then walks back to our small group, her short hair bouncing as she goes up the steps.

I hoist myself up, wiping the sand off my butt and rinsing my hands in the water. Remembering Grayson's lack of dishes, I make a quick trip to my house to grab two extra plates.

I notice a new chair on Grayson's back deck, one of his barstools. He brought it outside so we wouldn't have to share the seat. The three seem to be falling into easy conversation. Sarah is laughing at something Grayson says, and I can't help but realize how natural he fits in. Like he's been the missing link in our group all along.

When I'm within reach, I hand him the extra dishes. The four of us eat and talk easily, and I find myself laughing more than I have in a long time.

Once we finish, I take all the plates to Grayson's sink and wash them. He follows me inside shortly after, grabs a dirty dish and takes the sponge from my hand. He starts scrubbing, so I open his dishwasher to unload it, but there are only two mugs, a bowl, and a spoon. "Wow, you've really been living it up," I tease, grabbing the dishes and opening cabinets until I find the appropriate ones where they belong.

The sliding glass door squeaks open, followed by Elliot's voice. "Hey, Macy, do you remember when you and I won Manhunt and Sarah pushed me off my grandma's dock?"

I let out a laugh. "She was never good at losing."

"No one is *good* at losing," she recalls. "I want a rematch."

"Bring it on, Presley." Elliot says, calling her by her maiden name like he did when we were kids.

"What's Manhunt?" Grayson asks.

"You've never played Manhunt as a kid?" Elliot asks.

Grayson shakes his head.

"You can be on the winning team then." He smirks. "With Sarah and I."

"Hey!" I complain.

"Macy has to hide outside while we count to one hundred. It's basically hide and seek. The three of us will split up and find her. Once someone does, they have to hide with her and try not to be found. So as soon as you find someone, you join their team. The last person to find everyone loses."

Once we finish cleaning up, everyone gathers inside while I find a hiding spot. I already have the perfect one in mind. I sprint a few yards to the lifeguard stand, sand getting kicked up and hitting the back of my legs. There is a smile on my face when I duck beneath the stand and bring my knees to my chest to make myself as small and hidden as possible.

The sky catches fire and ignites the water beneath it, at least that's how it looks. Magical things happen at sunset. My skin tingles and a jolt of excitement shoots through me like it did when I hid as a kid.

The artwork hanging in the sky keeps changing and by the time I hear faint footsteps, the sun has just hidden beneath the horizon. Everything has a purple hue, and it won't be long until it's completely dark. I squeeze my eyes shut, hoping whoever it is doesn't spot me right away. I peek behind me to see if they left. My hand flies to my chest.

Grayson's breath trickles against my lips. "Caught you." His voice comes out low. I swallow and his gaze flickers to my throat. "Scoot over, Mace."

"Why?" I whisper.

He chuckles and the frequency of it touches every inch of

my skin. "Aren't those the rules? Once I find you, I get to hide with you?"

"Oh, right. Yes."

He's paradoxically too close, yet too far. His face gets impossibly closer, the tip of his nose skims mine. I suck in a breath when he climbs over and sits beside me, so he's hidden.

Painted in shadows, he looks nightmarish, except for the dimple peeking out of his cheek. It truly doesn't belong on such a sharp face, yet it makes my heart stammer.

He reaches out and brushes his thumb across the corner of my lip. "Sand," he supplies.

"How would there be sand on my—"

He interrupts me, pressing his pointer finger against my lips. "Keep quiet. You wouldn't want us to get caught, would you?"

I shouldn't breathe so heavily.

He takes his finger away from my lips and drags his knuckles along my jaw. He tucks a stray hair behind my ear.

Suddenly, I see a light getting closer. A flashlight. I hear Sarah's giggling and I stiffen.

Grayson reaches forward and grabs a bleached piece of coral from the sand. I don't have the chance to ask him what he's doing. It thuds off something in the distance, then Sarah's footsteps go toward the sound. Away from us.

I face him then. My eyes have adjusted to the darkness enough to see him, but everything surrounding us has turned black without the sun. I can see the stubble on his face and the veins pulsing on his temple this close.

He wears a serious expression. Gone are those heart-warming dimples. My stomach is flipping the way it does moments before the jump scare in a horror film. My heartbeat slams against my ears so rapidly. The second my eyes drop to his lips, his tongue swipes across them, leaving them glistening. His right dimple appears. Then the left. "You're staring at my lips, Mace."

"No, I'm not."

"You want to kiss me," he rasps.

"I would never want that."

"No, you don't *want* to want it." He's closer. "But you do." I gasp as his lips angle down to mine, making soft contact but not pressing. "I'm not going to kiss you, Macy," he whispers.

Warmth erupts in my stomach.

"I won't do anything to you unless it's your decision." His eyes flit to mine. "All you have to do is apply a little pressure and you can have me. Any way you want." He sounds desperately pleading when he says, "Just kiss me."

He lets out a deep sound when my mouth parts, and I flick my tongue across his bottom lip. He pulls back for a moment; every emotion one can feel seems to swim in his eyes. He slides his hand beneath my shirt, his callouses scrape against my back, and then he pulls me to him.

The warmth in my belly presses lower when he folds himself over me, my back against the sandy Earth and his weight pressing in all the right places. His lips skim over my jaw, and he nibbles my earlobe, coaxing a sound from my lips.

I want more.

I arch my hips into his, feeling just how much my feelings are reciprocated. He cups my jaw, his eyes waterfalling into mine. "So beautiful," he whispers.

"I think they're under the lifeguard tower." Elliot's whisper is loud enough for us to hear.

I push Grayson away and sit up right as the spotlight

lands on us. I squint my eyes against a flashlight, feeling the flush in my cheeks.

Another flashlight hits us, followed by Sarah's laugh.

Elliot says, "You lose, Presley. I found them first."

"Do you want to sleep on the couch tonight?"

Elliot clears his throat. He looks between us and his wife. He sighs. "Sarah won. Sorry guys."

I force a laugh, crawling out from under the tower and brushing sand off my butt.

Sarah brings her fingers to my waves. "How did you manage to get sand in your hair?"

My face heats down to my neck. "How weird."

"I think we're going to call it a night," Sarah says. "Thank you for dinner, Macy. And thanks for letting us use your grill." She aims the last sentence to Grayson.

"Any time. Nice meeting you guys," Grayson says like nothing is amiss.

Elliot hands him his phone to input his contact information. We say our goodbyes, and I watch my friends become smaller and smaller as they walk away. Once I'm alone with Grayson, I can't think of anything to say. It's as though a bucket of ice water was poured over our previous moment.

He sits down in the sand. "It's peaceful out here," he says. "If you're in no rush to leave, I'd thoroughly enjoy your company." He grins.

I can still feel his hands on my body. He's gotten under my skin from the moment we met but now I can't shake him. He covertly implanted himself within me, and I've realized too late because now I seem to burn everywhere, which is unacceptable.

Grayson is a maddening itch I can't scratch.

"I'm exhausted. Have a good night," I mumble. *Have a*

good night? Who says that after what we just did? I drag myself from him and pull all my clothes off the minute I'm inside my house. I turn the shower on cold, and the wind gets knocked out of me the second I will myself beneath the stream. I'm scrubbing away the fire from Grayson's touch, but it doesn't do anything to stop my swirling thoughts. Once I'm tucked in bed, my silly, stupid heart hijacks my brain. I dream of how good it would feel to scratch that itch.

Chapter 12
Grayson

I stand in my front yard, where Macy and I meet every morning. I hardly slept last night. I'd never felt more alive than when her lips were on mine, and it took every ounce of restraint to not knock on her door and pick up where we left off.

Usually she's here by now, so I decide to start stretching without her. I glance at her house several times. Minutes go by before the front door finally opens.

My grin quickly falls when I see wires hanging from her ears. *She's wearing headphones.* She merely glances at me before stretching, then she shoots off into a jog. I follow right beside her. "You seem chipper this morning," I say. She either ignores me or can't hear, which I realize was her intention of wearing the headphones.

This is our routine for three mornings.

I can't take the silence between us any longer. I grab her hand to still her running and she glares at me. I roll my eyes and grab the ear bud out of her ear.

She tries to grab it, but I hold it out of her reach. She

yanks on the wire which causes it to slip out of my hand, but she doesn't put it back in her ear, so I consider it progress.

"What's going on?"

She states the obvious and says, "We're running."

"I know that, smartass." She doesn't supply me with anything else, so I say, "I knew things would change between us after you kissed me." I don't want things to change, at least not in the way that they have.

Her eyes widen as if she never expected me to bring it up. "I didn't kiss you."

I grin. "I knew you'd say that."

She's squeezing her fists, the first sign she's getting irritated.

"I think we can both set our pride aside for a moment and acknowledge the fact that you did, in fact, kiss me." I look off into the distance, remembering it. "I mean, you *really* kissed me."

She turns from me and starts running, so I match her pace beside her. "You've hardly acknowledged me since." It feels like my chest has been punched out. "You regret it." I stop running. So does she.

"How could I regret something I didn't do?"

"Fine, Macy. You didn't kiss me. *I* kissed *you*. Does that make you feel better?"

"Slightly."

"Okay, if that's how you want to see it, but you kissed me back."

She shrugs. "What are you, twelve? Who cares, it was just a kiss."

I chuckle at the way she tries to downplay what happened between us. "If Elliot didn't find us when he did, we both would've had our clothes off and gone home with sand in some really awkward places."

Pink creeps into her cheeks and she looks away. "You…"

"Me?" I bite back another smile, remembering a similar conversation in New York.

That must set her over the edge because she faces me then, anger and distain pulling at her expression. She marches forward and pokes me hard in the chest. "You presumptuous prick! I would never have sex with you, let alone desperately beneath a lifeguard tower like some hormonal teenager!" she shouts.

"Okay, I'm sorry." I hold my hands up, but she doesn't look any less angry. "I shouldn't have said that—"

"Just when I was starting to think there were layers to you, you just proved that you're everything I assumed you to be from the moment we met." She marches past, her hair swinging behind her while she walks away from me.

I feel her words in every part of myself and it hurts. She despised me before, but now I've managed to make her *hate* me.

Chapter 13
Macy

I went online and bought a treadmill that morning because I'm not going to let Grayson take away my newfound love for running. *Wow. That's a sentence I never thought I'd say.*

Every time I'm able to run just a little farther, it gives me a sense of confidence. Plus, it helps my creativity, which is useful given that I'm an author.

I abhor how much I lust to feel Grayson's touch on my skin. I despise myself for how quickly my feelings are growing for him. I barely know him, yet I nearly turned into a puddle at the sight of his dimples, so much so that I *kissed* him. It's exactly the sort of thing I promised myself I'd never do after my relationship with Walter.

When I told Elliot about the treadmill I bought second-hand, he insisted on coming with me to pick it up. I didn't interject, since I had to go to a stranger's house to get it. I was glad to have Elliot with me to deter any weirdos from being, well, weird. And he has a pickup truck, so that helped.

Sarah met us back at my house and we drank wine while I set it up, and by set it up, I mean plugged it into the wall. We laughed and got wine drunk, playing games, and catching up on each other's lives.

Occasionally, I'll catch a glimpse of Grayson's house through my open windows, and deep down I wanted him to be here, drinking and playing charades with my friends. I blamed that silly thought on the alcohol.

The following week was spent in a similar fashion. I ran on my new treadmill, but it wasn't the same as running outside beside Grayson. I found myself missing his arrogant comments. I worked at the dinner table until my fingers cramped and my eyes ached. Then I'd hangout with my friends.

Tonight, I'm hosting Sarah and Tammy for a girl's night. We're sitting on my back porch and picking at my sad attempt of a charcuterie board. I even strung star shaped string lights along the porch to give it some life. One of the stars occasionally flickers, but I think it gives the space some character.

"Your grandma would be happy you are staying here," Tammy says.

"Yeah." I smile. "She would." I glance at the crescent in the sky, which was my grandma's favorite moon phase.

Later into the night, right as my guests are beginning to leave, the irksome pelican shows up on my porch railing. Tammy lets out a laugh.

"What?" I ask.

"I'm just surprised that bird still comes here."

"What do you mean?" Sarah asks.

Tammy shakes her head. "Macy's grandfather fed him like he was his pet." She looks at me. "Your grandma reprimanded him for it, but after a while, I think she started liking the bird. I caught her 'dropping' food off the porch a few times when it came by."

"How do you know it's the same one?" Sarah asks.

"It's injured," Tammy says.

I squint my eyes and notice he isn't putting his weight on his left foot.

"Your grandpa named him Ivin," Tammy says, grabbing her purse. She walks down the porch steps. "Thank you for a pleasant evening, ladies, but it's way past this old hag's bedtime."

"I think I'm going to call it a night too," Sarah says.

Once they leave, I grab the bottle of wine, three empty glasses, and my charcuterie board. I balance all the items and manage to open the sliding glass door, but once I'm inside, I have to set the bottle down or everything will slip from my grasp. I place it on the closest thing I can reach, the shelf of my grandparent's ocean treasures.

I jump from the sound of glass shattering. I slowly look down to find a pile of broken sand dollars, cracked starfish, broken glass, and spilled wine. I can't do anything besides freeze, as if I can stop time from moving forward.

My grandparent's favorite thing in this house was the collection, and in one fell swoop, I destroyed it. I bend down to see if anything is salvageable. The only item that didn't break is a bleached piece of coral. I flip it over and a sob leaves me. It's stained by the wine. I toss it with a frustrated cry.

I curl into the fetal position and weep, not caring how loud I'm being. I think about that summer before they died. How Walter told me to stay in Idaho and I listened. How my knees met the concrete of our garage four months later when I got the call that a drunk driver went eighty miles an hour into my grandpa's truck, who was sitting in it at a red light.

He was a minute from returning home to bring my grandma flowers like he did every Saturday for over fifty years.

I felt numb when I answered the phone the next day, and the person on the other line told me that my grandma had a heart attack from the news. I remember rushing to the airport, and right as I made it to my terminal, it was too late. She was already gone.

I'm unable to breathe past the splintering pain in my chest. My head throbs and I squeeze my eyes tight.

I startle when I feel a gentle touch on my cheek. My eyes shoot open.

Grayson is crouched in front of me. His eyebrows pull together, and I've never seen him look so serious. "Breathe, Mace," he says tenderly.

I try to take a deep breath, but I can't stop the sobs that leave me.

He pulls me off the ground beneath my arms and then folds me into the warmth of his embrace. My cheek presses against his chest and the rhythm of his heart beneath my ear soothes me, but I can't help but notice how fast it beats.

I don't know how long I'm in his arms, but eventually, once my breathing has slowed and I'm no longer crying, he asks in a voice that promises death, "Did someone hurt you?" He stiffens the longer I take to answer.

"No." My voice comes out as a broken whisper.

"What happened? I heard you screaming and I—" He chokes on his words. "I was *terrified*."

"I broke my grandparent's collection," I whisper, gesturing to the mess. "And then grief sort of took over," I say, hoping it is explanation enough.

I feel the pad of his finger beneath my chin. His touch is surprisingly gentle as he lifts my face toward his. His breath catches when he looks at me. "You're bleeding." He quickly picks me up as if I weigh nothing. He's careful to avoid stepping on glass.

He sets my butt on the counter and grabs a roll of paper towels. He spreads my legs, steps between them, and never removes his concerned gaze. I'm stuck in a trance as his face gets closer to mine, until I feel the warmth of his breath against my skin. His eyes are on my temple, then they meet mine for a moment before a sharp pain makes me cry out. I gasp, blinking at the small shard of glass he pulled from my skin, that he now holds between his fingers. He presses a bundled up paper towel to the spot.

"How did you get inside?" I ask.

"Your front door was unlocked."

I take in his appearance. He's wearing loose sweats and nothing else. He must've jumped out of bed. He doesn't even have shoes on, and I wince at the thought of walking barefoot on the tiny white rocks in our front yards. His naked chest makes a chill lick down my spine. His body is sculpted like he lives at the gym. *Beautiful.*

He removes the paper towel and inspects the injury. "The cut isn't deep. A bandage should take care of it."

"There's some in the cabinet." I gesture to the one directly beside my head. He reaches his arm past me, causing my face to be within an inch of his exposed chest. His woodsy scent wafts around me.

He pulls back and opens the package, and then places the bandage on my temple. "There," he says in a low, raspy voice.

I had no idea there was even a cut there. The glass must've pierced my skin when I curled onto the floor. "Thank you."

He gives me a tight-lipped smile and turns like he's going

to leave. I don't know what compels me to, but I say quickly, "Stay."

His spine goes straight, and the muscles in his back flex before they relax. He slowly turns to me. The night is draping over us like a cloak. Like we're in a dream, an alternate dimension. "Have you ever lost someone?"

His jaw sets and his eyes fill with a world of pain. He doesn't elaborate once he says, "Yes."

"Recently, or?"

His gaze is faraway. "A long time ago."

I want to ask a million questions. I want to look at the mystery before me and understand everything there is to know about him. The thought alone frightens me. "Does it ever stop hurting?"

His eyes rake over me. "No."

I glance at the ruins of my grandparent's collection. My eyebrows pinch together, and an overwhelming sensation takes over at the thought of cleaning it. At throwing away the broken bits of what once was invaluable to two people. Items they spent their marriage collecting. He follows my line of sight. "Come to my house," he says, as if he knows I can't deal with the mess right now.

Thankful, I simply nod and hop down from the counter. He freezes at the sight of my treadmill. He doesn't say anything about it when we walk in silence to his front door, which is ajar, like he was in such a rush he didn't bother shutting it. He switches on the kitchen light and leads me to his couch. I sit down, and he disappears for a moment, only to return wearing a shirt.

He sits down on the opposite end of the sofa and drapes an arm over the back. I lift my knees to my chest to get comfortable. Silence stretches between us before he says, "It doesn't stop hurting." He repeats what he said in my kitchen, looking thoughtful for a moment. "But I have this theory that if you fill your life with things that bring you joy, eventually happiness becomes bigger than the grief."

"And what brings you joy, Grayson?"

Shadows are covering him, but the light from the kitchen paints the edge of his face. I feel his gaze over my entire body. "I'm still figuring that out."

"Hence why it's only a theory," I surmise.

His head dips ever so slightly.

I take in his living room, the minimalism. Pictures of friends or family are nowhere in sight. The wooden coffee table rests only one coaster.

"What are you thinking?" he asks in a voice that borders on pleading.

Between what Sarah told me and the lonely nature of his house, I wonder if he's as wounded as I am after losing my grandparents. His isolation is telling, so perhaps more. "I'm thinking that this life doesn't let a single person pass without pressing in on them." The idea leaves me hopeless, but then I look at Grayson. Like *really* look at him. In defiance of the darkness that I assume once colored him, he's still standing. "We don't break, but bits and pieces of ourselves cave in. Our souls crack. Some more than others, but we're all marked with the fractures of this world."

His eyebrows are pulling together in concentration of my words.

"And I think—" My heart cracks and I will away tears that threaten to fill my eyes. "I think the biggest challenge is learning to smile with holes in our souls."

Grayson looks away for a moment, seeming like he's digesting every word. He scoots closer to me, blue eyes shining like a sea reflecting the sun. "Your mind is marvelous." His serious demeanor crumbles as his eyes soften and wrinkle at the sides. "You should put that in a book." He grins.

I laugh easily, and Grayson's answering smile is a rainbow in a gray sky. It's my turn to ask. "What are *you* thinking?"

His head dips and his eyes lift to mine. "That everyone has a story. We're all trying our best, but the world doesn't seem to let up."

"But we can be kinder to one another." The moment I say it, my heart sinks. I look at the man sitting across from me with a new understanding.

"Why so grim?" he asks quietly, no longer smiling.

I remember the look on his face after I snapped at him. How he looked gutted. "I was so mean," I whisper into the night.

"It's nothing I didn't deserve."

I shake my head immediately. "You didn't deserve it."

"You better not go soft on me, Mace." He's closer now. "I lied before. I do know one thing that brings me joy." He breathes, reaching out to tuck a stray hair behind my ear. "Arguing with you is my greatest rapture." He's impossibly closer. "Your fire is thrilling." His voice is like liquid dripping down my skin.

There is too much space separating us, yet not enough. I want to pull him close yet push him away. His eyes darken as if he can see the thoughts clearly on my face.

I break the wave of tension consuming us by looking away and saying, "It's getting late."

He simply says, "Sleep in my bed."

My eyes widen.

"No, I mean, you sleep in my bed, and I'll sleep out here on the couch."

I tilt my head. "That's ridiculous."

"The sheets are clean." He shrugs.

"No, I mean, why would I sleep here? My bed is right next doo—" And then the image of my grandparent's collection, ruined and shattered, comes to mind and I feel my expression fall.

"My room is down the hall on the left," he says, grabbing a throw blanket off the back of his couch and getting comfortable.

"I'll sleep on the couch if anything."

"No," he says definitively, rolling on his side and shutting his eyes.

I hesitantly stand and look at the hallway, then back at Grayson. "Are you sur—"

"Go," he all but growls the words.

"Fine," I mumble. As I enter the hallway I look back. "Thank you."

His eyes are still closed when he smiles subtly.

The door to his room is already open, the bed unmade since he was laying in it when he heard my cries. I shut the door behind me and take in the simple space. His bedding is light gray, and like the rest of his house, there are no decorations. My attention snags on his bedside table, and I realize there is a tiny picture frame. I walk up to it and see that it's not a picture, but a note. Written in childlike handwriting on a piece of notebook paper says, "I love you, Grayson." The "a" in his name is backward and it is written in purple marker. A child no older than five or six must have written it.

I climb into his bed. It smells like him, and when I wrap myself in his plush comforter, my heart aches. I realize as I stare at the framed note, it was angled directly at the bed, so he'd see it before falling asleep and the moment he woke up. *I know nothing about Grayson.* As slumber washes over me, I dream of blue eyes like the ocean raging with pain of the greatest storm.

I climb out of Grayson's bed and look for the bathroom, which is conveniently right across from his room. I comb my fingers through my hair and splash water on my face. I put some mint toothpaste on my finger and rub my teeth with it.

His living room is empty, and his throw blanket is folded on the back of his couch like it was never touched.

I put on my shoes and brace myself to go home. When I open my front door, my eyes go straight to the mess. I gasp. The shelf is hanging back on the wall. As I walk further in, I see my grandparent's collection resting on a towel on the dinner table. By looking at them now, you'd never know they were shattered into pieces the night prior. There is a note that says "Don't touch. Glue is still drying." Soaking in a bowl with bleach is the piece of coral that was stained in wine.

"Oh my," I breathe out the words. Grayson did this. Determination to find the man who did this thoughtful thing for me carries me out my front door, and I run.

I probably look insane, still in my clothes from last night and wearing flip flops. The strands of hair trailing behind me in the wind are an entity on their own. I follow the path we used to run together and then I spot him wearing shorts and sneakers with sweat gleaming along his bare back. He doesn't see me, and I can't catch my breath enough to call his name, so I push myself further until I can reach him. I all but slam into his sweaty back. He quickly turns around; his alert expression relaxes when he sees that it's me.

I hold up a finger while I catch my breath. He's taking in my appearance, and when his eyes fall on my flip flops, the corner of his mouth ticks up in amusement. "Looking for me?"

I throw myself at him, wrapping my arms around his waist and burying my head in his bare chest. He stiffens, then slowly wraps his arms around me. He holds me tight, resting his chin on top of my head. "I had to find you," I whisper. "Thank you."

"I have no idea what you're thanking me for," he says. "But you're being unusually nice to me, so I'll take credit for whatever it is."

I lift my face so I can see him. "Are you always so insufferable?"

"That depends. Are you always this tangled up with insufferable men?" he rasps. "Because if so, I can be intolerable."

I peel myself from him and cross my arms. "You are so weird."

He doesn't miss a beat. "You are so pretty."

Warmth creeps into my cheeks and I hope he thinks it's from running. I clear my throat. "Anyway, I came here to say thank you. So, thank you. I'm going now." I toss my thumb over my shoulder.

He grins. "See you around, Mace."

I remember how to move my feet and begin walking the way I came. Once I get a good distance away, I look over my shoulder to see him still standing there, watching me.

"Creep!" I call, but when I turn around, I can't control the smile stretching across my face.

Chapter 14
Macy

After hours of sitting to work, walking to The BARnacle makes my legs feel warm and fluid again before sitting for dinner with Sarah. It's amazing how much stronger my muscles are now that I've started running daily.

I spot Sarah instantly, sitting at the bar and flirting with her husband. I immediately recognize the back of the person sitting beside her. As if he can feel my stare, he turns and meets my gaze.

When I approach them, Grayson's eyes sweep over me. I decided to wear something out of my comfort zone. A tight black mini skirt, black high-top Converse, and a fitted black top. I'm wearing the color he always wears.

I pull out the barstool beside Sarah and she wraps her arm around me in greeting. "You look hot," she says.

"I second that," Grayson says from the other side of her.

I lean forward so I can see him. "I wasn't expecting you to be here."

"Don't look too excited."

I grin at him, and the three of us make light conversation

for a while. When Elliot returns to Grayson for the seventh time to talk and joke around, I realize that he probably invited him here. When Sarah saw Grayson sitting at the bar, she naturally sat beside him.

We place our orders and eat our greasy food. Once we finish, Sarah says to me, "Do you remember the boy you were in love with?"

I tilt my head.

"What was his name?" she says, snapping her fingers. "The one who lived next door to you? Remember?"

"Daniel." He was my best friend when I was five or six, but he moved away before I returned one summer.

Grayson sits up straighter, his eyes set on the TV.

Sarah laughs. "I remember one night after dinner at Tammy's, I found you outside all by yourself. You were focused on the sky, and when I asked what you were doing, you said you were waiting for a shooting star so you could wish to be his girlfriend."

We both laugh so hard, tears well up in the corners of my eyes. "He was probably my soulmate." I shake my head dramatically. "No wonder I have such shit luck with men."

Sarah pulls out her phone. "What was his last name?"

"I can't remember. Why?"

"I'm looking him up."

"He's probably married with kids." I think of my old best friend, how his hair would spill across his forehead after swimming. I never got a chance to say goodbye, and every night for weeks I wept in my bed.

I wonder where he ended up. I hope life has been kind to him. "I really did love that boy, though," I say quietly. "In the way a six-year-old can." I wonder what it would be like if he hadn't left.

Graysons eyes flash to mine, a divot between his brows.

"Maybe you can help us," Sarah says to him. "You live in Daniel's old house. Do you remember the family's last name you bought it from?"

"The previous owner was a single guy." He shrugs.

Sarah sighs. "Sorry, Macy. We'll never know where your soulmate ended up."

I try to remember that little boy, and imagine how he would look now, but I can't. My attention keeps snapping to Grayson, who I've caught watching me with deep intensity.

We move past the topic quickly, and the four of us bounce back and forth between easy conversation until the place is empty. We say our goodbyes once Elliot locks up The BARnacle.

It's only Grayson and I standing outside the restaurant. He glances at the parking lot, with only one car, then the empty bike rack. "You walked?"

I nod.

"Come on," he says, placing his hands in the front pocket of his jeans and sauntering to his car. When he sees that I'm not beside him, he faces me. "If you want to walk, then walk. But I'll be in my car right behind you."

I purse my lips together. "Creep."

"It isn't safe for you to walk at this hour. It's dark." He steps closer, eating away the distance between us. "Let me take you home."

His concern for my safety is warming. "Fine."

He opens the passenger door for me and is quiet when he pulls out of the lot and onto the road. His elbow is resting on the center console, his other hand holding the steering wheel loosely. We are silent the entire way home. I turn to him right as he's about to shut off the engine. I grab his hand and say,

"Thank you again for what you did. You have no idea how much it means to me."

His eyes go to our hands, and he runs his thumb over my knuckles.

My skin breaks out into a chill. I suck in a quick breath when he brings the back of my hand to his warm lips. Eyes glued to mine, he flips my hand over and kisses my wrist. A gentle sound escapes my mouth on its own accord, and his eyes widen slightly.

He's grinning when he pulls my arm, causing me to fall into him. "Don't make sounds like that around me, Mace, because once I hear one, I'll want to coax all of them from you," he whispers.

"Is that a threat?" I hardly recognize my own voice. Lust pulls at my vocal cords in a way it never has before.

"It's a promise."

My blood runs ten degrees warmer from the heat of his stare. He leans his forehead against mine and I erase the distance between our lips without a second thought. He wastes zero time to reciprocate the kiss. My hands seem to have a mind of their own when they grip his shoulders like an anchor. His tongue brushes mine and I can't control the soft moan I make.

Suddenly, he's turning off the engine and then stepping out of the vehicle. Before I can catch my breath, the passenger door opens and he pulls me out of the car by my hands, then lifts me so I'm straddled around his waist. He holds me as if I weigh nothing, tightly gripping the underside of my thighs. He presses my back against the hard surface of his front door.

There's nothing kind about the way I take his lips in mine. My fingers slip through his soft hair and then firmly tug the roots. The idea of tormenting him as much as he's done to me since the moment we met is what fuels me to roll my hips against the hardest part of him. His groan answers me.

"Open the door." My voice is low and raspy.

His eyes are holding mine as he pushes me past the threshold. He sets me down on the closest surface, which happens to be his kitchen counter. Big hands frame my face, then he slowly trails one down the side of my neck, over my shoulder, his callouses scrape my arm until he's holding my hand. His gaze is tender, too kind. Suddenly I have no idea what to do. Unease settles in my body, and I think back to my previous sexual encounters, all of which were with Walter.

He never kissed me like this. His hands never explored my body beside the parts of me that benefited him. He never cared to ensure I was physically and mentally ready for him. He just took what he wanted.

I can feel it now, him pushing into me when I wasn't aroused. How it hurt more than felt good. I'd have sex with him because if I didn't want to, he'd scoff and make me feel bad.

He never looked into my eyes to know that they were filling with tears. I'd roll over when he was done. I remember the way it felt to mute my sobs, how much my stomach hurt from trying to contain my pain so he wouldn't hear.

A thumb swipes across my cheek, bringing me back to the present. Grayson towers over me, and his eyes are no longer glassing over in arousal. They're searching mine in concern. "What did I do? Did I hurt you?"

"No, you didn't do anything." I look away in embarrassment, but he hooks his finger beneath my chin, so my eyes are on him.

"Tell me," he pleads.

"I've never been touched like this before," I say, gauging

his reaction. "It feels so *nice*. God, I can't believe I'm crying." He watches me intently, without any judgment, so I continue. "With Walter, this sort of thing was always just for him, so I've never actually been, I don't know—*caressed*, this way."

His jaw ticks and then he pulls me to him in such a kind embrace. It's easy to forget how much he once irritated me in this moment. After a few breaths, I'm not even sure who's holding who anymore.

"It's funny, you know? I'm a romance author, yet I've never experienced anything close to what I write, especially in *that* department." I laugh. "I don't think sex is as good as the movies and books make it seem."

He pulls out of our hug, pressing his hands against the counter so he's caging my hips. His head leans down, his eyes pooling with sympathy and pouring into mine. "If I were lucky enough to be with you, I'd make you feel so good. God, I'd *worship* you. I think with you it'd be better than the movies."

My breath catches from his words, and my pulse drops between my legs. "Lucky enough?"

"Yes," he breathes the words. "I'm lucky just hearing you laugh, Mace."

"Keep talking like that, and maybe you'll be lucky enough for other things." I nearly widen my eyes from my own words. I've never been like this with my ex, but Grayson makes me feel comfortable. Bold.

"Can I ask you a question?"

I nod.

He opens and closes his mouth, as though he's trying to find the right words. "Has anyone ever given you an orgasm?"

I reel back and my shocked eyes meet his curious ones.

Heat is creeping up my neck and into my cheeks, but he is being genuine. I shake my head no.

His expression flashes with something I can't place. "Can I?"

"*What?*"

"Let me make you feel good." He cups my jaw carefully, his eyes darken. "It will be just for you."

My chest is rising and falling so drastically from his words, from the forwardness to his question. Emotions bubble to the surface as I recall all the ways Grayson has showed he *cares*. The way he handled my emotions with care the other night when I felt as though I'd drown in grief. How he slept on his couch just so I'd get a good night's sleep, and then pieced every broken piece of my grandparent's collection together. The way he held me moments ago, and how his touch is tentative yet new and exciting.

I twist the front of his shirt in my hands and pull his mouth to mine. His fingers trail up my arms and then get tangled in my hair. He groans into my mouth, and I hook my legs around his waist.

He lifts me up and I can feel us moving through his house, but my eyes are shut and our lips never part. He drops me and I land in the comfort of his bed. I bury my face in his comforter and inhale his manly scent. He's staring down at me with a look of adoration. He moves down to untie my sneakers and carefully remove them.

"I'm going to kiss anywhere you point." He lowers himself on top of me but doesn't place all his weight down. "Point," he encourages with a low voice.

I swallow, suddenly unsure of myself. I tap my cheek, and just as promised, he kisses the spot. I smile and touch my lips.

He grins and kisses me delicately. I giggle when I bend my knees so I can reach my ankle.

Feeling slightly more confident now, I point to the places I really want his lips. The spot below my ear, my collarbone, the side of my stomach. The last one tickles, and I laugh. His answering smile is endearing, and his dimples make my stomach heat. I like that he put me in control of the situation, and how good it feels to show him exactly what I want.

My eyes never leave his when I reach for the hem of my shirt, slowly lifting it up to my chest. He kisses above my bra like I directed him to, below it, above my navel, the top of my thigh where my skirt ends. He takes extra-long there, sucking the skin and then swiping his tongue across it. I can hardly catch my breath.

I feel myself getting hungrier and hungrier for what he promised me. I lift myself up on my knees and pull my shirt all the way off. I turn my back toward him, and his lips take their time exploring my spine. My voice is a broken whisper when I ask him to remove my bra.

He does so carefully, and then I slowly face him. The blue of his eyes is hardly visible behind his dilated pupils. I tap the tender peak and he takes no time laying me down. He kisses my nipple and it's pure bliss. He uses his tongue and I've never felt more alive in my entire life. I cry out, and he grins up at me as he squeezes my other breast.

He takes his time in all the places that make me moan. His lips are music against my skin and his hands are a dance. He squeezes my hips pleasantly hard.

"My skirt," I whisper. "You can take off my skirt."

He blows out a steady breath. "Yes, ma'am." He wastes zero time pulling the tight fabric down my legs. He removes my socks and I feel delightfully exposed in only my underwear. He's fully clothed. Something about the sinful contrast makes it much hotter.

He's still for a moment, then I feel his fingertips trailing along my hip bone. "What's this?"

I look down at the spot he's focused on. My tattoo. "It's a sand dollar."

His eyes flit to mine. "Why a sand dollar?"

"It's stupid."

His eyes seem to shine. "Tell me."

I sigh. "I used to collect them with my friends when I was little," I explain. "I went with Sarah to get her first tattoo and she convinced me to get one too. When I didn't know what to get, she said to think of a good time in my life. The first few summers I spent here are the happiest memories I have."

He doesn't say anything else when he presses his lips against the ink. He's strangely thorough on this one spot. Then, finally, his mouth moves down my thighs, then up, until his face is hovering above the last piece of fabric on my body. His eyes lift to mine, as if seeking permission.

I slowly trail the tips of my fingers down my stomach and then tap the cloth. He grabs my hand and presses it against the mattress, then slowly kisses me. My underwear is blocking the feel of his lips, but the pressure has me arching myself against him. "You can take them off," I whisper breathlessly.

His grip tightens on my hand before he releases it to remove the fabric torturously slow. The air is cool against my bare skin, until I feel the warmth of his breath. I prop myself up on my elbows, eyes wide at the sight of his face an inch from the most intimate part of me. This man who I met only weeks ago, yet I trust with my life. He grins up at me. "Do you want me to kiss you here?"

I'm too aroused to feel embarrassed. I nod. He watches

me through thick lashes, slowly bringing his lips down. He does so passionately, as if he were kissing my mouth. A sound I've never made before fills the room and I turn my head into the comforter, pure bliss swimming through me. His tongue sweeps over the sensitive spot. I cry out. My head is spinning. His name leaves my lips as a moan.

"Yes, Mace," he encourages.

I feel something against my entrance. I look down and see that it's his finger. I nod quickly. He curls it into me, pumping the digit in a rhythm that makes the pit of my stomach heat.

"That's it, baby. Come on my tongue."

Oh my... His filthy words are sending me over the edge, and I *burst*. Pleasure is coursing through my body and my moans fill the room. The waves slowly subside until I'm heavy with relief and all I can feel is my heart beating rapidly. Everything is dark behind my shut eyes, and I know I'm safe when I feel his hands scoop me against his chest. His arms fold around me and I smile. "Thank you," I say.

He whispers against my ear, "The pleasure is all mine." There's a smirk in his voice. I listen to his breath, mine syncing to his. Exhaustion pulls my eyes shut.

I open them sometime later and realize I'd fallen asleep. Grayson is holding me loosely, and when I look at him, his mouth hangs slightly open. His soft snore makes me suppress a laugh. It's probably midnight.

I carefully lift his arm off me and creep out of his bed. I pick up the discarded clothes that scatter his room and escape to the bathroom to put them on. The girl staring back at me in the mirror has a smile on her face.

His care in every touch was something I'd never expect from Grayson. Perhaps I've only seen the outermost layer of my neighbor. But he peeled it back and showed me more of himself. For some reason, the gentleman from tonight makes me feel differently toward the shameless, arrogant man that I know.

I can't remember why I ever disliked him. It's all incredibly confusing.

Once I'm dressed, I go home and crawl into bed with a smile resting on my face.

~

My lower back begins to ache as I work on my laptop, hunched over with not the best of posture. I mindlessly sip my coffee, going through my manuscript and completing my edits. An email notification pops up, piquing my curiosity since it is addressed to Walter. A few months ago, he signed into his email on my laptop because he spilled juice all over his. I open his mail.

Your Twinkle verification code is: 128328.

I tilt my head while opening a new browser and searching "Twinkle." My chest squeezes. *Date, meet new people, make friends.* My hands are slick as I wipe them on my pants, hesitating with my curser over the website. I inhale a deep breath and click on it, searching Walter's first and last name. His picture pops up and bile rises to my throat.

I scroll through the photos on his profile, clenching my jaw at the familiar one of him with an arm wrapped around his midsection. *My arm.* But he cropped me out of the picture from our *engagement party.* My eyes land on a single sentence that has the power to knock the wind out of me.

Account created five months ago.

I completely freeze. Paralyzed and forced to stare at the

words over and over until they lose all their meaning. Until they are just sounds echoing in my mind. I numbly close my laptop and stare at the wall with my grandparent's sea treasures. I have no idea how much time goes by, but anger is bubbling up in my chest, desperate for an outlet.

I find the bottle of wine I bought from the store and pop the cork, not bothering to grab a glass. I put it to my lips, taking several swigs until it's nearly empty. I curl up on the couch with a blanket, feeling slightly dizzy. I'm not sure how long it's been, but suddenly I look up and it's dark out. My body weighs a ton as I stand. The floor rushes up to meet me. I let out a curse and push myself back up.

Screw Walter. Screw him and his cruel words and dumb blond hair. *I hate him.*

I step into my flip flops and stumble my way out the front door.

Chapter 15
Grayson

I'm smiling as I read the very last sentence of Macy's novel. I set it down on the couch cushion beside me when I hear a muffled voice from out front. I get up and peek through the window to see Macy on my front steps, appearing to be in a heated discussion with someone. She's all alone. I swing the door open, and she wobbles a little, looking up at me wide-eyed. "Gray-son!" she slurs.

I lift a brow. "Party a little too hard did we, Mace?" I grin.

Her eyes droop in an adorable way. "There's no party." She frowns. "Not a fun one at least," she mumbles.

I open the door wider for her to come in, and she does. I look down, she's wearing two different flip flops on her feet. I watch her struggle to kick them off, and once she does, she helps herself to my cabinet, grabbing a cup and filling it up with water from my sink. "I'd love some, thanks," she says.

I chuckle. "Is there anything else I can get for you?"

"Have you ever cheated on someone?" she asks, plopping down on my couch as if it were her own. She sprawls out completely, leaving no room for me. I sit on the coffee table across from her.

"I've never had someone to cheat on."

She frowns. "That's surprising."

"Why's that?"

"How have you of all people never been in a r-relationship?" she says slowly.

"Me of all people?"

"You're hot," she clarifies.

"You think I'm hot?" I grin.

"You're tall and muscled and have a good face." She shrugs and then shoots me a pointed look. "Don't let it get to your head." She sighs. "You can't help me then."

"Because I've never cheated on someone?"

She nods quickly, leaning to the side as if she can't control her own body. *How much has she had to drink?*

"Maybe I can still help you."

She stares at me for a while, her eyes tracing my features before she says, "I was going to ask what it was about your girlfriend that made you cheat on her."

My teeth ache as I tightly clench my jaw, trying to keep my composure. "Has someone cheated on you?"

She groans. "Don't remind me."

"Wally?"

"*Walter,*" she corrects. "But yes, he cheated on me." She looks thoughtful for a moment. "Do you think it was because of my eyes?"

"Your eyes?"

"They're so big. Maybe he wanted someone with smaller eyes."

I get down from the coffee table and kneel before her. "Stop. Your eyes are lovely. I could stare at them all day and never grow bored," I tell her honestly. "If Walter slept with other women, it's because he doesn't have an ounce of respect for you. And I'm sorry if that's harsh, but it has *nothing* to do with you and everything to do with him," I say with complete conviction. "That moron doesn't deserve such an exceptional woman by his side. And you certainly don't deserve to be with a fool."

"I let him disrespect me. *I'm* the fool."

I frame her face in my hands, taking in the pretty freckles lining her nose. "You are not a fool. You have a big heart, and I know enough about you to know you wanted to see the good in him. You can't fault yourself for loving someone. You just loved the wrong person, but now you can give that love to someone who deserves it." My eyes search hers, and I realize as I capture the expression on her face, that I want it to be me.

I want to be a man worthy of her heart.

She reaches for the hem of her shirt and struggles to pull it up. I still her hand. "What are you doing?"

She leans into me, and before I can tell what she's trying to do, she kisses me. I pull away. "You're drunk, Macy."

She smiles seductively, but her eyelids droop from the alcohol. "Fuck me, Grayson." Her lips curl around the words but they are all wrong.

"No."

She winces.

"I'm not touching you right now, Mace," I say gently.

"You don't want to?"

"I'd be more than willing to take you to my bed when you are sober and if you still want to." I brush my thumb over her cheek and then grab the water she got for herself off the coffee table. "Drink this."

She takes a single sip and hands it back, so I shake my head. "Drink all of it for me please."

She slowly gulps the entire thing, wiping her top lip when she's finished.

"Come on, I'll walk you home." I stand, holding my hand out to help her up.

She interlaces our fingers, and it makes my blood heat. Once we're in her house, I ignore the sight of her new treadmill and ask which room is hers, and then walk her there. I take in the small space. She has an accent wall covered with orange wallpaper and her bedspread is sky blue. Everything about the way she decorated is so true to herself.

She pulls off her pants as if I'm not standing here. I look away until she's beneath the covers. "I'll be right back," I say, then dig through the kitchen cabinets until I find what I'm looking for. She's already snoring when I return only a minute later. I put two Advil on her bedside table with a full glass of water. I shouldn't, but I press my lips against her temple before I leave.

Once I'm in my own bed, I glance through my window facing her house. My chest aches in a familiar way.

Chapter 16
Macy

I take the two pills and chug the glass of water sitting on my bedside table. My head is pounding, and I want to lift the covers over my face and never leave. I push away the images of Walter possibly in bed with other women when we were still together. Bile rises to my throat, but it's in this very moment that I appreciate the seven-month dry spell we had. At least I don't need to worry that he gave me an STD.

Dread tugs at me. Our house is in both of our names, and I'm certainly not living with him when I go back to Idaho. I'm packing up and leaving. Good riddance.

I hesitantly climb out of bed, my head throbbing with every step. I wince. I can't edit my manuscript in this state, so I give myself the day to rot on my couch and watch dating shows.

By the time the sun is hugging the horizon, someone knocks on the door. I groan and pull the hand-knit blanket off my body. I'm wearing a huge T-shirt, cotton shorts, and fuzzy socks. My hair is surely in disarray, and I'm certain the dark circles beneath my eyes are no better than when I glanced in the mirror this morning.

I open the door to find Grayson grinning down at me, wearing his typical dark colors and a hat. I remember being with him last night, but I can't recall anything that happened.

"Yes?" I bite.

"May I come in?" he asks in a jaunty voice.

"Why?"

"Because we're friends, and friends usually invite the other in."

"We are?" I tilt my head, studying him.

He touches his chest. "I'm wounded." He crosses his arms, then leans against the door frame. He's the image of cool indifference. "Maybe 'friend' is too innocent of a word for us. We can come up with a better one over dinner, which I'm cooking for you, by the way."

I glance at the paper grocery bag resting beside his feet. My stomach growls in a not so nice way. I haven't had a single bite to eat today. "Okay..."

"Thank you, Grayson. You are the most thoughtful man I've ever met. And handsome, might I add," he says in a high-pitched voice that sounds nothing like mine. His scent wafts around me as he passes by. Heat curls up my spine.

"I would never say such a thing."

"No, but you certainly think it." He winks.

I decide to retire from the couch and sit on one of the chairs at the dinner table. I point it so it faces Grayson in the kitchen, who pulls ingredients from the bag and opens drawers and cabinets until he has everything he needs to cook. He finds a floral apron hanging in the pantry and holds it up. "What's this frilly little thing?"

"My grandma got it for me as a teenager. We baked a lot." I smile at the memory of her with flour dusted on her clothes. I always managed to get the powder in my hair.

The pastel colors contrast his dark gray shirt and black joggers. He grins at me and ties it around his neck and back. "How do I look?" He curtsies.

I chortle, hardly able to contain myself at the sight before me. I quickly pull out my phone and snap a picture. Between his towering height and the apron being made for my teenage body, it stops at the top of his thighs.

His expression softens into something genuine as I wipe the corners of my eyes, a smile still plastered to my face.

"I like making you laugh," he says.

"You make me scowl more than laugh."

"I might like that better."

"What are you making?" I gesture toward the pan he has out.

"An omelet, and if you aren't retching by the end of the meal, I'll make you pancakes for dessert." *Of course. Because he only knows how to cook breakfast items.*

I replay the events of the prior night, but most of it is hazy. I sink into my chair. "I didn't do anything embarrassing last night, did I?"

He stares at me a beat too long. "Nope." He turns his back toward me.

I have no choice but to believe him, so I move past it. Grayson cracks eggs into a bowl, some of the slimy mess gets on the countertop. It's a strange thing to smile at, but this kitchen has been clean and lifeless for years.

The counters were in a constant state of organized clutter growing up, with baked goods bought from the store and random ingredients. The sink was full of dishes since neither of my grandparents believed in using paper plates, and my entire family ate three big meals every day. I always returned home with a few extra pounds at the end of summer.

"Tell me about your family," I say as he whisks the eggs.

He stills and his shoulders tense. He doesn't say anything.

"Grayson?"

"I don't want to talk about them." His voice is thick.

Fair enough. "Okay. Tell me something else about you."

He pours the whisked eggs into the pan and then faces me. "My favorite animal is a dog."

I smile. "How many dogs have you had?"

"None." He leans against the counter with his legs crossed at the ankles and his hands gripping the edge.

I sit up straighter. "None?"

"Zero," he annunciates the word, holding up his hand to demonstrate the number. "Now you have to tell me something about you." He switches my question back onto me.

"I won't bore you with details you probably don't care for."

"Oh, I care a great deal. Go on."

I roll my eyes before pondering for a moment. "Sometimes when I finish writing and have nothing else to do, I drive to the grocery store and sit in my car."

"Why?"

"I like to people watch."

He's focused intently, like that's the most interesting thing he's ever heard.

"It's your turn again."

He grins. "You're quite eager to get to know me, Mace. If I didn't know any better, I would call this the beginning of a friendship."

"I don't truly care to know the boring details about yourself, but your voice is distracting me from the hangover," I lie.

"So, my voice soothes you?" He grins. "Then I'll do you favor and keep rambling on about myself." He waits for me to protest, and smirks when I don't. "Once, I told a couple of vacationers on the beach that it's tradition to leave a cheeseburger by the front door of my house. I said it was abandoned and that it would keep a ghost from following them home and haunting them."

My eyes widen. "Why?"

"Look who's suddenly interested in my 'boring details.'"

"Don't flatter yourself."

"I don't have to. You do it for me, and it was because I wanted a cheeseburger." He shrugs.

"That's…a little fucked up."

"No," he says matter of factly. "They thought they were participating in a fun island tradition, and I had a delicious lunch." He turns and adds ham, cheese, and some vegetables to the omelet.

My turn. "I dreamed of how I would get engaged since I was a little girl. It was supposed to be something special that I spent my life anticipating. Well, Walter put a jewelry box on the dashboard of his car while we were sitting at a gas station parking lot. He didn't even open the box or put the ring on me. I had to do it myself. So, that night, I made him a milkshake with expired oat milk and he spent the night vomiting."

Graysons jaw is unhinged, and then he tilts his head back and laughs loudly. The frequency of it touches my entire body. "How did you want to get engaged?" He plates the first omelet, then does the same thing to prepare the other.

My heart aches at the shattered dream. "Fireworks always felt magical to me. I wanted to be cuddled up on the beach watching them light up the sky on the Fourth of July or New Year's Eve." Grayson's eyes never leave mine. "Right when the finale would start, the man of my dreams would present me with a ring and whisper his proposal in my ear." I look out the window, my eyes sting. "I never wanted a huge grand gesture, just something intimate. Something that showed he knew me."

"That sounds perfect," he says kindly. "Don't lose hope on that dream."

Our gazes catch and twirl between us like a dance. He's the first to break it.

He balances two dishes in his hands. His biceps flex and I take notice of the veins in his arms. Once he sets mine on the table before me, my mouth fills with water. Steam is rolling off the top. "If you're as good at making omelets as you are at driving me insane, then this seems pretty promising."

He gives me a sarcastic smile and sits beside me, apron still on. He probably forgot he was wearing it, and I wonder if I could get him to go out in public with it on.

I cut into my eggs, the cheese stretches and pulls until I rip it with my fingers. I take a bite and feel my eyes widen. This is the best omelet I've ever had. I feel his stare and shoot him a look.

"Good?" he surmises.

I'd rather not add to his inflated ego. "It's…decent."

"Lies."

I shrug.

"Your eyebrows raise."

I tilt my head.

"Just noting the tells of when you lie."

"Okay, weirdo." I take another bite. So does he. We eat in comfortable silence, like two people who have known each other forever.

Once we are finished, he rests his chin in the palm of his hand and watches me for a moment. "I don't have your number."

"Okay…"

He chuckles. "I'd like to have it. Should I ever find myself needing sugar, I could send you a text rather than walk all the way to your front door."

I roll my eyes and bite back a smile that threatens to overtake my face. I look at him pointedly with my hand out. Once I have his phone, I input my information and he takes it from me quickly, like I might change my mind and erase it.

"I'll need a contact photo, so I know which Macy Brookes this is."

"Because you just so happen to know another?" This time I do smile, and so does he.

"Perhaps." He points his phone at me, and I flip him off right as he snaps the photo. His lips curve as he stares at the picture of me. "Lovely." He sets down his phone and then claps his hands together. "Pancakes?"

I stand and take our empty plates to the sink, feeling his gaze on my back as I peek inside the bag he brought. "No chocolate chips?" I turn to him with a frown.

He shakes his head.

I trace his masculine frame. His long legs sprawl out, and as if he can feel my stare, he crosses them at the ankle. I ask, "Maybe we can go to the store and get some?" I don't care if we have chocolate chips or not, I just want him to go out wearing my apron.

His eyes narrow on me. "Sure," he says.

I bite back my smile and pad to my bedroom to change. I comb my hair and tie it into a ponytail, then splash some water on my face. Back in Grayson's presence, who waits patiently by the front door, like a dog waiting to be walked, I step into a pair of flip flops. I feel him behind me, his woodsy fragrance far too potent. I lean my head back a hair and it meets his hard chest. Warmth touches the shell of my ear as he whispers, "Do you want to walk or drive there?"

It's a simple sentence, but I'm suddenly breathless. In my silence, he trails the very tips of his fingers down my arm. The hairs on the back of my neck raise and I can hardly remember what he asked. His lips are so close to my neck, sending memories of his mouth someplace far less innocent. He sounds amused when he says, "Did I lose you there, Mace?"

I quickly turn around, so we are facing. "You can drive."

He smirks and leans down so his face is in front of mine. My quick inhale turns his grin into a full-fledged smile. My eyes touch every line and dip of his face like a paint brush to canvas. The corners of his eyes are creasing in a way that makes them look gentler. His pearly white teeth are close to perfect, but there's a hardly noticeable chip in the corner of his front tooth. My fingertips tingle at the sight of his stubble, imagining how it would feel to touch it. Being this close to him makes me feel like I'm sky diving.

I've spent my life in a constant state of desire. Longing to live someplace else, looking forward to summer in the dead of winter, and outright aching for *more*.

Within my very bones is the feeling I've been devoid of. I've chased it in every romance novel I've ever read and in every dream of something greater. It's right here in this very moment with Grayson. It has been since the moment I crashed into him at the airport.

He lights me on fire. I thought I hated him. But no, I don't hate Grayson. Not one bit. I hate that everything I've ever wanted to feel is right in front of me, yet I'll never be able to hold it. Like water slipping through your fingers.

My life isn't here. My house is in Walter and I's name.

And the man who embodies every want I've ever had is a mystery I can't seem to solve.

Grayson and I are as everlasting as this vacation, and when I'm thousands of miles away, I know that my heart will be beating right here in Sanibel, like it always has. But I won't just be dreaming of the sun on my skin, now his hands will be there too.

He looks down at me, still grinning, unaware of every-thing going through my mind. I follow him to his car. He opens the door for me and it's something I'm not used to. We peel out of his driveway, and I look out the window, staring at the overgrown foliage that makes up the island. I like that it hasn't been touched. Aside from some houses, businesses, and streets, the island's essence remains intact.

The grocery store isn't bustling, but as soon as we enter through the automatic doors, I catch a few workers' lingering stares. Grayson is mindless to it, standing proud and still wearing my floral apron that is ten sizes too small. He leads me to the section with chocolate chips. We are the only two people in the isle, and suddenly, both of his arms are caging me in against the shelves. "You think you're clever, don't you?"

I tilt my head and his eyes narrow at me, then he glances down at himself. "Very cute, Mace."

I can't help it. I laugh.

His eyes glimmer, staring down at me. "Did you think this would embarrass me?"

I shrug. "I thought it would be funny, which it is."

His eyes darken when they flit between mine, then he pushes off the shelves and grabs a bag of chocolate chips, seeming indifferent toward the whole thing.

He doesn't remove it, and when we checkout, the girl behind the cashier blushes as if his face is too much of a distraction to notice the ridiculous apron. He shoots me a smug smile and I roll my eyes, thanking the girl and walking ahead of Grayson. He's quick to catch up, thanks to his long legs.

I kick off my shoes once we are back at my house, the cold tile beneath my bare feet does nothing to cool the way I'm burning from within. Phantom sensations touch my body, and I'm reminded yet again of the other night.

Grayson puts the chocolate chips on the counter, and I pull out a big bowl from one of the cabinets. As I reach for it, my arm grazes him. I shiver.

Something about the way he's watching me makes me feel bold. I step into his personal space until we are pressed together. My palms drag up his chest, around his neck, and then I untie the apron. His gaze is intense, watching me with the care one would a captivating page in a book. I do the same for the part tied around his back, and once it's in my hands, I turn around.

My breath catches at the feel of him so close behind me. Electricity shoots through my body. I tilt my head back until it rests against his chest. "Will you help me put this on?"

He blows out a steady breath. His arms come around me to take the apron from my hand. He's careful tying it behind my neck, knuckles softly brushing my skin. My pulse beats rapidly as if calling to him, and he answers with a kiss to the spot.

His hand moves up my stomach, and softly runs over the column of my neck until his thumb swipes across my bottom lip. I kiss the pad of his finger and he lets out a breath. He gently pushes me forward, so we are an arm's length apart.

I face him and it seems to take him a moment to find his

voice. "Another second of that, Macy, and I wouldn't stay true to my word of making you chocolate chip pancakes."

As if nothing happened a moment ago, we make pancakes together. I manage to get flour in my hair, and Grayson's cheek is dusted in it. Each one I flip is a different shape, and Grayson's are annoyingly perfect. He insists on eating mine, leaving me with the masterpieces he made.

Chapter 17
Grayson

Macy is absentmindedly stretching before me, wearing leggings and an orange sports bra. Her hair is tied back, but a lose strand falls into her face when she bends down to touch her toes.

I was glad to find her waiting for me in my front yard, bright and early. I'm determined to sneak into her house one day and throw away that ridiculous treadmill she bought during our rift. Running on my own after being graced to run beside her is a new form of loneliness I never intend to experience again.

I want to pull her to me every time I see her. I want to kiss the tip of her nose and then the delicate skin between her eyebrows and finally her lips. *I want her to be mine.*

I'm no expert when it comes to relationships, but I know it will go up in flames if it's all based on a lie. I need to tell her. Right now.

"I might call Walter," she says, stealing me from my thoughts.

Change of plans. I lift a brow.

"I have these…moments in the shower—"

A grin stretches across my face. "Please tell me more."

She rolls her eyes. "I make up fake scenarios where I confront him about everything he's done." She tucks the loose piece of hair behind her ear. "I want him to feel all the pain he's caused me. I want him to hurt."

"If that's what you need to do, then do it. But do you want my opinion?"

She nods hesitantly.

"Your words are precious. Every single one that leaves your mouth is a treasure, and quite honestly, Wally doesn't deserve your pretty words." She doesn't correct me calling him the wrong name.

"The words I have for him are far from pretty."

"If they're coming from your lips, they are."

She lets out a long trail of vulgar words and then smiles at me as if she's proven her point.

"Sounded divine to my ears," I say.

Her eyes narrow on me and then she's off running. She guides us on a different path than the one we usually take along the beach. She runs toward the center of the island, on the wide sidewalk which is divided into two lanes by a line of yellow paint. One for bikes and the other for walkers.

Yellow wildflowers bloom on some of the bushes, there's even a swampy part that we pass with a sign that says *Do not feed alligators. $500 fine.* I'm running on the opposite side of Macy so I'm closer to the swampy water, in the rare occasion that one decides it's hungry for human meat.

I glance down at my watch. We've already ran a mile and a half, and she hasn't needed a break once. My lips split into a smile, full of pride for her. Her stamina has remarkably improved. She will no doubt outrun me soon.

We return the way we came, both of us occasionally slow to a walk so we can catch our breath. She leads me to the shoreline which is covered in thousands of shells. Her eyes are on the ground, a crease between her brows in concentration, then she kneels and picks up a bright pink scallop shell.

She's in deep concentration, unaware that I'm taking this opportunity to admire her beauty. The roots of her hair are painted with sweat and her cheeks are pink. I want to drop to my knees every time she picks up a shell and smiles, if only to embody the ground she's so fascinated by.

When she seemingly has the perfect collection, she leads me back to my yard. "It's time to liven up your house," she says, turning to me. She could paint it chartreuse, and I'd let her if it made her happy. "Could you hold these?" She places dozens of shells in the palms of my hands and then opens my door and heads straight for the drawers in my kitchen. She opens one after the other.

I chuckle. "Is there something I can help you find?"

She pulls out a bottle of super glue and marches up to me, grabs my arm, and leads me to my mailbox. She's on a mission.

"We'll start here," she says. "Your mailbox is the only one on our street that's plain white." She points to different mailboxes. "Look, that one over there is shaped like a dolphin. And the one next to it has flowers painted on it."

I bite back my amusement and nod my head like this is serious business we discuss. She grabs a shell from my hand and holds it up for me to see. Then, she demonstrates putting glue on it, then pressing it onto my offensively plain mailbox. She holds it for about a minute, then moves onto the next one. I set the bulk of shells on the ground, then grab one to glue. We do this for almost an hour until my mailbox has been fully decorated. She claps her hands together and nods her head with approval. Then she sighs. "I have to go work on edits now," she says, dreadfully.

I walk her to her front door, and she hesitates before going in. I haven't seen her this happy in a long time, and I don't want to let it go, so I say, "I'm calling in that favor you owe me."

She eyes me warily.

"I couldn't help but notice how nicely decorated your house is, especially your bedroom. So, I want you to decorate mine."

She cocks her head and asks, "When did you see my room?"

"How do you think you ended up in bed that night." I leave out the part about her being drunk.

Pink creeps into her cheeks and then she looks down. "Um, we didn't do anything, did we?"

"Of course not. You were drunk."

I pull open the door for her and she brushes past me. "I usually finish editing around three. I'll call you when I'm ready to go to the store." She grins up at me, and I smile. The expression was a rarity for me until I saw Macy at the airport, and now it's seeming to be a common occurrence when I'm in her presence.

Macy is a child in a toy store. She wizzes in and out of aisles, holding decorations up for me to approve. When she presses her lips into a firm line, I know the item she's holding is one she wants me to say yes to. I do just that. So, that's how I became the owner of a floral cookie jar. I can't remember the last time I even had a cookie.

She pushes the cart, despite me offering to do so a dozen times. We go down each and every aisle, but I notice that she skips right past the section of picture frames.

"I'd like to look here." I gesture to the frames.

Her eyes light up and she's eager to follow me. She looks at the simplistic ones, but I brush past her. One that looks as if it were meant for a child's bedroom catches my attention. The four sides are made of wood and are painted different colors. Purple, blue, crème, and pink. I place it in the cart, feeling Macy's curious gaze.

She is the jauntiest person standing in the checkout line. She smiles at each item she picked out as it moves along the conveyor belt. My eyes widen at the new set of pots and pans I hadn't realized she put in the cart. *What the hell do I need new ones for?* The cashier scans a simple white vase, an artificial plant, and the strawberry scented candle Macy picked out with an adorable grin. The worker struggles to find the barcode on my new ginormous rug. Macy points to it, and I catch sight of her yellow nail polish.

She helps me load everything into the trunk of my car, and she's extra careful with the fragile items, like my new lamp. I turn to her. "Are you okay with making one more stop?" I ask.

She shrugs and then nods her head. If I didn't know any better, I'd think Macy is starting to enjoy my company. I grin.

"What?" she asks, eyeing the expression on my face.

I suppress it enough to appear nonchalant. "Oh nothing."

"I still don't like you," she supplies. Her eyebrows raise. *It's a lie.*

I grin even wider. "Keep telling yourself that, Mace," I say as I slide into the driver's seat, a wide grin on my face.

Macy shoots me a curious look when we walk through the automatic doors of a home improvement store. I lead her to the section filled with hundreds of paint colors. She turns to me with a smirk. "And here I thought we were taking baby steps but you're ready to enter the big leagues."

I glance at her painted fingernails. "Is yellow your favorite color?"

She shakes her head. "It's a close second, but I like a certain shade of orange that looks like the sunset."

A memory blurs my vision. Macy's eyes glittering in the setting sun, edges of her hair glowing from the sky. Her kissing me beneath the lifeguard tower.

I think orange is my favorite color too.

I saunter to the section of orange, overlooking the neon shades, and glancing at a row of pastels. I find one called "Sunset Orange" and pick it up. Macy's eyes widen and she doesn't try to conceal her surprise. "You're painting your walls my favorite color?"

"No," I say. "I'm painting *a* wall *my* favorite color."

By the time we are back at my house, I'm starving. "Want to go grab a bite to eat?"

She reels back as if she's been insulted and then gestures to the countless bags of décor. "We haven't even started yet."

I raise my brows at her when my stomach rumbles loudly. I dig around my fridge, gathering everything I need to make an egg sandwich. Macy claims she isn't hungry, but I make an extra one anyway. Once I set it down in front of her, she eats it rather quickly.

After she washes her hands, she plays music on her phone and sets the volume on high. She pulls out a stack of books from one of the bags. I told her at the store that I was never going to read them, but she claimed they were for decoration and that no one ever reads them. After arranging them on my coffee table, along with a vase of greenery, she steps back to appreciate her work.

"Looks good," I say before digging through the bags to find my picture frame. "Be right back." Macy doesn't even look up, and I doubt she heard me since I'm of little interest to her at the moment. I chuckle when she starts lip syncing to the music, and then I disappear down the hallway and tuck myself in my bedroom to put away the frame.

Once I'm back in the living room, she eyes me with an expectant look on her face. "Are you going to sit around all day or actually help?"

I hold up my hands in surrender. Feisty thing she is. With everyone else, she's an unlit match. Being around me ignites something within her, and there's something thrilling about being the exception to her niceties.

I bring the bag of throw pillows to my small couch and place them where I think they look good, but then Macy clicks her tongue with the shake of her head and then rearranges them. It looks ten times better, and I question how anything gets done correctly if not for a woman's touch.

She hands me a small wooden shelf, then points to a spot on my wall. "Hang this."

"Yes, ma'am."

Once I do so, I grab the three copies of Minerva Day

books scattered throughout my house and display them on my new shelf.

I help her unroll the huge rug, lifting the corners of my coffee table to slide it beneath. Once all the bags are empty, I take in my house. There's not a corner that she hasn't touched. I realize how bare it truly was. I can't help but compare the space to myself. My life was colorless until Macy stepped into it. I've been numb to the world around me, but she taught me how good it can feel to *feel*. And God, Macy makes me feel everything.

I take her face in my hands and kiss her forehead. "It looks great, Mace. Thank you."

Her cheekbones pinken and my lips tingle like I need to kiss her blush.

"Which wall did you want to paint?" she asks, her voice soft.

I gesture to it. It's the one closest to her house, and it's not that big. We can paint it tonight. She must realize the same thing. "I'll be right back. I need to find an old T-shirt."

"I have one you can wear." I don't. I own less than ten shirts, all of which I wear regularly, but I want to see her in my clothes, even if she stains them with orange paint.

I return from my bedroom a moment later and hand her a black one. She puts it over her tank top. The hem reaches just above her knees, and she glances up at me. "You're huge," she says. I slowly grin, and her face flushes. "Don't make it dirty."

I feign innocence. "No clue what you mean."

She rolls her eyes and then throws her hair into a knot above her head. A few strands come loose, falling into her face. Sometimes it's excruciating to look at her, like my gaze alone could taint something so perfect, like spilled ink on a white tablecloth. But she is marvelous, and I can't help but look. Maybe that makes me selfish.

She pries open the bucket of paint and then pours some into the tray. I cover the floor and put tape over the outlets, baseboards, and the part where the wall meets the ceiling. By the time everything is prepped, more strands have found their way into Macy's face, and my shirt is so baggy on her that her legs look like two toothpicks sticking out from beneath it. I grab my phone and snap a photo of her. She's shooting me a glare, and I take another. It takes us a little over an hour to cover the wall in paint, and once we are done, we're both shiny with sweat.

Both my shirts are ruined—the one I wear and the one I gave to Macy. I set the paint roller down and pull her to me by her hands. The smallest bit of paint is dried in her eyebrow. I rub it away with my thumb and her eyes fall shut. She ever so slightly leans into my touch.

Every moment spent with her is a new experience. Simplicities, like having someone to enjoy the feel of my touch, is unfamiliar.

I admire her standing in front of me, letting me hold her face. Her eyes open. Her chest heaves as if she's been running, and her vanilla scent is stronger when she steps closer to me. I'm pleased that she hasn't shied away from me. My touch is featherlight as I run my thumb over her jaw.

With my eyes glued to hers, I kneel steadily. My knees touch the floor and her throat bobs. I suppress my grin and feign confusion for her sudden breathlessness. "Why do you look so scared, Mace. I was only picking this up." I hold my phone up for her to see, then stand to my full height, towering over her once again. I put the device in my pocket.

A crease forms between her eyebrows, and then she moves

to step away from me, but I grab her wrist and pull her mouth to mine.

She claims my lips with the same fire she always gives me and I'm feverish because of it. I quickly throw my hat off, my hair probably looking as disheveled as I feel. She runs her hands beneath my shirt, and when I nip at her bottom lip, she digs her nails into my skin. I groan and she answers me with a lovely sound that I etch to memory. This kiss is a duel, and right now she's winning because I will yield to her every want.

She backs us up until she's pressed against my sliding glass door. I remove my hands from her body and press them against the cold door, framing her face.

She places her palm over my racing heart and then descends it down my body teasingly. The muscles in my abdomen are flexing against her touch, and I'm completely at her mercy when she reaches the top of my pants. She's watching me with intent.

Like a moth to a flame, I'd willingly burn just to be closer to her.

When her hands stroke me over the denim of my jeans, the friction causes my head to fall between her shoulder and neck. It shouldn't feel this good with so many layers between us. "Reluctantly, I need to ask you to stop doing that or this is going to end far too quickly."

She covers her mouth to stifle a laugh. Even if it's at my expense, I'll gladly be the cause of it. "You find this funny, do you? Your touch is going to be my defeat."

Her cheeks go crimson and this time I do kiss them. "Do you trust me?" I ask.

She nods her head, and then gasps as I guide her hips to turn her around, so her back is to me. I grab her hands and press them against the glass, covering them with mine. No one can see us. I've had these windows tinted for privacy. I breathe against the side of her neck where I know she likes being kissed. I'm pleased by her shiver. I've mapped out every sensitive point on her body.

I drag the tip of my finger down the back of her neck. "I'd like my shirt back now," I say, toying with the collar. She slowly lifts it over her head, tossing it somewhere behind us.

She puts her hands back on the glass. I place mine beside hers, my thumbs brushing the back of her littlest fingers. My bottom lip feathers down her pulse and over her shoulder. I press closer until we are flush together. I move a hand from the door to drag it over her lower belly, slowly inching beneath her tank top until I'm right below her breast. "Can I touch you here?"

Her head lulls back and she's hasty with her nod. I grin and say in an amused voice, "You don't seem sure. Perhaps we should sto—" She steps on my toes with such force that I hiss out a breath. "Feisty," I purr, and then squeeze her, pleasantly surprised to find she isn't wearing a bra. I take the sensitive peek between my thumb and index finger. She squeezes her legs together and lets out a breath.

With my other hand, I feel the button on her denim shorts. I slowly peel them open, then take her chin between my fingers so I can see her face. "Is this all right?"

"Ye—" I kiss her before she can finish the word, and her lips form a smile against mine.

I dip my hand into her shorts, palming her over her underwear. My forehead falls into her vanilla scented hair. "You're enjoying this more than you're letting on," I say in a grainy voice. I pull her shorts down her legs. She turns her head to look at me. "I'm not going to be the only one losing clothes this time."

I smirk. "If you want to see me naked, Mace, all you need to do is ask." I pull my shirt off. She's impossibly closer than before. We're both breathing heavily. She places her hands over mine as I explore her body. I trail the tips of my fingers down her torso, playing with the hem of her underwear until she squirms against me. She squeezes my hand.

I whisper against her ear, "What do you want?"

"You know."

I want her to beg for my touch. "Say it." I catch her reflection in the glass. She's shooting bullets at me. I grin, then lift my hand higher, away from what she craves.

"Maybe I'll just leave." She mimics my expression in the glass.

I dip my hands in her underwear, making her head turn in surprise. I'm quick to kiss her parted lips. "You win," I whisper, but I'm the one who's truly rewarded by the delightful sound she makes.

I swirl the tips of my fingers over the most sensitive part of her, entranced by the hazel globes staring at my reflection. I memorize the way her eyebrows pull together. It's truly cruel to be so beautiful.

I press against her back so she's flush with the glass. Her head turns and I hover over her lips. Our gazes never part, not even when I press my finger against her entrance. Her eyes darken and I push in, slowly curling the digit, which earns a new sound from her. "That's it, Mace. Sing for me." I quicken the pace and kiss her fervently. Our lips meet and break apart, like the clash of two swords. It's a battle and we're on opposing sides because she doesn't want to want me, and I want her to be my center of gravity.

I slip another digit in. "Does that feel good, Mace? Fingers of a man you despise, filling you and coaxing those sounds from your pretty lips?"

She cries out, pulsing around my fingers. Her hands curl into white knuckled fists against the glass, as though she needs something to hold onto. I grab them with my empty hand, and she pierces me with her nails.

Once her moans quiet, I place a soft kiss to her hair and pull my hand out of her underwear, my fingers glistening. I turn her around, and smile at the sight of her rosy cheeks. Her eyes shine and when she stares up at me, I realize that she'll never be my center of gravity because she is an asteroid rocking my entire world. She's equally my undoing and my salvation. She's heaven, and I'm hell.

She'll either go up in flames with me or be the rarity that smothers them.

She slowly moves down until she's on her knees, eyeing my zipper. Right now, she's lighter fluid about to burn me alive. I take her chin between my fingers, with my clean hand, so she meets my eyes. "Don't worry about me, Mace."

"But you've made me…" Her cheeks go red. "Twice."

I go on my knees, still towering over her, so I crouch down until our foreheads touch. "You say it as if I don't get any enjoyment from it."

"But no relief." She eyes my zipper again, and the evidence of that statement is clear.

"I have plenty to think of tonight." I grin.

She deserves to think of sex as something beautiful. At herself as divine. Not an object for someone else's pleasure, the way her ex-fiancé made her feel. I can tell she was only going to do that out of obligation, and if Macy is going to touch me, it needs to be because she wants to. I intend to make up for all the wrongs I didn't commit. For her.

I softly brush my lips against hers, and it's kind. Like we're finally on the same side, embracing one another as if we've won. The way she makes me feel burns brighter than anything I've ever lost, and then I realize, my theory proved true.

"If you fill your life with things that bring you joy, eventually happiness becomes bigger than the grief."

Chapter 18
Macy

"When are you coming home? You can't ignore Walter forever." My mother's voice comes through the receiver of my phone.

After last night with Grayson, I can't imagine leaving. He's starting to grow on me, the way barnacles take over the underside of boats. Nonetheless, I don't want to leave the sunshine and my friends. "I don't know."

My father speaks, and I can picture my parents now, sitting at their round dinner table with the phone placed in the center, shooting each other looks. "We are worried, honey. This behavior isn't like you."

My mom speaks. "And you need to stop ignoring your fiancé."

"He's no longer my fiancé because I'm not marrying him."

"I don't know what happened between you, but I'm sure you will talk it out. Just come home," my mom says.

"This isn't something talking will fix," I mumble.

"Then help us understand." My dad.

"I hate to break it to you, Macy, but you're not going to find anyone else like Walter," my mom says. *Thank God for that.* "I strongly suggest you get home and fix this before it's too late."

I sigh, pinching the bridge of my nose. I slide open the back door and sit on the swinging bench.

My eyes automatically go to Grayson, who sits on his porch, holding one of my books in his hand. It feels like fireworks go off inside my chest. He's wearing glasses which is new, but they complement his features and make him look sophisticated. The black frames nearly match his dark hair.

"Are you there?" my dad asks.

"Yeah, sorry. Bad connection," I lie. "All you guys need to know is that Walter doesn't make me happy."

It's silent. I'm pretty sure they put me on mute. My mom eventually says, "Macy Brookes, if you don't get your ass home this instant…" I don't hear the rest because Grayson's eyes meet mine and the rest of the world falls away.

He smiles and it's all dimples and paperwhite teeth. The glasses raise slightly from his cheeks pressing them up. It's not his usual smirk or grin. It's him without his arrogant mask. A person's smile shouldn't have the capability of stealing my breath. Its dreadful to know that no site will compare to him.

I hang up on my parents.

An invisible string tethers me to him, and right now our distance pulls it taught. Tension ripples in the air between us. In the back of my mind, I dare anyone to try and break it.

I lift my hand in greeting, and he dips his head in response, a gentler smile playing on his face. Then, he closes the book in his hand and gets up from his chair. His black shirt hugs him in all the right places, and I don't need to imagine what's beneath, because I've seen him without a shirt. He looks like a statue carved from marble. He's not wide and bulky, he's tall and sculpted to perfection, and I can only conclude it's because he lifts weights in addition to his daily runs. He crosses the distance between our yards.

"Macy," he says as way of greeting.

"Grayson."

"Lovely morning, isn't it?"

Now it is.

I push the previous phone call with my parents from my mind. It's simple because I'm not leaving, at least not for a while. For once, I feel like my life has meaning. Like I'm finally doing what I want.

He sits beside me on my porch swing, making it rock slightly. His shoulder is touching mine, and the entirety of my side burns as if I'm sitting beside a fire. But there's no fire, there's only Grayson. "How did you sleep?" he asks. It's an innocent question that makes me think back to last night. My face heats down to my neck.

I slept better than ever, but I won't admit that it's because of him. "Tossed and turned all night. You?"

He grins and the glasses soften the hard angles of his face. "Perhaps you would've slept better if I had been there beside you."

I roll my eyes, despite the appeal of him in my small bed. There would be no space between us. His legs would hang off the end, and everything about him would look out of place in my bedroom.

"Those new?" I change the subject, pointing to his glasses. And impossibly, his cheeks pinken. Perhaps it's the lighting because Grayson doesn't blush.

"Yes."

"Interesting," I say. "I like them."

"I'm marking this day in my calendar. That might be the

nicest thing you've said to me. And I got them because I was having a hard time seeing the words in your book."

He got glasses just to read my writing.

I feel my chin begin to quiver. I will away the emotion, but not before Grayson notices. There's a crease between his brows and suddenly my thumb tingles. I want to rub it away.

Swept up in the moment, I reveal a glimpse of myself. "No one's ever cared about my books."

His gaze is full of something I can't place. "I care."

"I know," I whisper.

He tilts his head and it's like he's teetering on the tightrope between us, trying to reach me. To understand. I find myself doing the same most of the time. But I can never tell what he's thinking. Every time he reveals something about himself, it makes it ten times harder to understand him.

"I'm bored," I say to change the subject, and whatever fell over us seems to have moved past. Like a small cloud blowing by, shading what's beneath it for only a moment.

His expression remains serious, as though he's having a hard time moving on from what I said. "What are your plans for today?" he asks after a few moments, like he needed to find his voice again.

I shrug. "Nothing. I give myself the weekends off from editing."

"Great. I'm not working today either. Get dressed, I'm taking you somewhere." Not bothering to hear my reply, he walks back to his house without a second glance and disappears inside.

I pick up my phone and call him. He answers on the first ring. "Miss me already?" he asks, voice smug.

"Where are we going?"

"You'll see when we get there."

I bite the inside of my cheeks. *What am I supposed to wear if I don't know what we're doing?* "Well, will we be inside or outside? Should I dress nice or comfortable? Will we be sitting or standi—"

"Wear something casual." He hangs up.

I roll my eyes. *How helpful.*

I'm curling the last section of my hair when I hear a knock on my front door. I unplug the curling iron and then run my fingers through the curls as I walk through my house. I open the door to find two agonizing dimples and a towering man sporting his usual hat. No more glasses.

He blows out a low whistle, taking in my appearance. I'm wearing a bright coral baby T-shirt and a pair of denim jeans. He takes a strand of my brown hair between his index finger and thumb, eyes roaming over my face. "You look lovely." He steps out of the doorway, gesturing for me to join him outside.

I expect to find out where we're going, but he doesn't say anything about it. He drives us over the bridge that connects Sanibel to the mainland.

I shoot him a questioning look, but his lips curve, and he pretends to zip them shut. He opens the window and tosses away the invisible key, which makes me laugh at how playful he's being, and right as the sound touches his ears, he glances at me. The look in his eye is one I've only seen once from him. When he saw his first shooting star. I thought it looked like peace. A chill trickles down my body, and I tell myself it's because I'm cold.

I plug his charging cord into my phone, and a mischievous grin takes over my face when I realize my music connected to his car speakers. I play an old Taylor Swift song and start singing her lyrics.

So does Grayson. He sings every word, attempting to turn his deep voice soft and instead it comes out scratchy. At first glance, his frivolous smile looks out of place, but the more I watch him, I realize he's shed another layer. I laugh so hard, I'm tempted to pull out my phone and record the moment, but I'm afraid he'll stop and slip his mask back on. So, I brand it to memory instead, for only me to see.

I've always hid parts of myself in the presence of others. I want to protect them from the harsh opinions in this world. I can tell Grayson conceals more of himself than I do. Bravery manifests in a million different ways. So, when he reveals something new to me, I recognize the trust he has to do so. There's intimacy in his vulnerability.

Another song plays, and like the previous one, he knows the words. By the fourth one, I turn to him. "I never pegged you to be a Swifty."

He lifts a shoulder. "I've been listening to her since I was a kid." His expression changes ever so slightly. Do memories of his childhood make him sad?

I try to get his mind off whatever it is. "Where are we going?"

He grins but doesn't answer.

"Are we almost there?"

No reply.

"Can you at least tell me how much longer we have?"

Nothing.

"Are you playing The Quiet Game or something?"

Silence.

I take it as a challenge. "Fine, don't say anything. I'll just sit here and keep myself entertained."

His lips tick at the corners, like he's trying to suppress a smile. Then, I sing in the loudest, most obnoxious voice I can muster. I shoot him a glance, but he doesn't crack. Fine. "You know, I can remember exactly what I thought the first time I met you," I say, and his face changes to curiosity. "Too bad we aren't talking to one another, because maybe I'd tell yo—"

"We'll be there in fifteen minutes," he says.

I grin, then seal my mouth shut.

"Touché," he says. "I remember what I thought of you the first time we met. Perhaps I'd be open to sharing if you were."

Now *I'm* curious. I can't read him now any more than I could then. "Fine," I say. "I thought you were an arrogant prick who was undeserving of such luscious eyelashes."

His laughter is husky. "Your first impression was that I didn't deserve eyelashes?"

"Did you miss the 'arrogant prick' part? And no, you just don't deserve *those* eyelashes. Do you know how much money I'll probably spend in my lifetime on mascara?"

"What's mascara?"

I roll my eyes. "Exactly. Undeserving."

"Anything else?"

"Yes," I say. "You were the bane of my existence."

He grins. "You done?"

"Yes. You're turn."

His face loses all amusement, he turns serious. "When I first met you, I thought you were the prettiest girl I'd ever seen."

I tilt my head. Perhaps I took it a step too far when I called him the bane of my existence.

He continues. "You embodied the rays of a thousand

suns. You were joy personified. I thought you were lovely, Mace."

Is he being sarcastic? I was a grump who had just left her terrible fiancé and found out her flight was canceled. "Were you in a parallel universe that day?"

"Perhaps," he says, but there something hidden beneath the word, and I can't explain why, but I feel like I should know what it is. I rack my brain for a clue but come up empty. "We're here," he says. I was so focused on him that I hadn't looked out the window. We're parked in a grassy field, along with countless other cars.

Before I can ask where we are, he climbs out of his car and rounds the front to open my door. The sky is naked, with only the sun to keep it company. Not a single cloud. My skin warms but it's not too hot out today. We must be experiencing our first cold front, and by cold front, I mean it's probably sixty-eight degrees and sunny.

He links our arms and walks toward a crowd of people. There's a labyrinth of pumpkins. The air smells of fresh cider and hay, and there's children with face paint running between the legs of adults. He leads me to a wooden booth. "Two tickets, please," Grayson says after we wait in line. The lady gives us bright green wrist bands and Grayson hands her his credit card.

We walk through an arch made of flowering vines. A black and yellow striped butterfly flutters past me. This place feels magical, with families and their jubilant children together. "What is this place?"

He finally answers me. "It's the annual fall festival."

"You come here every year?"

"No." He doesn't elaborate.

There are colorful booths made of wood, painted to represent what they are. I pull Grayson over to the spiked cider and buy us both a drink. It leaves a foam mustache on his lip after he takes a sip.

I spot a sign with an arrow pointing toward the corn maze entrance. I tug Grayson, walking fast enough that the contents of my cup spill over the edge, making my hand wet and sticky.

At the mouth of the maze, I meet his eyes and chug the rest of my drink. He takes my empty cup and stacks it with his.

"Close your eyes," I whisper.

He looks at me with beautiful curiosity and then shuts them. His lashes cast a crescent shadow on both his cheeks, and a part of me wants to stay like this forever. With his eyes closed, unaware that I'm learning every detail of his face.

I take off running into the maze. A thrill of anticipation shoots down my body. My hair is flying behind me, and the wind caresses my face.

I try not to contemplate why I want him to catch me while I run to escape him, why the idea of him finding me is exhilarating. I don't want to understand why I can't fathom ever hating him, how the idea seems ridiculous now. I go to bed every night with excitement, knowing I'll see him first thing in the morning on our runs. I see his eyes when I gaze up at the full moon. I seem to find him everywhere, even when he's not around. I try not to pay attention to my body, the way it feels as if I'm falling down a wishing well, hoping I'll find him at the bottom. I'm a liar when I convince myself I'm not having these thoughts, these feelings.

I don't look behind me, I just run until I meet a dead end, then I turn back and go another direction. The rows of corn are a blur as I whiz past. I haven't seen a single person yet.

I hear the crunch of hay beneath someone's shoes nearing behind, until a firm body presses against my back, and two arms of steel wrap around me.

His breath is warm against my racing pulse, as he whispers, "You think you can hide from me?" He slowly steps in front of me. "It's me who can't escape you, darling." Lips feathering mine, he says almost to himself, "I've already tried."

Then he kisses me. Hard. Passionate. Dizzying.

It's the kind of kiss you read in a story and wish to experience at least once in your life. The kind in a fairytale before you read the words *they lived happily ever after.* This kiss is a maze in itself, and I'm lost. Nothing exists other than Grayson and his devouring lips. As if they could ever be mine, he steals them away, and then there's just his eyes. And I think of a full moon hanging in the sky, shining light on everything.

"You're looking at me differently," he says. There's no smirk or grin. It's just him and I without our masks, getting closer and closer on that tight rope.

"How am I looking at you?" My voice doesn't sound like mine. It's too breathless, too choppy.

"Like you don't hate me."

"I don't," I whisper.

His eyes shut when I say it. Moments pass before he says, "Promise me something." His eyes open again, but they are sad.

"Okay." I breathe.

"Remember it," he says with so much weight. "Remember this. Not hating me. Just—" his voice cracks and I want to fix it. Fix whatever it is that's making the full moon frown. "Don't forget it. Okay?"

He's scared I'll change my mind? I feel an intense need to remedy it, so I say, "I won't forget. I promise."

He kisses me but it's different. This one feels like goodbye. Like an apology. Like he's trying to savor the last bite before it's gone. Maybe he's right to feel this way. I mean, I live across the country.

He lifts me easily, and I hook my legs around his waist. The kiss changes to something hungry. Breathless, until we're both starving for something forbidden in a place like this. Where anyone could walk by. His lips graze my neck, and I grip onto the back of his and let my head hang back, exposing the column of my throat to him. He runs his lips over it, and the unexpectedness makes me sigh out a moan.

He's so warm that every place we are connected heats, making me think of a fire so hot that it burns blue. And then I realize that his eyes aren't ice-cold glaciers, nor are they the full moon. They're blue flames.

"Mace, you've gotta stop me."

"Why?"

"When it comes to you, my inhibition seems to evaporate, and I'm moments away from tearing both our clothes off." His words shouldn't make me *want* so much. He sets me down easily and places a gentle kiss to my temple. "Sorry," he says. "I lose myself a little bit in you."

I laugh. It's loud and joyful and something unexpected, and it lights up *his* face. This is not what I was expecting today when I woke up, but I'm loving every second of it. The spontaneity is something I've always starved for. It's a need close to breathing for me, and Walter never cared to meet it. Grayson doesn't try. He just *is* spontaneous. From the moment we met, he went with the flow. His flight was canceled but he wasn't stressed, he made the most of it. He made it fun. He makes everything fun. I don't even think he realizes it.

The cold, rude man I met in the airport was yet another mask. Grayson is warm and kind. He's fun and playful. He's sweet and tentative.

I take his hand and run, our laughter chases us, hay crunches beneath our shoes. My heart races and it feels as if it's saying *mine mine mine.* We reach countless dead ends until we make it to the end of the corn maze. It spits us out to a different part of the field with bubbles filling the air and children chasing after them.

A dog barks somewhere in the distance. I search for it, until I see a sign that says *Pet Adoptions.* There's a giant dog in a crate, wiggling its butt and howling at Grayson and I when we get closer.

"Would you like to see her?" an old woman asks, wearing a purple T-shirt that says she's a volunteer for a pet rescue.

I quickly nod.

The woman opens the crate and quickly clips a leash on the dog. The husky darts out and jumps on Grayson, trying to kiss his face but he's too tall to reach. He crouches down and the dog licks his cheek and makes winy noises, as if it can't contain its excitement. It looks at me and howls. I crouch down beside Grayson and run my fingers through its soft fur.

"Her name is Daisy. I foster her," the woman says. "Sad story of how we got this sweet girl. The couple she was with since she was a puppy both passed away. Such a tragedy. A friend went to clean out their apartment a week later and found her in the bathroom drinking from the toilet bowl." She looks between Grayson and I. "She's two and a half, which is the perfect age to me. She's potty trained and won't chew on your shoes or destroy your home, but she's still young and energetic. She'd be perfect for a young couple like yourselves."

Neither him nor I correct her assumption. Daisy is so happy; you'd never know how she ended up in a foster home by looking at her. She's so precious, I'd take her in a heartbeat, but I have no idea what I'm going to do with my life, and she needs stability. I hope she finds a loving home.

The laughter bubbling in the air is one I haven't heard before. The joyful sound is coming from Grayson. Daisy's licking the palm of his hand. His dimples are deeper than I've ever seen.

He continues to play with Daisy, patting her side and saying, "Who's a good girl?" He looks reluctant when he stands and thanks the lady fostering her. She gives us a tight-lipped smile, then puts Daisy back in her crate.

Grayson flicks his head, gesturing me to follow him, and as soon as we begin to walk away, Daisy howls and my heart breaks. The bright smile on Grayson's face has vanished.

I'm too focused on him to realize where he's led us, until we're showing our wrist bands to a worker and getting on a hay bale ride. There are two young girls sitting across from us. They have the same blond hair, and one looks about three years older than the other. I assume they're sisters. They have excited smiles on their faces.

We go along a trail, weaving through rows of hay and some trees, until suddenly a person wearing a Halloween mask pops out from a divot in the hay. I screech and so does the youngest girl in front of me. Her big sister starts laughing, which immediately makes the little girl relax. I look at Grayson, who's chuckling at me. "You didn't tell me this was a *haunted* hayride."

He leans down to whisper in my ear. "I know. I just like watching you cause a scene."

The ride is only about five or so minutes, and each time someone pops out, I jump a little, which makes Grayson laugh. The sisters in front of us don't even flinch, and they join Grayson in laughing at my expense. I can tell the little girls look out for one another by how the older one's presence comforts the younger one. Growing up, I'd see how my friends were with their siblings, and a part of me always envied them. It would be nice to have someone constantly by my side. By the time it's done, I've scooted as close as humanly possible to Grayson out of pure instinct.

We walk around the festival until Grayson suddenly freezes. I follow his line of sight to a booth selling stuffed animals. It's as though he has tunnel vision, not hearing me when I ask, "What is it?" He tensely walks over to the booth, picking up a blue stuffed dolphin and staring at it solemnly.

"Shopping for a kid at home?" the chipper old man behind the table asks.

"No," Grayson says in a dry voice, which causes the worker to wince at his rudeness. I want to remedy the situation, but before I can make it to them and say something polite, Grayson pulls out his wallet and tosses a fifty-dollar bill on the table.

He walks toward me, as though he doesn't care about getting his change back. He puts the stuffy in my hand. "For you," he says in a faraway voice, like he's in a trance. *What's gotten into him?*

"Um, thank you."

We continue to roam the fair in silence. I glance at Grayson several times, who is even more impossible to read in this moment. There's an angry gray cloud in the sky and most people have left by now since they don't want to get caught in Florida's unpredictable weather.

I spot a face painting booth and luckily there's no line, so I tuck away my mischievous grin as I walk up. Grayson mindlessly follows me, and I can only hope that my plan rids him of this grim mood.

I spot the wall of designs and find the perfect one. Grayson eyes me but doesn't say anything. I shove him into the chair and tell the artist which design I want her to paint on his face.

Grayson narrows his gaze at me. His gaze runs down my body and then focuses on my feet. I go up and down on the tips of my toes in excitement. He sighs and lets the lady get to work.

I can't help but laugh as it comes together, and when the artist hands him a mirror, he rolls his eyes at his own reflection. She painted a black circle around his right eye, a black nose, dots on his cheeks, and a red tongue hanging out of his mouth. I chose a dog since it's his favorite animal. He doesn't seem to appreciate the sentiment.

When he stands up, I can't fight the hysterical laughter that leaves me. It's a hilarious sight to see such a tall, chiseled man with child's face paint. His eyes soften and the grouchy mood he was in finally dissipates. I pay and then Grayson says in a dry voice, "I think it's time to go."

I laugh and take a picture of him, right as I feel a sprinkle of rain hit my shoulder.

"Okay, now it's really time to go," he says.

I follow him toward the parking lot but then tug on his hand. "I'll meet you at the car, I'm going to run to one of the porta potties," I lie, shove the stuffed dolphin into his hands, then take off into a sprint since the sprinkles are turning into a full-on storm. When I glance back, he is rubbing his face clean with the help of the rain. I can't even be upset because the photo I captured is priceless.

I try to remember exactly where I need to go, back-tracking my steps, until I finally spot the woman in the purple shirt, who is in a hurry packing. "Did Daisy get adopted?" I ask with water starting to drip down my face.

Kneeling as she puts things in a duffle bag, her eyes meet mine and she gives me a gentle smile. "Sadly, not yet. One of the volunteers brought her to my car while I packed up. Didn't want her to get all wet."

"Can I take your phone number?" I ask. "I'm not promising anything, and if another family wants to adopt her don't wait on me, but I'd like to think on it and maybe give you a call soon."

She digs through her bag until she finds what she was looking for. She stands and hands me a card with her contact information. "Thank you!" She gives me a quick nod before getting back to work.

It's in this very moment, as I'm sprinting to the parking lot, I realize how much my stamina has improved since running every morning. If I made this exact attempt a month ago, I'd be on the brink of death by now. My feet sink into the soggy grass with each step, making a sloshing sound. My attempt to open the passenger door is futile since Grayson doesn't make a move to unlock it.

I pound at the window, my clothes sopping wet and hair sticking to my cheeks. *So much for curling it.* His muffled laughter makes my chattering teeth grind.

"This isn't funny!" I pull again, and this time, the door swings wide open and I don't waste time climbing in. I point a threatening finger into his chest. "You—"

"Motherfucking cockbucket?" he surmises.

I grin and lean over the center console, bringing my lips within an inch of his. His demeanor instantly changes to something primal. And then, with his focus on my lips, I ring my hair out onto his lap, and he hisses the moment the water soaks his crotch.

"You're evil," he says with his eyebrows raised.

I lean back into my seat and cross my legs with a pleased shrug.

He blasts the heat and the only sound while we drive is my teeth chattering and the windshield wiper at full speed. Ten minutes in, Grayson is completely dry since he made it to the car before it poured. However, my long hair drips down my back, and the denim of my jeans certainly won't dry any time soon.

"You don't need a GPS?" I ask when he gets on the highway.

"My job is in the area. I usually do everything from home unless I have a meeting or something."

"What made you want to live in Sanibel?" I ask. It's a small island with expensive houses. Most people want to visit the island for a weekend and then leave. And the ones that do buy a place usually use it as a vacation house.

"I wanted to be close to the office. It's only a thirty-minute drive, sometimes forty-five depending on traffic." He shrugs. "I didn't want to live in the city, so Sanibel it was."

"What about your family. Where do they live?"

There's a long stretch of silence. I almost think he won't answer, but eventually, he says, "I don't like to talk about them."

Here I am again, balancing with my arms out along the tightrope between us. "You aren't close with them?"

I take his silence as a yes.

"I see," I say. "Maybe one day you'll patch things up." I squeeze his hand that holds the steering wheel, and when he glances at me, I give him an encouraging smile. I don't know what happened between him and his family, but I hope for his sake they work it out. He doesn't deserve to have no one.

He clears his throat. "Tell me about your family."

"My mom is a little…high-strung, but she means well. At least that's what I tell myself. My dad just goes with whatever my mom wants. They are day and night, but hey, they make it work," I say. "I'm an only child, but I've always wanted a sister." I sigh. "I was closest with my grandparents. I mean, I could tell them *anything*. They would never judge or lecture me." I focus on the raindrops on the window, watching one pool into the other until it gets so heavy it drips. "The summer going into my junior year of high school I told my grandma I was ready to have sex for the first time and she slipped me a pack of condoms to bring home." I laugh to myself, picturing her buying them at the store. But I never used them, because when the opportunity presented itself that year, I realized I wasn't ready. And that was okay too. I look at Grayson to gauge his reaction, and smile at his wide eyes. "My grandpa was pretty go with the flow…a lot like you. You would've liked him," I say.

"Your family sounds great," he says. "I already like them, and you're very fortunate to have them."

He's right. It's easy to take what you have for granted until you look at those who aren't as lucky. I think of those who have negligent parents or even abusive ones. I close my eyes and take a moment to appreciate what I have. Who I have. Even though it aches knowing I'll never see my grandparents again in this lifetime. The memories and time we shared are a privilege in themselves. "Yeah. I guess I am."

It's nearly the end of daylight. We sit in comfortable silence and the melody of rain pounding at the car nearly puts me to sleep. Right as I'm at the cusp of a dream, Grayson curses beneath his breath.

I crack my eyes open. We aren't moving and there are countless taillights before us. It's raining impossibly harder now. I look farther and that's when I see red and blue lights blocking anyone from entering the bridge to Sanibel. *The one and only bridge.*

Grayson picks up his phone and calls someone. "Hey man," he says. He laughs at something the person on the other line said. "You know what's going on at the bridge?" He listens for a while, then says, "All right. No worries." He listens for another moment, then hangs up.

Car horns blare and then a white pickup truck makes an illegal U-turn, making its way out of the standstill traffic and away from Sanibel. Grayson makes the same move as the truck, earning several honks of his own. He takes us onto the highway, farther away from our houses. I can hardly see past the wind shield, even with his wipers at full speed.

"That was Elliot," he says. "There was a bad accident on the bridge. Five or six cars piled up. Probably from the storm. It won't be cleared for anyone to leave or enter for hours. Possibly even tomorrow morning." He doesn't take his eyes off the road for even a moment to gauge my reaction.

I bite my bottom lip, something I tend to do when I'm worried. "Where are we going?"

"There's an inn by my office."

I pictured taking a bath tonight and then curling into bed with a book. I steal a glance from Grayson. His body isn't tense, and his face is relaxed. It dissolves some of my anxiety. *He makes me feel safe.*

Once we get to the Inn, the rain has slowed to a drizzle. It's a small two-story building with a neon sign in the parking lot. We walk empty handed to the office to check in, no bags or clothes to change into. The jingle above the door makes the sleeping old man behind the desk stir awake, then he smiles warmly at us. "I was just resting my eyes," he lies. "Need a room?"

"Two, actually," Grayson says.

The old man looks down at a piece of paper, then worries his lip. "You coming from Sanibel?"

I nod.

"I'm afraid a few people already beat you to it. We have one room left."

Great. "We'll take it," I say.

He hands me a key and directs us to room thirteen. I walk behind Grayson, who climbs the stairs slowly. We've shared a room before; this isn't anything new for us. Once he opens the door, any lingering amusement on his face falls away. I drag my eyes away from his expression to see what made him so upset. Once I look at our room, it's evident.

One bed. No couch.

I've written this exact scenario before, but now that it's happening in my real life, rather than a fictional one, I regret putting my characters through such a compromising situation. Perhaps this is karma.

I feel the heat of his stare. I'm exhausted, hungry, and the chill from my wet clothes hasn't left. I want to get into a warm shower and order something to eat, so I walk in and say, "We'll make it work."

Grayson follows, shutting the door behind him. He

removes his shoes and sits on the bed. "Do you like pizza?" he asks.

"I love it." My stomach rumbles.

He makes a quick call to order a pie. Once he sets down his phone and meets my eyes, he slowly rakes them down my body. "You go shower and hang your clothes to dry. You can wear my clothes," he says, which brings me back to the night we painted his wall. I wore his shirt, and it smelled like *him*. I vividly remember what happened shortly after, how he asked for it back and then touched me in such pleasant ways. My face must be crimson, because Grayson grins up at me, as if his thoughts took the same turn as mine. I look away and tuck myself in the bathroom. I remove my clothes and hang them to dry. Luckily, my underwear isn't wet.

The shower is pleasantly hot, slightly burning and making my skin red. I let the water pelt at my back for what feels like forever, chasing away the chill in my bones. I unwrap the bar of soap and rub it over my skin.

Once I've used up all the hot water, I take my time drying off. After turning the towel into a dress and slipping on my underwear, I glance in the foggy mirror. I swipe my hand across it. Once I see the leftover mascara beneath my eyes, I rub it away until my face is bare.

Steam follows me into the cold room, and my gaze immediately locks onto Grayson, who is standing by the door holding a pizza box.

He doesn't glance at my towel-wrapped body, but his eye contact is making me feel entirely bare. He sets the pizza on the bed. His next action changes the atmosphere when he reaches behind his neck and lifts his shirt over his head.

My eyes trace every exposed inch of him, from the hard lines of his abdominals to the delicate veins twisting through his arms. I promised myself I wouldn't turn into a puddle at the sight of anyone, but I know Grayson. I know his heart and I'll allow him to be the exception to my rule, because if I melt, I know he wouldn't abuse my puddle on the floor.

His body is a work of art that I wouldn't mind looking at for a while, but his smile is a spell, and I've been bewitched. Everything about him is masculine. Nothing boyish remains, except for the two shadows in his cheeks. His dimples are sprinkles of sugar, making him look oh so sweet.

"Here." He extends his shirt to me.

The heat beneath my skin makes me want to look down, but I don't. "Thank you." The fabric is soft in my hand. I put it on in the bathroom and wrap the towel around my wet hair. When I step out, he freezes with a slice of pizza in his hand, mid-bite.

I glance down at myself. His shirt stops above my knees. "What?" I ask, a bit self-conscious.

"You. In my clothes." He blows out a steady breath. "Second best to that outfit you wore the other night at The BARnacle." The night I told him how much his touch contrasted Walter's. I would think he was making fun of my appearance, but his gaze is gentle and seems to admire me as if I'm exquisite like something in a museum. "Come to bed," he gestures to the pizza box resting on it.

I lean against the headboard and pull the covers over my bare legs. Once I finish three slices, I lick my fingers clean and sigh with relief.

I go to the bathroom to brush my teeth and am pleasantly surprised to find two toothbrushes wrapped in plastic, and a travel sized bottle of toothpaste. Grayson taps his knuckles on the opened door. Our eyes lock in the mirror and he saunters in with his usual grin. Our eyes never seem to stray from the other's reflection as we brush our teeth. He smiles when I get toothpaste foam all over my lips. Once we're finished, he turns and peers down at me, but I still watch his reflection. His features relax, and his gaze softens, then, he turns and leaves.

I turn the facet and splash cool water on my face. I grip the countertop firmly and inhale a deep breath. I step into the room, which is only lit by a single lamp, casting shadows on the walls and ceiling. Grayson is on the carpeted floor, head resting on a single pillow and a thin sheet draped over his tall body.

"What are you doing?" I ask.

He lifts his head, then rests it on his arm, as if he can't get comfortable. "Going to sleep. What are you doing?" His voice drips with sarcasm.

I sigh and move directly above him and pull the sheet off his body. His muscles tense from the cool air. "Get up."

He rolls over so he's on his back, eyes lifting to mine. "Why?"

"You're not sleeping on the hard floor."

"Are you volunteering for my place then?"

"Neither of us are sleeping on the floor," I say, stretching out my hand to pull him up. He's eyeing it for only a moment before he nods and takes it. I pull with all my might, and he doesn't budge. He chuckles and stands on his own. *Rude.*

I try not to overthink as I climb into bed, making myself comfortable at the very edge. I feel the mattress dip beneath his body weight. The comforter ruffles as he gets settled. He turns off the lamp closest to him. Darkness falls over us.

I drift to sleep before I wake up sometime later in the middle of the bed, curled against a warm chest with a solid arm draped over me. It feels as if my belly is full of wine, my blood running comfortably warm. *I should move.*

I nuzzle my face even more into his chest. He smells like strawberries and a hint of sea salt caught in the breeze on a summer day. He smells like home.

I startle from his voice, which vibrates through his chest. "Are you sniffing me?"

"No," I say immediately, lifting myself up on my elbow to move back to my side, but his palm presses me back down.

"Macy," he says in a broken whisper. "I don't want to play." His voice rasps over my skin and sinks into my pores, making my heartbeat too quickly. "Just for one night, can we stop pretending we're indifferent toward one another." His callouses delightfully caress down my arm.

My stomach cartwheels and I interlock our fingers, hidden away in the dark. I can hardly see him, but I angle my face until I feel the silk of his lips. I speak against them. "Only for tonight."

He's kissing me like he's moments from drowning and I'm the breath of air he needs to survive. Suddenly, I'm beneath him, and his weight eases an ache I hadn't realized was there. My legs wrap around him, and my vision adjusts enough to see him. His eyes darken as if the midnight sky has swallowed them whole.

The comforter cloaks us from the rest of the world. I lock my fingers behind his neck, and he turns his head to the side, his soft hair is tickling my face as he presses a kiss to my wrist. The big T-shirt bunches up to my waist, and his knuckles are a soft caress against my torso as he slowly removes it. Then his skin touches mine. His subtle chest hair is grazing the peeks of my breast with wonderful friction. His grin is a secret against my lips. I gasp against his mouth when he pinches the sensitive bud. He does it again to the other one, making my hips buck into his.

"Feel good?" I can hear the smirk in his voice.

I begin to pulse between my legs. "Yes." It comes out breathless.

His face is no longer above mine. I cry out when he kisses the places he pinched, and then swirls the tip of his tongue. He palms my chest, and his empty hand draws lazy patterns up and down my thigh, leaving gooseflesh in his wake.

I grip him over his pants and we both let out a pleasurable sound. I cup his jaw to bring his face back to mine. I move my lips over his neck, and he kisses my bare shoulder. The heat of his sporadic breath does nothing to tame mine.

I want to explore his body as he's done mine, so I slowly shimmy down beneath him, kissing the hard planes of his pectorals. He's planking over me. I press a kiss to the soft skin of his forearm with a giggle, which turns into a gasp as he slides off me and shimmies us around so that I'm laying above him. It makes it easier to kiss his abdomen. His muscles tense and relax beneath me, and once I get close to his navel, he squirms, and I grin. "You're ticklish here."

"Don't abuse that knowledge."

I do just that, digging my fingers into his skin and making him tense. He's quick to still my wrists, the size of his hands swallows them whole, as if he were holding toothpicks.

"Very cute, Mace."

I paint an innocent smile on my face.

"That smile is going to be my demise."

I crawl up the length of his body. He's hooking his finger beneath my chin so his gaze can burn into mine. "It's unfair," he says so closely to my mouth.

"What is?"

"For someone to look so divine." His lips touch mine, and he lowers his voice, making it come out deeper. "There are flecks of gold in your eyes, did you know that?" *There are?* "And your hair beneath the sun shines golden. It's heavenly, really." He sighs, like the beauty he describes is painful. "I think my favorite color might be gold."

His words are a drug, turning my blood molten and liquefying my heart to something that feels as pure as gold. His laugh comes and this time it's childish. Innocent. The cadence of it feels familiar, like a dream tugging at the edges of my mind that I can never fully grasp. "What were you like as a kid?" I find myself wondering out loud.

"Happy," he says, then lays flat on his back, pulling me down so my head rests upon his chest. "And sad."

"What made you happy?" I ask.

The dark room is devoid of sound, save for the hum of the air conditioning, for eleven heartbeats until he responds. "The sun."

I nearly ask what made him sad, but I want him to hang on to the sun. I want him to lay here with me, only remembering how it feels to be happy. After several minutes of focusing on his breath, it slows and becomes even. Each rise and fall feels like waves rolling over sand. Shortly after him, I fall asleep too, head on chest, skin against skin. It's one of the most intimate things I've ever felt.

It's easy to be bold in the dark, with shadows adorning you. But in the morning, with daylight pouring through the window, I glance down at my shirtless body and hurry to throw my clothes on, which are fully dry after hanging up all night.

Grayson stays asleep until I'm dressed, or he does a good job pretending. Once his eyes crack open, he smiles at me. It's a real smile, wide and cheeky, showing nearly all his teeth. I feel myself returning it, and it's as if the room at the Inn is floating in space, far away from the world.

My phone is dead from the day prior, so I plug it in the moment I'm home since Grayson was using his charger in the car. It's flooded with missed calls from my mother, but I don't bother returning any of them. I want to exist in a bubble, if only for today, and perhaps I'm naïve to believe nothing can burst it.

I'm combing through my wet hair after taking a shower, the vanilla scent of my shampoo hanging in the air. I roll my eyes when I hear a demanding knock. I quickly wrap my hair in a towel and throw on denim shorts and a cropped tank top. I don't bother looking out the window, assuming it's Grayson here to demand I eat dinner with him. My smile slips as I swing open the door to find my parents standing there, side by side.

My dad turns to my mom. "I told you she was okay."

My irritated mom barges past me to enter the house, revealing what I had missed before. The man I begrudgingly agreed to marry and then effortlessly dumped over text.

Chapter 19
Macy

"Macy," Walter says curtly, rushing past my dad. Then, his mouth is on mine and it's wrong. His tongue is sweeping in without permission and his hand are claiming me as if I belong to him. *How many other girls has he kissed while we were together?* My lips are unmoving, yet he continues to assault them. Bile rises to my throat, and I shove at his chest.

He feigns hurt. His eyebrows come together but his nostrils are flaring when I wipe my mouth with the back of my hand.

My dad clears his throat in discomfort and awkwardly passes us, following my mom into his parent's house.

I hold up my hand, so Walter doesn't come any closer, but the idiot smiles and interlocks his fingers with mine. I quickly tug my arm back. "You need to leave."

His eyes flash with disbelief, and then my mom calls. "Walter, honey, bring Macy in here. You two don't need to stand out in the heat."

He grabs my hand again and it's so different than when Grayson does it. Everything about Walter is a stark contrast.

He tugs me inside and my mom says, "We'll leave you two to talk." She turns to my dad, who is quick to open the sliding glass door and leave.

I'm frozen in disbelief. The man I detest is standing in the living room of my grandparent's home. He is making himself cozy on the couch, kicking his feet up on the coffee table, not even bothering to remove his shoes. He drapes my grandma's hand-knit blanket over his legs. "Come sit next to me."

I pinch the bridge of my nose and let out a steady breath. "I have nothing to say. We're broken up."

"Sweetheart." I wince at the endearment. In the beginning, I loved the pet name. Funny how three years later I never want to hear it again. "I know you're mad about our video call. I *like* your small tits, so you don't need a boob job. I was just annoyed when I said that, okay? Why don't you start packing and we'll leave in the morning?"

"Oh my God, you are so vapid!" I grip the back of a chair that's tucked into the dinner table and say in a voice so calm it unnerves me. "Get out."

He reels back and stares at me with pure shock. He opens his mouth to speak but then stops. I never peel my gaze away. I just watch him stumble over my rejection and then he finally speaks. "I was trying to be nice before, but you're clearly on your period. Let me put it to you this way. You're getting on a plane with me, you're going to put my ring back on your finger and stop acting like a brat." He's off the couch and moving toward me.

"Get away from me," I say through my teeth.

He doesn't. His mouth is on mine again and this time I won't let him *happen* to me. I take his bottom lip between my teeth and bite down as hard as I can.

"You fucking bitch!" he growls, bringing his finger to his

lip to find it dripping scarlet. I almost crack a smile from the shock on his face.

"You need to leave. Right now," I demand for the third time.

"This isn't your house." His lip splits into a sardonic smile, blood staining his teeth. "And your mom invited me to stay." He sucks his injured lip to appear thoughtful. "I think I'll go grab my luggage and put it in *our* room."

This house embodies a version of myself I've been striving to return to, and it's in this very moment, standing with Walter in the space, that I realize he turns everything in his vicinity to gloom. I never knew misery until I met him. His pessimism rubbed off on me, and I haven't been myself in three years. I used to frolic through this very living room as if it were a field of flowers. I danced my way through the day and saw the world for every bit of beauty that it is. The glass was always half full until he taught me to see the emptiness.

This vile man is going to corrupt my corner of heaven, and there's nothing I can do to stop him, but I can leave.

He goes out front to grab his belongings from the driveway, where the Uber left it. He's using one of *my* suitcases since he doesn't leave the five-mile radius of our house to need his own.

I step into my sneakers, not bothering with socks. I knock on Grayson's door, hoping he'll answer before Walter sees where I went.

"Well, *you* aren't Amazon." All six wonderful feet of him greet me with dimples and an endearing grin. I glance at my house with unease which is quick to sober his expression. He steps aside for me to enter.

"What's going on?" he asks in a fleeting voice, like he's

ready to fix whatever it is. His hands are on my face, cupping it tenderly. "Talk to me, Mace."

I don't want to. Once I voice it, it becomes real, and I'll have to accept that everything I've been avoiding chased me here.

He stiffens from my silence. "Did someone hurt you?"

"No." I sigh. "Walter is here with my parents," I say with dread.

His lethal gazes set on the front door, blue eyes flaming with something terribly cruel. He is furious. I've never seen such a strong emotion from him. His pure hatred is aimed at a man he only knows for disrespecting me. Looking at his expression now, I'd never guess he'd have the capability of smiling, let alone possessing dimples.

"Hey," I say, softly touching his cheek. His burning eyes touch mine and everything on his face melts away until he's *my Grayson* again.

I mean, until he's *himself* again.

"Are you okay?" he asks, voice so gentle it contrasts the way he looked only a moment ago.

"I don't know how to answer that."

He runs his thumb over the seam of my lips, and it feels as if he's washing away Walter's kiss. "You bring out a lot in me, Mace, but murderous is a new one." He lifts me and sets me on the counter, like when he tended to the shards of glass in my skin. But these wounds cut much deeper. "What are we going to do?"

We.

"I told him to get out *three* times, but he just smiled at me and put his suitcase in my room." I want to cry. "My mom invited him in. Told us to talk it out. She has no idea how awful he is, and it's my fau—"

Grayson cuts me off before I can finish the word. "Don't you dare say it's your fault."

"But she doesn't have a clue. She thinks I'm being dramatic over a small argument or something."

He rests his hands on my hips, not bothering to step back to an appropriate proximity. "Then perhaps we can show her."

"How?" I ask.

"Assholes like him can only pretend for so long. I'm sure we can break him in front of your parents if you give me some details about his personality."

I sigh. Walter hasn't cracked in front of them thus far, so I doubt he will now, but I say, "He looked pretty angry when I wiped his kiss off just now."

His eyes flare with hatred yet again. "I might actually kill him." He slowly collects himself. "Anything else?"

"When I said I wasn't coming back to Idaho anytime soon, he told me I was begging for attention and that if I wanted it so badly, I should've gotten breast enlargement surgery."

His grip tightens on my hips. "Torturously slow," he says.

"His true colors show when he's pissed off," I say.

"I can work with that."

Everything he's ever done is tumbling from my lips. "You know, he never congratulates me when I accomplish something in my career? He treats my job as if it's a joke." I shake my head. "He never takes me anywhere either. It's like he wants me to stay the same forever. Like the twenty-year-old girl I was when we met." Relationships shouldn't hold you back. They should inspire you to grow in every way a person can, like sunlight for a tree. But Walter isn't the sun, he's a weed shading me, so I'll never touch the light.

"I'm no expert, but it's obvious that he's intimidated by

your success. He wants you to feel small to compensate for *his* shortcomings."

He treats me the way he treats *himself*, so I'll never leave him. Because why would I leave when he's led me to believe I'm worthless on my own? That he's better than me in every way and I need him to thrive. He keeps me in the dark because he knows that once the lights are on, I'll realize he was below me all along. A small part of me pities him, but he hurt me. He manipulated me. But most importantly, he lied every time he said he loved me.

Someone who loves me will cheer me on from land as I touch the sky, and if I'm ever in a dark place, they'd show me the stars.

Grayson is watching me patiently, and I think back to the first day we met. He ordered my books, and now he has them displayed in his house. I saw him read words I've poured my soul into. I've heard the names of my characters on his lips. He held me as I cried the night I broke my grandparent's ocean treasures, and he glued them back together the next morning before I woke up. He hosted my friends with no warning. His face lights up when I laugh, and he touches me like I'm something divine.

"Why are you so nice to me?" I ask.

His head tilts. "Why wouldn't I be nice to you?"

"Because I certainly wasn't. I acted like I hated you."

He lifts a brow. "Acted?"

I glance at his orange wall. "We both know you never gave me a true reason to warrant hatred. You did, however, supply me with several to dislike you, but that's neither here nor there," I joke. "But the reasons you've given me to like you win by a landslide."

"Don't—" he says, holding up a hand. "Please don't say any more. Walter doesn't deserve you, but neither do I."

"Why are you saying this?" I whisper.

"Because it won't be long until I give you a true reason to hate me."

I open and close my mouth, but nothing comes out.

"Let's focus on getting rid of Walter, okay?"

No, it's not okay, but what can I say right now? "Okay." My voice is small.

Chapter 20
Grayson

When I was a kid, my mom took her wedding ring off a lot. Before swimming, doing the dishes, even riding her bike. It was diamond, the most durable stone, but she treated it as if it were as delicate as glass. Yet, I'd notice her holding her hand out and watching it sparkle in the light. I didn't understand how she could love it yet hardly wear it.

Macy reminds me of my mother's ring. She's a diamond I want to keep tucked in a drawer because I'm afraid I'll ruin everything. It's not illogical. It's a simple truth.

I don't know what I'm doing when it comes to Macy. I wanted to hang on to happiness so bad that I put off telling her the most important truth, and now, telling her would ruin everything good between us, because I waited too long. I *pretended* for too long. I *lied* for too long.

I watch her leave and disappear to her house. I try to busy myself by reading, but my mind is next door, wondering if she's okay. But she's strong. As durable as my mother's precious stone.

Forty-five minutes later, I'm out the door and crossing the

distance between her and I. As promised, Macy's house is unlocked. I let myself in to find four sets of eyes staring back at me.

Macy, her parents, and Wally—*or whatever his name is*—sit at the dinner table, eating the meal she made. It smells heavenly. The only person who isn't eyeing me like I'm an intruder is Macy. *God, she's so beautiful.*

"Mr. and Mrs. Brookes!" I say in a cheery voice that sounds foreign to me. I remove my shoes and set them neatly by the front door. I'm using every bit of willpower not to slam my fist into Wally's confused expression. I shake her father's hand, who has a firm grip. I attempt to do the same with her mother, but her eyes snag on my features. "I'm Grayson," I say. It takes her a moment to shake my hand.

I take the empty seat at the head of the table, right across from Macy. "Smells delightful," I tell her, trying to ease the tension I can clearly see in her shoulders. I would go over to her and massage them if it was deemed appropriate.

"Grab a plate." Her lips pull taut in an attempt to smile, but it looks more like she's baring her teeth. It takes everything in me not to glance at Wally, who's eying us and gripping his fork in my peripheral vision. It feels as though he's seconds from shoving the prongs into my carotid. *Exactly as planned.*

I take a paper plate from the stack on the table and fill it with Macy's spaghetti and meat sauce. I lock eyes with her as I blow on a forkful.

Her mother clears her throat. "Who's this?" She aims the question to her daughter.

"This is Grayson. I told you he would be joining us."

"And how do you two know each other?"

"He was at my layover in New York. It turns out he lives

next door." She forces herself to laugh. "I invited him for dinner tonight, but I didn't realize we'd have more guests."

I feel Wally's gaze on me, and this time, I finally meet his eyes, as though I'm only just now noticing him. "Oh, I'm sorry. Macy didn't mention she had a brother," I say earnestly.

His nostrils flare. "I'm her fiancé," he bites out rudely, which causes Macy's dad to whip his head in his direction. Wally clears his throat and steels his expression. "My girl is too polite to ask you to leave, but this is a family dinner." His eyes set on the front door, as if he could will me to exit.

"If I wanted someone to leave, I'd say it to their face," Macy says. Silence and tension stretch across the room.

"Hey, the more the merrier. Right, Walter?" her father says, which the moron tenses at.

I bite back a grin.

Macy claps once. "Dig in. The food's going to get cold."

Wally glares at me while we eat. Macy doesn't look away from her plate. Her mom's eyes linger on my features for too long, while her dad looks at ease.

Once my plate is clean, I say, "Thank you for cooking, Mace. This was delicious."

Her eyes meet mine and it's as though an invisible string wraps around my heart.

"Mace?" Walter says with disdain. "What is she, pepper spray?" He looks around the room for someone to agree.

The only sound is the squeak of my chair sliding against the floor as I stand to take her parent's plates. I lean over to grab Macy's, inhaling sweet vanilla. I take Wally's last, and he's the only one who doesn't say thank you. I toss them in the trash and take my seat once again. "You have a lovely daughter," I say to her parents, straying from our plan, which causes Macy to tense.

I selfishly want to talk to them, and Macy is my favorite subject.

"She's something," her mom says, which has Macy rolling her eyes.

"She is," I say. "You know—" I chuckle. "When we were at the airport, she bought coloring books for two kids whose flight was canceled, so they wouldn't stress their mother out." I meet her eyes then. "She already had her own stress to deal with, with her flight getting canceled too. I realized quickly that she's selfless and kind." I grin. "She has a way with words, your daughter." I smile and it's not for show anymore. "I have one book left until I finish them all." I feel flecks of gold pouring over me. Macy's gaze is akin to the way I find myself looking at her most of the time. "Though, I'm sure you've already read them all," I say to Wally.

"Of course, I have."

"So, you read the one where a girl finds her ex-fiancé with thirty-six stab wounds?" I ask, completely making it up. It's not far off from the fantasies I have swirling around when it comes to him.

"I said I read them all, didn't I?" he sneers.

"What's it called again?" I ask.

He opens and closes his mouth.

Macy clears her throat, pretending to look hurt. Or maybe she really is. "You haven't read them," she states.

"Don't lie in front of your parents, sweetheart."

"Why would I write a book about someone getting stabbed? I don't write murder mystery." She scoffs. "Do you even know the genre I write in?"

"Why are you quizzing me all the sudden? And who is this asshole to question me?" He points to me. This is all going so well. I nearly grin.

"Answer the question, Walter. What genre does my daughter write?" her dad says, the friendly tone absent from his voice.

Wally gives him a smug smile when he answers. "Fiction."

"What kind of fiction, specifically?" Macy asks.

When he doesn't answer, I steal a glance from her dad, who is narrowing his eyes on her ex-fiancé. "Do we need to step outside, son? Because if I'm hearing this correctly, you haven't been supportive of my daughter's career, and now you're lying, and that certainly won't do."

Macy's eyes widen in shock, and based on her reaction, I'm assuming her dad's never spoken to someone like that before.

"I—I'm just so busy at work, you know how it is. Gotta keep a roof over this one's head." He reaches under the table to grab Macy's hand, who quickly pulls it away. She sets her palm flat on the table.

"You think I'm not aware that my daughter bought that house? Cut the crap."

Her mom's looking at Wally like she's in denial. Like everything she believed about her daughter's perfect fiancé is crumbling to pieces and she doesn't want to accept it.

"Did you ever tell them how you proposed to their daughter?" I ask, leaning back and crossing my legs at the ankles.

His jaw ticks. "Of course," he says slowly, like this entire conversation is ridiculous. "They know I did it at the top of a Ferris wheel."

"I thought you said you proposed on top of a mountain," her mom says.

"I think I'd remember my own engagement." He laughs.

"I remember the mountain story too," her dad says. *Can't even remember his own lies.*

Macy's eyes are on the table, shoulders pulling forward, and I immediately feel like an idiot. She hates the story of their true proposal. I wish I didn't bring it up.

"Enough," she snaps, eyes flaming. "Walter's biggest crime wasn't that he never read my books or even that I found out he's been cheating on me." She looks at her parent's angry, awestruck expressions and says, "He treats me no better than a piece of gum stuck to the bottom of his shoe, and when I told you guys that I broke off our engagement, you sided with *him*." She points to the pathetic excuse for a man, who looks like he's about to defecate himself. "The fact that you brought him here—" She shakes her head, full of anger. But I see through her mask. Beneath it, she's hurt. "I shouldn't need to tell you about the gruesome details for you to support me. Yet, here we all are, in the uncomfortable position *you* put me in." She gets up and leaves, disappearing to her bedroom.

Her father's face is beet red when he says to Walter, "Get the *hell* out of my house."

Wally opens and closes his mouth, then looks at Macy's mom for backup. Her nostrils flare, which is the only tell that she's pissed. She points to the door, and whatever guard she held up crumbles. She's livid when she says, "If I ever see you again, so help me God, I might kill you." I guess I'm not the only one who's murderous when it comes to Macy.

The asshole gets up to leave, but not before he knocks his cup over, spilling water all over me like a child throwing a temper tantrum. He slams the front door behind him, and several moments go by, the only sound are our angry breaths.

"I'll leave you to talk to your daughter," I say, and then follow Wally out the front door.

Chapter 21
Macy

A knock sounds from the outside of my bedroom door. It slowly creeks open and carries my parents inside. My mom sits at the corner of my bed and my dad is standing in the middle of the room.

"I want to know why you allowed a random man to stay for dinner. We haven't seen you in over a month, and you think it's oka—"

"That's enough!" my dad interrupts, both our heads snap in his direction. "Let her speak."

I dip my head and an involuntary smile tugs at my lips. I wipe the expression from my face when I meet my mom's gaze. "Grayson is not a random man. He's my friend, and he's nice to me." I shift, feeling the heat of her eyes on me, ready to pick apart and judge everything that leaves my mouth. I feel like a child. "I invited him over for dinner way before the three of you barged in here unannounced, which you already know. He was *excited* to meet you. He was kind to you, mom, yet you sit here and call him 'strange'."

Her head tilts in a predatory manner. "So, you'll spread your legs because he was *nice* to you?"

"Mom!" I gasp. It feels as though I've been stripped bare and picked apart piece by piece, her demeaning gaze set upon my bloodied frame.

"You won't be part of this conversation if you're going to behave this way," my dad says.

"Am I wrong?" she asks. "I saw the way you two looked at each other."

If I bite down any harder, my teeth will shatter. "What I do or don't do in my *private life* is none of your business."

My dad shifts, clearly uncomfortable by my statement.

"Your precious Walter has been cheating on me. So don't reprimand *me* for the suspicions you have when I'm a single woman who is free to do whatever I want."

She goes silent, arms crossed in a way to protect herself from the truth. In her mind, Walter could do no wrong, and I was never in a rush to change that until now. She saw him the way I wished he was. But I'm done settling for anything less than what my grandparents had.

"You want to see his profile on the dating app? I can pull it up in less than two seconds."

A beat of silence is hanging between the three of us. My dad clears his throat, and then my mom whispers, "No. I believe you."

The weight of the world glides off my shoulders. The thick tension thins and suddenly it's as though we can all breathe a little easier.

"I painted a perfect picture so you guys would see him the way I wanted him to be." I look at my ceiling fan. Memories of our relationship bubble to the surface. "But he's awful," my voice stumbles and breaks over the words.

"I need to go take care of something," my dad mumbles, leaving me alone with my mom.

Silence drapes between us. She stares too intently at her nails, pushing back her cuticles as if nothing has been said. I shift my legs, crossing them and lifting the covers higher over myself.

"I—I'm sorry," she says. I can't suppress the shock on my face. Apologizing is foreign to a woman who can't admit when she's wrong. "You know, I dated some *horrible* guys before I met your dad?"

My eyes widen at her vulnerability. "I didn't know that." It's hard to imagine your parents' lives before you were born. It never occurred to me that either one of them dated anyone but each other.

"I remember what it was like to lie to my family. I wanted something awful to appear shiny to everyone but me." She looks at me in the eyes. "I'm ashamed that I never saw what was happening in my daughter's life. I know you're capable of hiding it well, I was too, but if anyone would see through it, it should've been me."

"It doesn't matter now."

Her gaze is on the wall, appearing deep in thought. The only sound is the breeze flowing through the house. She sighs and reaches for my hand above the comforter. "You had no one to talk to about all of this for so long. Talk to me, sweetie. You're not alone anymore."

I've never opened up to my mother. When it came to my emotions, I always brought them to my grandma. She handled them with a certain care that my mother always lacked. But now, years of heartbreak pour from my lips and tears drip along *her* cheeks. I tell her everything, including the way Grayson is Walter's opposite.

Horrible experiences bring people together. As much as I wish I never put up with Walter's shit, it led to this moment. One where a mother and her daughter finally see each other.

Hours have ticked by, and we steer off topic to more simple things. She tells me about drama she overhears in the gym locker room and then I tell her how Elliot proposed to Sarah. We bond and laugh, and later into the night, she says, "I think I like Grayson."

"Yeah?" I grin.

She nods. "He looks familiar," she says. I shrug, but she doesn't see because her thoughtful gaze is on the window facing his house. She yawns and it's contagious. I look at my alarm clock, realizing it's just past midnight.

"Goodnight, sweetie," she says when she follows my line of sight. "I love you."

"I love you too, Mom."

Chapter 22
Grayson

As soon as I leave Macy's house, I catch sight of a figure not far off in the distance, walking on the sidewalk. I catch up quickly, grabbing his shoulder so he turns around. Wally's eyes meet mine and before he can anticipate what's about to happen, my fist is connecting with his nose. Bone crunches and blood sprays.

"That was for Macy," I seethe. I wind up my fist and pack a powerful blow to his jaw. "That one was just for fun." I'm turning around, about to walk away when he latches onto my shoulder. I spin and twist the appendage in a way that makes the motherfucker cry out.

My voice is lethal when I say, "Pray I never see you again, because the longer I sit with my hatred toward you, the more it's bound to grow. I might not be as pleasant if you cross my path again." I take a step back, the metallic smell of his blood making me queasy. "You never deserved her," I say as a way of farewell.

"And you think you do?" he calls from behind me.

I stop walking for a moment. "No one does," I say, clenching my jaw. *She's too perfect for the scum in this world.*

"But I'll become a man worthy of her, even if it kills me." I leave him where he stands, not giving a damn where he stays tonight, or if he finds a doctor to fix the nose I broke.

I startle when I see Macy's dad walking toward us. *How much did he see?* His gaze goes to Walter, and then settles on the bruised fist I hold. He gives me a subtle nod. I return it and then leave him to get whatever revenge he sees fit for his daughter.

I attempt to get some sleep, but I toss and turn in my bed. I go into my living room and prop open a Minerva Day book, hoping her words can relieve the stress of tonight.

Chapter 23
Macy

Once my mom goes to her room, I step into my sneakers and cross the distance between mine and Grayson's house. I send her a quick text. *Going to a friend's house.* My heart is drumming in my chest and I wipe my slick hands on my shorts. I try to tell myself it's from the conversation with my mom, but I can't deny what's happening any longer.

I was wrong before when I thought it felt like I was falling into a wishing well, hoping to find Grayson at the bottom. Falling is simple. You jump and eventually you land. This is different. It feels as though I've been pushed into that well, clawing at the walls with bloodied nails, fighting to never reach the bottom.

It's not the impact that I fear. The water will break my fall. It's not knowing what else lies in that water. How will I climb out? Will I find bottomless gold? Will I drown?

Fear is an angel in disguise, perched on our shoulder, whispering in our ear to keep us safe. We often judge fear, pick it apart and criticize it. We never ask fear "why?"

Why am I so scared to simply allow myself to fall?

It's simple really. I don't want to get hurt, and the way I feel for Grayson… The intensity will burn me alive if something goes wrong. Walter hurt me, that much is certain, but it was a mere sting in comparison to the catastrophe Grayson could leave me with.

This fear is loving. It wants me safe. But comfortability will only get me so far in life, and if I allow Fear's whisper to dictate everything I do then I'll never truly live. The thought alone is a nightmare.

And so, with shaky hands, I bring my fist to the door and tap ever so slightly. And maybe that's fear, deep down hoping he won't hear my knock so I can go home believing I tried. But he hears, and the door creeks open.

Chapter 24
Macy

Fright is delicious when it greets me with flaming eyes, a crooked grin, and hair in disarray. An alarm sounds from my chest, pumping blood in my ears. *I see you, fear. But I'm doing this anyway.*

It's hold on my heart releases, falling away until it's just a girl standing before the boy she's falling for, stomach in knots and blush in her cheeks.

"Hi," he says, his midnight voice is hoarse.

"Hi."

"Is everything okay?" he asks.

I shake my head. "No."

His expression shifts to something slightly alarmed.

"Grayson?"

His eyebrows pull together. "Yes?"

"Invite me in."

He steps aside, allowing me to pass the threshold. Strawberries and a scent which can only be described as *him* fills the dim space, only lit by a single lamp in the corner.

"I'm tapping out," I say. "I can't play nonchalant any

longer or pretend to dislike you." Eyes on the sunset wall, I whisper, "You win."

In his silence, fear is raging like an angry sea. But I remain still, despite everything happening within. I feel him behind me, like standing too close to a furnace. Closer and closer the heat gets, until my wrist is encompassed by his hand, and it feels like flames licking up my arm. His breath is against the shell of my ear. "I lost the moment my eyes set on you, Mace. I've been at your mercy for what feels like my entire life." His words hold a certain power, turning my skin to gooseflesh despite the heat.

The tips of his fingers are trickling up my arm, knuckles delicate as he moves my hair over my shoulder and kisses the back of my neck. He's pressing his nose against my hair. "So sweet," he purrs. His hands dig into my hips to spin me around, which forces a gasp from my parted lips. He backs me up until I'm pressed against a wall. *The sunset wall.* "You've invaded my mind and now my home," he says. "You consume my every thought." He eyes my lips. "If we're done playing, if this is *real*, then kiss me," he says.

I take in his face, the pure wonder in his eyes and the hint of trepidation swimming in the blue pools. His eyebrows pinch together, forming a single line of worry between the bold arches. I still believe he is undeserving of such luscious eyelashes. An orange hue from the lamp in the corner of the room is casting sharp shadows across his face, making his features appear as if they've been honed from rock. He looks like something nightmarish, something I shouldn't want. His eyes have been swallowed by black ink, and a thrill runs down my spine.

When I bring my delicate hand to the sharp edge of his face, it somehow softens, and a new shadow appears in his left cheek. I touch the dimple, and the other appears. Then, I hover my lips above his, torturing him with patience. I move closer, my mouth feathering his. I pull back for a millisecond, and then I'm kissing him.

His hands tighten on my hips, and he groans. It's such a beautiful, masculine sound, that makes every intention I had of taking this slow fall away. I press my hips into him and the only word that comes to mind is *desperation*. Perhaps the spell of his lips on my neck explains my lack of vocabulary. And then, every thought I've ever had, every bit of hurt I've felt in my life is melting away like cotton candy on my tongue.

It's beautiful to get lost this way in another person. To let yourself be vulnerable with someone you trust. To be wanted in such a way that makes someone's body react like his does to me. I can't imagine ever believing sex was bad or that it was wrong. *This isn't wrong.*

Our clothes tangle together on the floor, both of us stripped down to our underwear. Suddenly I'm flying in his arms through the hallway, my bare back meets the door to his bedroom, and I'm soaring when he opens it and drops me onto his bed. The mattress bounces and squeaks and he takes his time watching me this way. With my laughter echoing off the walls and a smile stuck on my face. I feel my hair fanned around me, my bare chest cold and peeked.

The dim light leaking through his open door is enough for me to notice his eyes sparkling with adoration, as if I'm the most beautiful site he's ever beheld. I want to shy away, cover my breasts and tuck my face into the thick comforter, but I don't. Maybe it's okay to be confident and a little scared too.

"Macy," he says like my name is a prayer. "I know I should probably play it cool right now, but I can't. I love this.

You, in my bed, lips pink and swollen from mine." He lowers himself so he's above me, elbows propping him up. "I loved opening the door to find you standing there, knocking on it in the middle of the night. I love knowing you feel comfortable coming to me at any time of day. I want you to wake me up at three in the morning because you're hungry for a snack and nothing in your pantry looks good. I want you to come to me. For anything."

"That's…quite neighborly," I tease.

"I mean it."

"You can come to me too," I whisper.

He looks at me for a few moments and then nods ever so slightly. A grin slowly spreads across his face right before he grabs me and quickly maneuvers us, so his back is against the headboard and I'm straddling him. I feel every inch of him pressed against me this way, only the thin fabric of our undergarments separates us. I realize in this moment how empty I am without him. "I want you," I whisper.

Simply looking him in the eye and expressing my wants is empowering. It shouldn't be something I'm unused to, and right here in this moment, I promise myself I'll never do anything I don't want ever again.

His eyes lock on mine, not straying for a moment when he slides his hand between our bodies, cupping me over my underwear, and then letting out a hiss once he feels the moisture. "I would've thought I imagined those words leaving your pretty lips but…" He glances at the spot we meet. "I'm going to try not to let that go to my head." He grins, then slips his hand beneath the soft fabric, coaxing a moan from me.

He's swirling the tips of his fingers over the sensitive nerves, skillful in his pattern, like he's paid attention to what feels best for me. My lips part and I glance at his hand disappearing beneath the only piece of clothing left on my body. He leans forward and circles my nipple with his tongue. *Oh my…*

My gasp is loud when he pushes his finger inside, curling and pumping it so my back arches, causing my chest to press into his face. He uses his thumb to stimulate the bundle of nerves, applying just enough pressure. My moaning becomes sporadic.

Like a symphony halting to a stop, his fingers still. "Don't finish," he says gravelly. I stare down at him breathless, the back of my neck sticky with sweat.

"Why?" I ask, desperately moving my hips to gain relief.

"Because I'm not done with you." He starts again, and it's just a few moments until I'm close to bursting with relief.

But he stops. *Again.* I glare at him.

He gazes at me through thick lashes, lips parted in awe as though I'm his center of gravity. "I love when you look like you loathe me," he says.

"You seriously need therapy," I say between breaths.

"Perhaps." He chuckles and then angles his face, so his lips touch mine. He whispers, "I'm going to work you so close to relief, and just as you're on the cusp of finishing, I'll steal it from you, until you're writhing for *me*." His bold words have my lips parting in utter shock, which he takes as an invite. His tongue sweeps inside my mouth, lips locking on mine.

I slow the pace until it's delicate like a kiss between lovers, and then he pulls back, placing his forehead against mine. His hand cups my jaw and he whispers, "This might be more torturous for me." I smile and he kisses it, and then he shimmies us around until I'm beneath his weight, and all I see are his eyes, the color of midnight waters.

He sprinkles tender kisses all over my body, and when he

reaches the side of my abdomen, I squirm and giggle. He kisses the only piece of fabric left on my body, then slowly removes it, baring me to him. His warm lips are touching me in such an intimate way. Tasting me, he groans like I'm something delicious. He gets me so very close, I can see the sharp glare of relief, but it quickly turns dark as he steals it away, just as promised. Once my breathing has slowed a fraction, he starts again. He doesn't stop this torturous pattern until my head is spinning and I cry out. "Please!"

He's gazing up at me with a raised brow, his lips glistening, when he says, "Please, what?"

"Stop…doing that. It's torture," I whisper.

"What is it you want?" he asks in a voice nearly as pleading as mine.

"You."

He's suddenly reaching over, opening the drawer to his nightstand to grab a condom. He gently places his weight on me. Then his lips.

He deepens the kiss, and that's all we do for several minutes. His innocent touch moves over my body, yet it feels incredibly intimate. He threads our fingers, lifting my arms above my head, kissing his way up to my wrists. He gazes down at me, eyelids heavy with lust. "I want you too," he whispers. The way he says it, the intensity of his gaze makes his statement seem entirely separate from sex.

He frees himself from his boxer briefs, moving them down his legs, then kicking them away. "This is what you want?" he asks.

"Yes," I whisper.

He tears the wrapper with his teeth, rolling the condom on and lining himself against me. His eyes search mine for permission, to which I smile and pull him down so his lips are against mine. I kiss him as I lift my hips, a gasp escapes the both of us when he starts to fill me.

I think of that magical moment when you take off in an airplane. When the future is a blank canvas of possibilities. When I left Idaho, I never imagined *this*. Grayson is a dream I never once dared to hope for. Because hope is dangerous, it leaves you vulnerable to a world of hurt if it never comes true. He's everything I always deemed as fiction. But he's real. He's my fairytale come to life.

Mine. *He's mine.*

He slowly fills me all the way, gazing at me as if I'm his too. We come together, and he cups my face. His thumb touches my lips, so I kiss the soft pad. His eyes darken when I suck the digit into my mouth, swirling my tongue around it.

"You have no idea—" he starts, then buries his face between my neck and shoulder. "How long I've waited for you."

My thoughts swirl, I can't grasp a single one to understand what he means. Everything in my mind parts like a sea until Grayson is at the very center, and it hits me like stars aligning.

I've landed in that wishing well to find I am inescapably in love with him. There's no rope out, only the one tying us together. I want to live and die here.

I am in love with Grayson.

Words don't leave my lips, but I send every feeling of love through that invisible rope between us, and suddenly it feels as if I'm on fire, those blue flames flashing over me. I bare my heart to him. I let him fill every inch of me. My mind, body, and soul.

I don't want this to end. I press my hand against his chest, and he pulls out of me, eyes burning with wonder. I push him so he's on his back and then straddle him. His eyes are ping ponging between my face and the place he disappears inside me.

His lips are beautifully parted, and suddenly I wish I was an artist so I could capture the look on his face. I would paint the way his eyes seem to shine yet darken at once. Like night and day in a duel. The way his cheeks are flushed, and his hair is wild, flying every which way. I've made him look so unkept. I would name the painting "Unveiling his Final Mask."

I pour everything I feel into the rhythm of my hips. His gaze drips over me like a soft rainfall. "I can't last much longer with you moving like that," he says through his teeth like he's pained.

Burning light takes over my vision until I'm blinded by it, caught in a wave so strong I might never break the surface. It's pure ecstasy. My moans are faraway. His movements beneath me become jerky. That wave slowly eases me to shore, until I'm washed up, trying to catch my breath. Grayson's chest is heaving like mine, and I slowly pull myself from him. His arms come around me and pull me to his chest.

We lay like this forever. Me listening to the rhythm of his heart, the way it starts to slow, along with his breath. He draws lazy circles on my skin. "Write me a story." His chest vibrates with his voice.

I feel myself smile. We're writing a story right now. A beautiful one.

"What kind?"

Three beats go by before he says, "Something wildly dramatic." His hand waves in the air as he speaks. "Make it depressing enough for me to cry."

I could never write a story that doesn't have a happy

ending. "When was the last time you cried?" I ask, wondering out loud.

He counts on his fingers. "I don't know. Maybe ten or fifteen years ago."

"What?" I all but shout at him.

He shrugs, the movement raises and drops my head.

I say with an edge of seriousness to up the dramatics, "Something you should know about me, Grayson, is when I see a challenge, I'm determined to overcome it. I vow right here to break that ten-year streak of yours."

His chest vibrates beneath my ear with laughter. "Good luck with that, Tato."

I roll my eyes. "We're back to that one, are we?"

"What would you prefer I call you?" The question reminds me of a story. A rivalry between an angry girl and an arrogant prick, set in the JFK airport. Nonetheless, I smile at the memory. It's *our* story.

"Mace," I whisper. "I like when you call me Mace."

"It's settled then," he says with a smile in his voice. "Dream of me, Mace."

"Still as arrogant as ever." *And just as charming.*

His chest is my pillow, and his breath is a melody that puts me to sleep.

Chapter 25
Macy

"Sleeping Beauty," a deep voice coos.

I squint open an eye and lift the covers over my face. Grayson pulls them all the way off the bed, exposing my naked body to the crisp air. I groan and sit up, my hair a wild entity against my back. "What do you want?" I ask through my teeth.

He clears his throat and mumbles, "I mistakenly awoke the beast." Then his eyes are raking down my body, and clear images of last night take over. I don't shy away from the memory or my nakedness. I embrace it with a smile, then climb out of his bed and make my way to his bathroom to brush my teeth with my finger and take a much-needed shower. I rub his sandalwood scented soap over my skin, his aroma potent in the steam.

Grayson is in the kitchen flipping pancakes while eggs cook on a separate pan. As though he can sense my presence, he says, "You snore, by the way." He turns to me and frowns at the clothes I put on, as if he wished I had come out here naked.

"Well, you talk in your sleep," I lie.

"About?"

I walk further into his kitchen and sit on a barstool. "Puffins."

He eyes me with amusement. "Puffins?"

"You heard me."

"So, you're saying that I went on and on about puffins the entire night?"

"Yup."

"Interesting," he drags the word out, appearing thoughtful with his eyes narrowed on the sunset wall.

"Why is that?"

"Because I have no clue what a puffin even is."

We stare at each other for several moments until I'm breaking out into laughter. The kind that hurts your stomach and causes tears to trickle from your eyes. Suddenly, Grayson is right before me, his mouth is on mine.

His hands find their way into my hair, and I deepen the kiss by parting my lips and sweeping my tongue across his. A *zing* drops between my legs when he groans. I blink open my eyes when I smell something burning. He doesn't notice until I gently push him back. His gaze is entranced on my lips until he inhales. He rushes to the stove and grins at the black circles that were once pancakes. "The world could be burning down, and I wouldn't have a single clue." He faces me. "I am enthralled in you."

After we eat our eggs and split the only pancake that didn't burn as much as the rest, I peel myself from him and go home to find my parents sipping coffee on the couch and watching the morning news like always.

"Where's Walter?" I ask.

My dad merely glances at me. "He won't be coming back." He doesn't elaborate.

I'll have to see him again. My belongings are in the house we own together, well, that's if he hasn't set them on fire or donated everything I own to a thrift store. Although, both of those options would be too much of an effort for him.

My mom's gaze drags over me, then she glances toward the direction of Grayson's house. "Did you have a good time at your friend's house?" The corner of her mouth lifts ever so slightly before she turns back to the TV.

My cheeks flame and I nod.

"Our flight is in three hours."

I feel myself freeze in place. "*Our* flight?"

"Your father's and mine. You seem…settled here, so we didn't book you one."

"I'll drive you!" I exclaim, glad they aren't going to give me a hard time or try to drag me to Idaho.

I drive them to the airport, and we talk like any normal family would. Right as my dad is leaving my car, suitcase in hand, he says, "I saw one of your books in the airport on the way here. Someone was buying one and I told her Minerva Day is my daughter."

I hug them goodbye and a sense of peace washes over me. For once in my life, I feel truly seen by my parents. Everything is falling into place like the world is wholly on my side. Tears that resemble something akin to joy sting my eyes as I drive home. *Home.* That's what Sanibel has always been to me. But now, I don't just think about palm trees and salty waves curling over my toes. I picture *him* waiting for me.

I've spent nearly every moment away from the island wishing I was there. I refuse to spend my life dreaming that I live a different one.

I'm not engaged anymore. I don't have a job in Idaho. My true friends are here, but most importantly, so is Grayson. I'm free to do whatever makes me happy. It's as if the clouds have dissipated to reveal a serene sky.

As I pull into Grayson's driveway, there's a smile stretched across my face. *I'm going to move to Sanibel.*

I rush to his house and swing open the door, grateful to find it's unlocked, so I wouldn't have to wait for him to let me in. I can't imagine sitting still right now. I have thousands of words on the tip of my tongue, begging to be let out. He's not in the living room, and as I search his house for him, my heart speeds as if I'm running, and when I find his bedroom empty, I conclude he's not home. But I am so pent up, I can't just sit and wait for him, so I make myself busy and tidy up his room.

After I make his bed, I find the pack of condoms from last night sitting on his bedside table and blush. I pull out the drawer to put them back, finding a sand dollar and a picture frame face down. I shouldn't rummage through his things, but what would it hurt to look at a photo? I pick it up and turn it around with anticipation.

I smile when I see it's the childish picture frame he bought when we went home décor shopping together. My eyes fall to the picture. Something booms loudly in my ears, and I realize it's my heart, like the beating thing in my chest recognizes him before I do. Everything seems to fall away, as if a vacuum has sucked the air from the room.

In the picture, Daniel, the boy who once lived in Grayson's house, grins widely in his mom's lap, who sits on a beach chair. His dad stands behind them, a little girl on his shoulders.

Arms twist around my waist and I yelp, dropping the photo onto the bed. Grayson's body tenses against mine, and he whispers in a terrified voice, "What are you doing?"

My heart was beating so loud that I was unaware he came back. He turns me to face him, his eyes wide and alert as he takes in my expression. I exhale a steady breath. "You scared me," I whisper, then wrap my arms around him and tuck my face against his chest. *Home.*

He's slow to hug me back. His heart beneath my ear beats as quickly as mine did a moment ago.

I pull away to pick the photo back up and trace my index finger over the boy I once swore I loved. "Where did you get this?" I ask, still staring at the familiar face in the picture.

I look to Grayson, waiting for his response, but when my eyes land on his, a feeling of déjà vu washes over me. I glance down at the printed little boy and his grin.

That grin.

The world tilts on its axis. The dimples in the photo, the eyes, and the nose—they belong on Grayson's face, yet they're right here on someone else's.

"Macy—" His voice stumbles over my name, breaking on the last syllable.

"Where did you get this?" I demand, trying to make sense of it.

His expression is full of sorrow. Of pain.

"No," I say, shaking my head in denial. "No, no, *no.*" My chest feels exposed, like a hole ripped through it, exposing my heart to the airless room. I turn from him without an ounce of control over my body. My head still shakes, as if I have the power to deny what's happening right now. To make it less real.

"Mace, please—" His arm touches my shoulder and I brush it off and cross the room.

"How?" I ask. I can't believe I didn't recognize him. It's so clear. "Daniel," I breathe his true name.

Hurt crosses his face like he's been gutted, but that can't be true. Maybe I'm seeing my pain projected onto him.

"Did you know who I was?" I wonder out loud. "You read my name on my boarding pass. I told you I was going to my grandparents' house in Sanibel—of course you knew," I whisper. My heart somersaults at the prospect of finding him again, yet my mind sees the betrayal. *He lied.* The organs battle between what I should do in this moment, if I should wrap my arms around the boy I once loved or let myself hate him.

"I'm *so* sorry." His voice shakes and he holds up a hand. He looks moments away from crumbling.

"For pretending we were strangers? You were there when Sarah and I were talking about you, and you didn't say anything!" I'm so deeply wounded that anger disguises my pain to protect me from it. "You kissed me, knowing exactly who I was. We had sex!" He's a blur behind my tears. I hate how I cry when I'm mad, because he crosses the room and wraps me in his arms as if I need comfort.

I push him away which causes his face to fall. "You lied about your name!" I realize now that he never once told me his last name, and I never bothered to ask. This entire time, I only knew him as Grayson. A fake name.

He struggles to speak, and I realize he's crying too. *For the first time in over a decade.* "Macy, please—" His voice comes out fragmented. I can hardly understand him. His chest heaves as if he can't breathe. "Let me explain." He shakes his head. "Grayson is my m-middle name."

I feel like a paper target, my very center punched out by a thousand bullets. I thought he was different. As close to perfect as someone could get. I thought he was mine, that I unveiled his last mask. I was so wrong. So blind. *So stupid.*

"Why lie?" I ask in a soft voice.

"I want to tell you, b-but I can't manage to say it—*damn it*!" He squeezes the roots of his hair.

"You made me feel so special," I say, trying to wrap my mind around him being Daniel. They're separate people in my mind, and now I need to merge the two. His last name is Wright. I remember now.

"You *are* special to me, Mace."

Now, I realize, beneath all his masks, Daniel Grayson Wright is a liar to his very core.

"Then why didn't you tell me?" I snap. "In the airport, when you saw me, why the hell wouldn't you tell me who you were? Why pretend to be someone else?" I squeeze my hands into fists, the familiar bite of my nails brings me back to the morning I left Walter. It's like I'm reliving the memory, only Grayson has hurt me a million times worse than my ex-fiancé ever could've.

"Because I don't want to be Daniel." His voice breaks. "I wanted to tell you so many times, and I was going to, but I kept putting it off because..." His jaw clenches. "You have no idea how long it's been since I've been *happy*, and it's selfish, but I didn't want those lose that feeling, and being Daniel certainly would've chased it away."

"You're making no sense."

His eyebrows pull together. "You make me *happy*, Mace, and suddenly all this time had passed, and I knew it'd ruin everything good between us if I told you, because then you'd think I was a liar—"

"You *are* a liar!"

"I'm not a li—"

"You lied about who you are!" I shout at him. "God, you might be worse than Walt—"

"Don't," he snaps darkly. He fists the roots of his hair. "I'm not Daniel anymore."

I laugh dryly. "What the hell does that even mean?"

"That happy boy you knew, the one you told Sarah you loved? He's gone, Macy. He died the day his family did!" The man standing before me crumbles to the floor, as if he can't hold himself up anymore.

Chapter 26
Grayson
18 Years Ago

The first thing I see when I wake up is a mop of dark brown hair hanging from the top of my bunk bed. Two blue eyes identical to mine stare at me. Delilah giggles and her hair disappears, and then a stuffed dolphin flies at me from the top bunk.

"Lila!" I laugh, rolling out of bed and climbing the latter onto hers.

"Are you ready for the best day ever?" she singsongs, grabbing another one of her stuffed animals and hugging it to her chest.

Dread tugs at me. "No," I say. "Macy is leaving today, remember?"

Her smile flips, but when she looks down at her stuffed animal, it returns. "Yeah, but Mom and Dad are giving us *twenty dollars* to spend at the festival! I'm going to buy a new stuffy." She grins at the one in her arms. I wish I was as excited as her.

Everyone jokes about how different we are even though we're twins. Delilah was born first. It's like those extra minutes in the world made her so much wiser than me. The grown-ups like to say *she* could babysit *me*. "Do you think Mom and Dad will let me stay home?"

"I don't know, but I really want you to come," she complains. "The festival only happens twice a year! Do you know how long a year is?" Her eyes widen.

It's only open at the end of summer, and around Halloween. There are bounce houses and toys I can buy with the money Mom and Dad are giving me, but I want to play with Macy one last time before she leaves. I *do* know how long a year is because that's how long until she's coming back.

"I don't want Macy to go either." She frowns. "When we get bigger, you have to marry her. Then her and I will be sisters and she'll have to live here all the time. Not just in the summer."

"Married people kiss." My face scrunches up.

"You're going to have to kiss *someone* when we're bigger. Every grown-up kisses, so you might as well kiss her. You think she's pretty, don't you?"

My face gets hot, but I lie and say no.

"Delilah! Daniel! Come eat, we gotta go soon," Mom calls from the kitchen.

Delilah grins at me. "I bet we're having strawberries." She loves the fruit. Me not so much. We just learned what a bet was last week. "I bet we're not."

She lifts her chin. "Okay, then if we do have strawberries, you have to eat them *forever*." She emphasizes the last word. Forever sounds like a long time.

"And if we don't have strawberries, then you can't eat one ever again," I say.

She puts her hand out for me to shake, and then we race to the kitchen to find two bowls of cereal. "Ha!" I point a finger at her, but she doesn't look like she lost. She smiles proudly. I follow her gaze to the bowl and realize we're having cereal…with sliced strawberries mixed in.

I slump my shoulders and frown. I'm really not going to like the outcome of this loss.

Delilah sticks her tongue at me right as dad comes up from behind us and kisses both of our heads. He ruffles my hair and then takes a seat across from us at our dining table. "Let me guess, you two already made a bet for today."

"Yup! And guess what, Daddy?" Delilah beams.

"What, pumpkin?"

"Daniel has to eat strawberries forever."

"Whatever," I mumble. "I'll win tomorrow's bet." I take a bite of cereal, milk dripping from my chin.

My mom's perfume fills the room and suddenly my chair is being pushed closer to the table with a loud squeak against the wood floor. "How many times do I need to remind you to push yourself in? Look at your lap," she says. I glance at the milk staining my pajamas with a shrug.

She kisses my head just like dad did, then sits beside him with a mug of steaming coffee. Her smile is wide and contagious when my dad presses his lips into her cheek and whispers something in her ear. "Hurry up and finish breakfast so you two can get dressed," mom says. She takes a long sip of coffee and shuts her eyes like it's the most delicious thing she's tasted.

"Mom," Delilah says.

"Yes, sweetie?"

"Can we *please* listen to Taylor Swift on the way to the festival?"

"We've heard every single song in her album a million times," I mumble my complaint.

"So? You don't even want to go."

"You don't?" dad asks with a frown.

I shake my head.

"But you love the festival. It won't be open again until the fall, you know?" Mom says.

"Does this have something to do with a certain brunette girl leaving this afternoon?" Dad eyes me.

"I want to play with her one last time," I say. I take a sip of my apple juice and glance at her grandparent's house through the window.

My mom sighs. "There's no one to watch you, sweetie pie. I'm sorry."

I look at the floor.

"What if we asked the Brookes's to watch him? We can make it home before they leave for their flight," Dad says. I pipe up.

My mom looks considerate for a second, then says, "I'll call and ask." I want to hop up and down. She talks on the phone for a little while, and when she puts it down, she says, "Finish eating so you can get ready."

I smile widely, but when I look at my sister, she's frowning.

I scoop cereal into my mouth until there's only red fruit and milk in the bowl. I stand to take the dish to the sink when Delilah yells, "Stop!" She peeks inside my bowl. "You have to eat all of them."

I groan and eat one. She laughs at the way my nose scrunches in disgust. I put them all in my mouth, nearly choking as I chew. Once I finish, I run to the bathroom we all share and brush my teeth as fast as I can. I put on my clothes and when I run back into the main living area, my dad laughs. "Daniel, come here." He pulls my shirt off and turns it around. "You put it on backward, goof." Oops. I sit on his lap for a minute while he fills out his daily cross word puzzle. My mom and sister are both getting ready, so it's just the two of us. I grab the pencil out of his hand and write my name in one of the rows since I just learned how.

"Very good, buddy."

I touch the face of his watch. The glass is cold against my finger.

My sister calls my name from our room.

"Sounds like you're being summoned," he says.

I climb out of his lap and ruffle his hair like he always does to me, making him laugh. He reaches out and does the same to me.

Delilah is sitting on the floor, emptying her sparkly back-pack. She has a twenty-dollar bill resting beside her. "Do you want me to get you a toy with your money?" she asks.

A lot of my friends from school fight with their sisters. I don't. Not ever. She's my best friend. So is Macy. I would never fight with either of them. "Yeah." I grin.

"What do you want?"

She always picks out cool toys. "You choose."

Her eyes light up and then we slap our hands together in a familiar way. It's our secret handshake. "Gotta go," I say, rushing to the hallway. "Bye, Lilah!" I call over my shoulder as I race to my parents' room.

"Love you!" she calls.

"Love you too!"

I knock on their bedroom door so my mom can walk me to the Brookes' house. She comes out of her room with a knowing smile. I always catch her watching Macy and I play with the same look on her face. She pinches my cheek and I laugh. "Are you positive you don't want to come with us today?"

"Yes, Mom," I mumble.

She laughs and it's bright and happy. "All right. Come on, I'll walk you there."

I reach up and hold her hand with a wide smile on my face when we cross the yard between my house and Macy's grandparents'. I try not to feel sad waiting for someone to open the door, knowing it's going to be a year until I see Macy again. *A year sounds like forever.*

Her grandma greets me with a warm hug like always, and then I wave my mom goodbye and dart inside the house.

Macy's hair is wild in the mornings before she brushes it, and today is no exception. She sits at the table, dancing in her chair and eating pancakes. Once she notices me, a bright smile overtakes her face. She takes one large bite before leaving her plate and running out the sliding glass door. She calls over her shoulder, "You can't catch me!"

I laugh and chase her, but she's much faster than I am. She gets smaller along the shoreline. I stop to catch my breath, my hands on my knees. She peeks over her shoulder and runs my way. Once she's within range, she says, "Slow poke."

"When you come back next summer, I'll finally catch up to you. I'm going to practice every day."

She looks at the sand, using her foot to draw random shapes in it.

"Are you okay?" I ask when she doesn't say anything else.

When she nods, her chin quivers. She angles her face down so I can't see it. I reach for her hand and squeeze in encouragingly. She slowly meets my gaze with tears in her eyes.

My chest squeezes. "What's wrong?"

She sniffles. "I'm scared to leave. A year is a really long time."

My throat tightens again, but I won't cry. I'll be strong for her, like my dad always is for my mom. I notice something round washed up, so I walk over to it and see it's a sand dollar. I hand it to her, but her frown deepens.

"What's the matter?"

"I can't take this with me. It'll break."

Oh. "Well, I'll hold onto it until you come back. Okay?"

"You promise?"

"I pinky promise." I hold out my smallest finger and she wraps hers around it.

"Riveting! I can't wait to see it when I return."

Riveting? She always uses vocabulary I don't understand. I try to hang on to her pretty words until I can get home to ask my mom for help looking them up in the dictionary. I repeat "riveting" several times in my head, so I don't forget.

"Macy!" her mom calls from the house. "Come put away your plate!"

Macy looks at me with wide eyes and runs back to her house. By the time I make it there, her dish is already in the sink and she's dancing in the living room, jumping on the couch cushions.

"Get down," her mom says.

"She's fine. Let her have fun," Macy's grandma says, which just makes her mom sigh.

Macy hops off the couch to grab my hand, then pulls me up on the furniture and starts jumping. I copy her and she chuckles. My stomach tickles whenever I hear the sound. I like being the cause of it. So, I dance with my arms flailing around, which makes her head tip back with heavy laughter.

"Hey there, kiddo!" her grandfather comes into the living room.

I wave at him mid-jump. He shakes his head at the site of us with an easy smile.

I overhear the grown-ups say they need to leave in two hours for the airport, meaning my family will be home before that.

Macy and I play inside so she doesn't get all dirty before leaving. I count to twenty while she hides, catching sight of her mom glancing at her watch.

We play at least thirty rounds of hide and seek when I hear her mom say to someone, "We needed to leave twenty minutes ago. Where are they?"

Has it already been two hours? I glance out the window and only see my dad's car in my driveway since they took my mom's car to the fair. "Oh, they're back!" I lie, knowing Macy's family is waiting on me, and I don't want to make them late for their flight.

"Great!" Macy's mom says. "We don't have time to go over but tell your family we said goodbye!"

I nod, but no one sees, because everyone is grabbing luggage and rushing out the door in organized chaos. Macy turns to me with tears in her eyes. "I'm going to miss you." She wraps her arms around me. I try not to, but my throat tightens, and my vision goes blurry. I squeeze her tightly. "I really hope this year goes by fast," I whisper into her wild hair that she still hasn't brushed. She smells sweet. Like cake at a birthday party.

"Come on, Macy. Time to go," her grandfather says, practically prying her away from me.

I follow them out the front door and then her grandfather locks it while everyone else piles into the car. Macy's grandma rolls down the driver's window and tells me to go home, so she can see that I made it there safely.

"Bye!" I call with tears falling down my face. Macy waves at me frantically from the back seat.

I drag myself away from the Brookes. My chest aches.

I go through the back door since we usually leave it unlocked, and then I wait in my empty house for my family to return. I open the pantry for a snack and eat it on the couch since no one is here to tell me not to.

I turn on the television with crumbs covering my fingers. I lick away the evidence and put on my favorite cartoon. Countless episodes play until my stomach growls again. During my second trip to the kitchen, I glance out the window only to see one car in the driveway. *Did they forget about me?* I find a package of cheese from the fridge and eat the entire thing.

I hear a car pull up and run back to the window, only to find its Macy's grandparents returning from the airport.

I go to the room me and Delilah share and find a page in my dinosaur coloring book to work on. I color six whole pictures, working extremely hard to stay in the lines, by the time my room starts to darken. It's nighttime. My heart beats fast, and I run to the living room. Maybe I didn't hear them come home. But like before, the house is empty, and terrifyingly quiet.

I'm starving. Again. I eat gummies. I hope they bring fast food home. Maybe that's what's taking so long. But fast food is supposed to be *fast*.

I plop onto the couch with a loud sigh, ready to watch even more cartoons when red and blue light up my walls. There's finally a second car out front when I look at the window, only this one belongs to a police officer. *Am I in trouble?* Someone knocks on my door, and I freeze. I'm not supposed to open it for anyone but my mom and dad.

I run and hide beneath a barstool when a second knock comes and a muffled voice calls from the other side of the door. "This is the police. Please open up."

I squeeze my eyes shut and try to wish them away.

"Daniel, buddy, come open the door," a familiar voice calls. Uncle Ron?

He lives in Fort Meyers, but I only see him on holidays. I know I'm only supposed to open the door for my parents, but I don't think they would want me to leave my uncle outside, so I climb out from beneath the stool and unlock the door.

Uncle Ron doesn't smile or give me a hug. His eyes are red, and he looks scared. A girl police officer with long brown hair follows him inside. I don't know why I'm shaking, why my heart is beating so quickly. They ask me to sit on the couch with them.

"Daniel, something happened when your family was driving home from the festival," Uncle Ron says. He looks like he might cry, which shocks me because I didn't think grown-ups ever cried. "They were in a car accident."

I gasp and cover my mouth. "Is my mom's car okay?" I ask. She was so happy when she bought the vehicle, I remember the pink in her cheeks when she jumped up and down in our driveway to show it to us.

"Have you heard of heaven, Daniel?" the police officer asks.

I nod my head. Heaven is where old people go. It's where my grandparents went.

She looks down for a moment, and when her eyes meet mine, they shine. "Your family went to heaven today. I am *so* sorry," she says in a broken voice, then gets up and leaves the room. I look at my uncle who isn't crying, and then I laugh when I realize the cop was making a joke.

My mom and dad are much younger than my grandparents were when they went to heaven, and Delilah is only six like me. She wouldn't leave me because we're best friends, and my mom and dad love me, so they wouldn't leave me here either.

"Good one, Uncle Ron." I smile.

He clears his throat and shifts. "This isn't a joke, kid."

I laugh a little more.

"*Damn it*! It's not funny, Daniel!" I flinch from how loud his voice is. He sniffs and looks at the wall angrily. His jaw ticks and then he says in a low voice. "Everyone in the car died."

"Stop!" I shout. "That's not funny!" I slap him repeatedly in the chest, trying to make him take back his cruel joke.

He grabs my small hands and looks at me without a hint of a smile. There are two creases between his eyebrows when he says firmly, "They are gone, Daniel."

I'm screaming the word "no" repeatedly, shaking my head, and running down the hallway. I slam the door to our room behind me and click the lock into place. I pick up Delilah's stuffed dolphin and hug the plush toy to my chest, inhaling the smell of my twin. *Please come home.*

Uncle Ron tries to open the door, and I shout at him to leave me alone. Eventually he does, and in the silence, I wonder if he was telling the truth.

Delilah was just here, throwing this very toy at me. Laughing and making bets about strawberries. She isn't old enough to go to heaven. Mom and dad take care of me. Where would I go if they all left me here and went to heaven?

~

I hardly remember what happened after that. It's like a fairy came and stole my memory because it hurt too much. I remember glimpses of a woman talking to me. "I help kids like you," she said. "Your Uncle Ron will become your legal guardian. He's going to take care of you." I didn't bother listening.

I waited for my mom, dad, and twin sister to get home every day. I watched cartoons to pass time. I pictured Delilah's laugh as she darted inside. My mom would likely tell her she needed to take off her shoes and my dad would ignore the chaos to kiss my head.

Uncle Ron slept in my parent's bedroom that week. Most of the time he stayed inside the room with the door closed. Silence raged on and on every day, and I wondered how a home could become a house in a matter of seconds.

One night after dinner, I sat in front of the TV but couldn't bring myself to turn it on. Because distractions were like sleeping, and the second I woke up, everything would come crashing back to me and it hurt all over again.

I watched my reflection in the dark screen. Nothing moved in the background.

There was only me.

I lifted my arm and flapped it in the air and my stomach began hurting. So badly. It was a different stomachache from when I'm sick. This one felt like I might die and go to heaven too.

The pain moved to my chest, through my arms, and down my legs.

The realization was the loudest thought I've ever had. *They aren't coming home.*

I would never see my twin again. She'd never eat another strawberry. I remember, before all of this happened, how I thought a year was long. I'd give anything to wait a year in comparison to a lifetime to see them again. As I saw the emptiness behind my reflection, I realized how permanent forever was.

I curled into myself and cried harder than I ever had. If I had gone with them to the festival, I'd be in heaven with them. Instead, I'm left alone in a huge world without parents or a sister who I called my best friend.

I climbed the ladder and slept on the top bunk, hugging Delilah's stuffed animals. I wonder if she bought a new one like she said she would. I wonder what toy she was bringing back for me. I had a million questions for her, but they would go forever unanswered.

Are there strawberries in heaven? Can you see me lying in the top bunk and crying myself to sleep every night? Do you miss me as much as I miss you?

Uncle Ron made me move to his house in Fort Meyers. I even had to start a new school, since he wouldn't drive me forty-five minutes every day to my school in Sanibel. I was the only kid in the first grade without a best friend. Mine was in heaven and I had no interest in finding a new one. During recess every day, I sat on the bench by myself, and when my teacher tried to get me to play with the other kids, I acted as if I couldn't hear her.

My uncle picked me up in car line daily. He made sure I did my homework and woke me up every day so I wouldn't be late. But he never spoke about my family. He didn't give me hugs or kisses like mom and dad did. He didn't read to me before bed. He pretended not to notice when my eyes were red and swollen.

Every day I lived in deafening silence. Every day hurt. Every day I wished I'd gone to heaven too.

A year had come and gone.

Uncle Ron took a week and a half off work that summer. My old house was in his name, so he brought me there for the short amount of time.

I was in my old room the moment Macy hopped out of her grandpa's truck with her bright yellow backpack. She bounced up and down on her tippy toes and lifted her face toward the sun. She looked at my house and a huge smile overtook her face. I was suddenly less alone in this huge world, until she ran to my front door, and I stupidly hid inside my closet.

I never told anyone what happened to my family. I can't say the words. I never will. Everything was so different from last summer, so much so I decided staying away from the only person I had left was easier than voicing the truth.

Macy's voice was muffled, but my uncles carried since it was so deep. I sunk to the hard floor, and me and Delilah's clothes covered my pained face when I heard him tell Macy that my family and I moved away, and that he was a stranger who bought our home. When the front door closed, I ran to the window to see her walk to her house with her shoulders slumped. She lifted her hand to her face and wiped her cheek. I was crying too.

Chapter 27
Grayson
Now

No, no, *no.*

I can't believe this is how Macy found out I am Daniel. I was so happy to see her in my room, I wrapped my arms around her waist and inhaled her sweet scent. When I saw the picture, she was holding, it was like the world ended.

I was paralyzed as I watched the gears turn in her beautiful mind. Her face fell with betrayal and pain. I was to blame for the tears in her eyes. *I hurt her.* As if she realized it too, her gaze turned lethal with hatred until I blurted out the truth.

Now, I stare at her worried face, unable to move. Because I'm back there, eighteen years ago, when the only word I could speak was "no."

The summers growing up, my uncle took a week or two off work to take me back to Sanibel. I spent that time looking out my bedroom window to see Macy. I just watched her. Because, while I wasn't out there dancing beside her, I could close my eyes at night and imagine I was.

One afternoon, while I watched Macy chase seagulls, her

laugh carried to my window by the wind, I realized she's always happy. I forgot what that felt like. I figured I'd never feel it again. She looked at my house and her whole body seemed to frown.

I miss you, Mace, I thought. I spoke to her in my mind sometimes. I liked to imagine she'd appreciate the nickname I'd given her, since she'd never had one before.

The school years were black and white. Dark as a charcoal drawing. But when the warm season came, Macy lit my world up with color. She was taller each year. When we were ten her hair had grown to the bottom of her back. When we were thirteen, she began looking like a teenager, and at nineteen she looked like a woman.

I had grown up too. I did online college and started working, eventually saving enough money to buy my house from my uncle. I took down the wall that separated my room from my parents, turning it into a master suite. I got rid of the bunk bed and donated most of my family's belongings. They weren't using them, and someone else needed them more than I did. I found a note in Delilah's sparkly backpack that said "I love you, Grayson" in her childish handwriting.

She called me Grayson to tease me since we only heard our middle names when we were in trouble. I decided to go by my middle name from then on. I didn't want to be Daniel anymore, and this way, no one from town would ever guess I was the boy left behind.

I framed the note and put it next to my bed, because even after all these years, I needed to see her before I fell asleep, and the moment I opened my eyes.

I blink back to the present, glancing down at my pathetic self, crumbled on the floor, remembering what it was like to have my entire world ripped away. I can only say a two-letter word over and over, covering my ears like I am a six-year-old boy again.

She needs an explanation but can't bring myself to explain. I haven't even said their names since I was a kid. I never needed to. I told no one, and my uncle never spoke of them.

I'm a shell of a man, breaking before the woman who unknowingly saved me just by being outside my window. I squeeze my eyes shut, trying to suppress the pain rocking through me, but my heart booms heavily in my chest.

With eighteen years between me and that day, I realize time doesn't matter. Not when I can feel every exhausting sensation I did back then. I close my eyes and pray to whoever will listen to take away this pain. Somewhere in the midst of my silent pleas, I fall asleep, like the emotional event is too much for me, so my body simply shut off.

Chapter 28
Macy

With his knees to his chest, back against the wall, Grayson is a mess on the floor, like he's in some sort of trance. *"That happy boy you knew, the one you told Sarah you loved? He's gone, Macy. He died the day his family did!"*

When I was a kid, the summer Daniel and Delilah were gone, I overheard people in town talking about a car accident that killed a local family. It couldn't have been the Wrights. Someone would've told me. Besides, the man who bought their house told me they moved.

But how is he living in the same house he lived in as a kid? Why did he move back? Where did he go, all those years ago?

I sink to the floor in front of Grayson. It doesn't even seem like he notices me here, like he's someplace else entirely in his mind. "Grayson?" I whisper.

"No, no, no," he mutters, eyes unseeing.

"Sh. It's okay." *Is it, though?*

Was I just a pawn he played with for the mere purpose of

entertainment? Was any of it real? My hands shake, and I try to process what's happening, unsure of what to do.

Chapter 29
Macy
18 Years Ago

"You string it through the bead," Delilah says, demonstrating how to make a friendship bracelet. I follow her directions and she claps in approval, causing her to drop the bracelet she was nearly finished making. Beads scatter across the table and fall to the floor. "Not again!" she complains, as though this is a common occurrence.

Daniel sets his grilled cheese on his paper plate and crawls beneath the table. He gathers all the beads, one by one, and hands them to his twin. Once the mess is cleaned up, he hops back in his seat to finish his lunch.

"Can you roll your tongue?" Delilah asks me.

I stick my tongue out and wiggle it around.

The twins laugh.

"Can you?" I ask, which causes both to demonstrate that they can, in fact, curl their tongues.

Delilah remakes her bracelet, creating a pattern with teal and purple. I thread yellow and pink on my string, replicating a sunset.

"Making friendship bracelets?" Mrs. Wright asks, coming into the kitchen and grabbing an apple to snack on.

"Yup!" Delilah says.

"You know what they say about friendship bracelets, don't you?"

"What?" Daniel asks.

"When you give your friend a bracelet you made, that means you are *best* friends."

Daniel frowns. "How come Lilah gets to be Macy's best friend? That's not fair." His lips curve downward dramatically.

"You can make her one too!" Delilah singsongs.

Her brother smiles, two deep dimples appear in his cheeks. My stomach cartwheels when he moves his chair so it's right next to mine. The three of us spend the afternoon making bracelets for one another. Mrs. Wright ties them since we nearly lose all our beads when we try to do it ourselves.

Later that afternoon, the three of us sit in a circle on the beach. The sun is a bright fiery thing as it sets, making me have to squint to look at Delilah, who sits with her back toward it.

"What's it like being a twin?" I ask.

Daniel looks at Delilah, who is looking at him. They shrug in sync. "What's it like *not* being one?" Daniel asks.

"Boring," I say, looking at the sand on my feet. "You guys are lucky. You always have someone to play with."

"Yeah, but you can always play with us," Delilah says.

I shrug. "Not during the school year."

Daniel frowns. "I wish you lived here."

"Me too," Delilah says.

"Me three."

I glance at the purple and teel bracelet on one arm, and the green and blue one on the other. I'll never take them off. I look between my best friends, at the bracelets on their wrist. Even when we are thousands of miles apart, we'll be connected in this small way, as long as we never take them off.

"Best friends forever," Delilah says.

"Forever," I say. *That's a really long time.* Good. A smile spreads across my face.

Daniel's eyes meet mine, and then he reflects the happy expression.

Chapter 30
Macy
Now

He fell asleep curled up against the wall, as if whatever overcame him leeched all his energy. I don't bother waking him up, knowing deep down he needs the rest, and I need this time to myself. To think. To try to make sense of why he lied.

I pull out my phone, and type Delilah Wright into the search bar on Facebook, hoping to find some answers. I bite my thumbnail as I scroll through several people who share her name, but none of the profiles belong to Grayson's sister. I search him next, since he probably follows her, but neither of the twins are searchable. But my search for their mom's profile is successful, and I eagerly click on her page.

"Aug 2nd, 2024

It's been eighteen years since we lost a beautiful soul—"

I scroll.

"Eighteen years later and I still can't believe you're gone—"

I scroll even further down, finding hundreds of posts she was tagged in, all of them expressing their grief. I scroll until I find posts from August 2006. Eighteen years ago.

"I am saddened by the news of my dear friend's untimely

passing. She, her husband, and six-year-old daughter were killed in a car accident. I am still in shock. I can't believe such a beautiful family was taken from us. May the Wright family rest in peace."

I'm going to be sick. I inhale an unsteady breath, trying to get my emotions under control, but despite my best efforts, tears well in my eyes and my heart sinks to my stomach. *It's not true*, is my first thought. Delilah, my very first friend in Sanibel, can't be gone. If she were, that means she's been gone this entire time. And that would mean that while I was growing up like a normal kid, Grayson was grieving his entire family. And if that's true, it would mean the man I fell in love with has experienced more pain than I could possibly fathom.

I look at my phone, eyes dragging over the words repeatedly until they truly sink in. *It's all true.* It feels as though tragedy has swallowed all that was once beautiful, and I can't imagine ever smiling again. I can't begin to wonder how Grayson manages to so much as laugh. I wrap my arms around him and bring his head to my chest, slowly running my fingers through his hair. "I thought I loved you then," I whisper, even though he's sleeping. "But if *that* was love, then we need a new word for what I feel toward you now."

A peaceful snore fills the room, and I imagine for him, peace is hard to come by. I hold his sleeping body for what feels like an hour. My arms and legs tingle from keeping them still. My heart shatters for the boy who lost his family, and for the man who couldn't bring himself to tell me. He begins to stir, and then his head shoots up, eyes wide and alert when he looks at me. "Macy," he breathes. "Oh my God. I fell asleep?" A divot forms between his brows. "There's an explanation. I'm trying to find the words, bu—"

I bring my index finger to his lips. I tilt my head down so

our foreheads rest against one another. It's the only thing I can do to bring either one of us comfort. Even if it is in this small way. My heart feels as though it's cracking in my chest. "You don't need to say anything." I hesitate to say the words, and when I do, my voice breaks. "I know what happened to your family."

He pulls away, his gaze searches mine and his eyebrows pull together. "You...know?" he whispers, and I never thought his voice could sound so sad. The cadence of it weighs me down.

"I know." I hold my phone up. "Facebook," I say sadly, as way of explanation. I press my lips against his, as though I have the capability to take his pain away with something as trivial as a kiss. "Daniel," I breathe his name. "I am *so* sorry for your loss." I try to hold it together, but his presence is comforting in a way that makes me forget to show up with a mask at all. As much as I try to fight it, to be strong for him, a tear slips, and his thumb catches it.

All the despair falls away from his features. "I didn't know how to tell you. To even *say* it." He reaches for my hand, interlocking our fingers as though he needs to hold onto me in some way.

"That's why you pretended not to know who I was? Why you called yourself by your middle name?" I try to understand.

"That's part of the reason."

"And the other part?"

He looks away, opens his mouth like he's about to speak and then closes it.

"Talk to me," I place my hand tentatively on his cheek and angle his face, so his focus is on me. "Please."

He nods but takes a moment to himself. To gather the

words or perhaps the courage. He sniffs and then says, "You're going to think I'm so weird."

"I already think that," I joke, trying to make him feel comfortable.

He forces a small smile, but it's absent of anything resembling happiness. "Macy." He hesitates, and then steels his expression. "I've returned to this house for a week every summer." He speaks each word considerably slow.

Time seems to still with that one sentence, and the silence that follows is sizable. I feel my head tilt, my eyes looking between his as if I can decipher everything within those blue flames. The truth is a heavy thing, filling my chest like cement around my heart. "But—" I shake my head. "I came to your house… There was a man there," I say more to myself. "He told me that you and your family moved."

"I know," he says. "I remember." His eyes twinkle with wet tears. "That was my uncle. He became my legal guardian after everything. I don't know why he lied, perhaps he also couldn't voice the truth." He shakes his head. "What matters is that I hid when you came to my door because I was terrified to tell you what happened. I didn't want to accept it myself."

My eyes dart back and forth as I think. "But… I never saw you."

"I stayed inside." He shrugs.

I'm pelted with stones of what could have been. Would we still be friends if things were different? Would I fall in love with him regardless of the circumstances?

I'm hit over and over, until my body seems to go limp with exhaustion. Grayson must feel the same. We comfort each other like two dominos, leaning on one another to keep from falling.

"I'm so sorry I kept this from you. I tried to tell you, Mace, but I couldn't find the words."

I press a kiss to his cheek. "I get it. You don't need to be sorry," I promise. "And I never exactly made it easy for you. God, I've always given you such a hard time, I'm *so* sorry for not being the safe space you needed to open up to me."

"You've been perfect, Mace." He brings his hand to the base of my head, gently grabbing my hair. "Does this change things?"

"Yes," I say, which causes him to flinch. I quickly add, "Because now I need to figure out what the hell to call you." I smile which seems to ease the tension in his body.

"When I moved back here years ago, I decided to go by Grayson. I didn't want anyone to realize who I was. I couldn't handle being treated like the boy who lost his entire family, it would be too painful of a reminder. But you can call me anything you want, Mace."

I nod understandingly.

"I need to get off this floor," he says. I stand, trying to be a strong force for him. I hold out my hand, which he takes. I pull him up, and once he's towering over me, he scoops me into his arms and breathes in the scent of my hair. We hold each other for several minutes, until it hurts a little less, and then he whispers, "I really need a shower."

I chuckle. "I was wondering what that smell was." He pulls away and flicks my forehead, then kisses the exact spot.

I lay on his bed while he cleans up. My eyes are on the ceiling, but my mind is someplace else entirely. I'm experiencing pain for the man I love while simultaneously grieving my very first friend, and his parents who were always so kind.

I try to process Daniel being here this entire time, isolated in a world of pain I'll never fully know. I hadn't noticed I was crying until Grayson is suddenly above me, wiping away the tears. His hair is damp, and his towel is wrapped around his waist.

"I had a crush on you when we were kids," I say. Seeing how he overheard my conversation with Sarah at The BARnacle, he already knows this.

"I've had a crush on you my entire life."

I peel my back off the bed and sit up on my elbows, my head tilting back to meet his gaze.

"I saw you every summer. My window faces your house." He gently rests his weight on me, using his arms to hold himself up so he doesn't crush me whole. "You were the sun, Mace." I remember a conversation we had at the Inn. *"What made you happy?"* I asked, wanting to know what he was like as a kid. He answered, *"The sun."*

My stomach warms like the star we speak of. "I wish I could've seen you grow up."

"I wish I had let you," he says, then looks away. "Do you remember my sister? Delilah?"

"Of course, I do. She was my best friend."

He points to the framed note I spotted weeks ago on his bedside table. I remember when I first saw it. It was the night I broke my grandparent's ocean treasures and grief swept me up. I thought I'd drown in it, but then Grayson came and took me to shore. I asked him if he ever lost someone, and he said yes. I remember the first shooting star he saw. He described it as, *"Like I'm looking up at heaven and it's looking right back, waving hello."*

I glance at the framed note, then back at him.

"I've seen you look at it a few times," he says. "I wanted to tell you my sister wrote it, but then I'd have to tell you that I lost her. That—" He closes his eyes, and when they open again, they're glistening with fresh tears. "The note was special because it was all I had left."

My chest squeezes. I carefully push him off me and then gesture for him to sit against the headboard. When he does, I rest my head on his chest, inhaling the scent of his soap still potent on his skin.

"You want to know what she always said to me?" I ask, looking up to find him nodding. "She told me I had to marry you when we got older, so that her and I would become sisters."

He laughs, the beautiful cadence filling the room and chasing away the heaviness. "She said that to me too."

Then it's silent for a while. I listen to his breath and the miraculous rhythm of his heart. *He's alive.* "Where were you that day?"

He stiffens beneath me, then says in a gravelly voice. "With you."

"What?" I whisper.

"I stayed with you that day because you were flying home in the afternoon. I needed every minute with you." My face must reflect a thousand questions because he continues. "Your family was waiting for mine to return home, and I could tell that your mom was starting to stress about getting to the airport on time. So, I lied and told them my family was home. I waited all day for them—" His voice breaks off and his eyes are squeezed tight. I see how brave he is in this moment. How hard it must be to speak about something he's never told anyone before.

"Hey," I whisper, bringing my fingers to his cheekbone. "You don't need to tell me everything today unless you want to. Or tomorrow. Or even months from now."

"Won't you be gone months from now?"

"Oh," I say, realizing I never got the chance to tell him. "I was going to tell you, but then…" I let that part of my sentence trail off. "I'm moving to Sanibel."

His wide eyes meet mine and he lets out the most beautiful sound I've heard. He laughs. His arms twist around me tight enough that I let out a huff of air. "Thank God. I was beginning to worry about how much I was going to miss you." He kisses me powerfully, then lifts us out of bed. He spins us around. My laughter echoes off the walls, adorning the room where everything seemed to hurt minutes ago.

It's nearly midnight when Grayson suddenly says, "I'm taking you somewhere." After the exhausting emotions from the day, we stayed in bed and showed each other our comfort movies, only leaving to grab our dinner from the delivery person at the door, and to occasionally use the bathroom. It was a much-needed distraction for the both of us.

"It's like the middle of the night," I point out, which he ignores.

He climbs out of bed and stretches his limbs, then he interlocks our fingers. He guides me down the hallway, stopping to grab a sheet from his linen closet on the way out.

It's nearly pitch black outside. We walk in the sand for a few moments before he stops and lifts me off the ground. I wrap my arms around his neck and nuzzle my face in his skin. "I'm glad we're not pretending anymore, because I've always wanted to smell your skin shamelessly."

"I've wanted to do much more improper things with you, shamelessly."

I laugh. "You've made that pretty clear."

"Have I? And here I thought I was doing a good job concealing how attracted I am to you." The hand that's holding me up slides to my butt and squeezes. I bite his neck hard enough to leave a mark, but he chuckles as if a mosquito bit him. "We're here."

I open my eyes to find ourselves beneath the lifeguard tower. He sets me on my feet and then spreads the sheet over the sandy ground. He sits and leans against one of the posts. I do the same. I trace his profile with my eyes once they adjust to the dark.

"Ask me," he says.

"What?"

"I know you have a million questions, and I know you said I don't have to talk about it today. I'll let you know if something is too much for me, but I'm going to try. I want you to understand me. So, ask."

So brave. "Okay… Tell me about the first time we met."

His gaze snaps to mine like he wasn't expecting my question. I give him a smile which erases his hesitancy. "Okay." He nods. "Delilah always woke up before I did. It was the first week of summer break, and I took advantage of the time to sleep in. I had finished breakfast late one day, my dad was at work and my mom was on the back deck watching my sister play with another girl. I remember the moment I walked out the back door, you were mid-laugh, shoveling sand into a bucket when my eyes caught yours. I was terrified in the way that most boys are of pretty girls. I had every intention of turning around and hiding inside. Delilah called me over and I didn't move. She stalked toward me, grabbed my hand, and dragged me to you against my will."

I laugh, picturing it. He smiles in return. "I was too scared to speak, but Delilah said 'This is Macy, our new friend. Macy, this is my brother, Daniel.' You smiled so bright; it was like staring at the sun." I remember our conversation on the way to the fall festival, when we shared our first impressions of each other. *"You embodied the rays of a thousand suns. You were joy personified. I thought you were lovely, Mace."* There's a smile in his voice when he says, "You hugged me and then ran off along the shoreline. Something in my mind clicked, and I chased you. I could never catch up to you back then."

"Now look who's faster," I whisper.

"Not for long. You're already making me work for it."

"I remember that day." I smile but it slowly fades into a frown now that I know how the story ends. The kind boy I had met that day lost his family shortly after, including his twin sister.

There's a bond between twins unlike any other. The moment he twinkled into existence, she did too. She was the first person he ever met, even before his parents, and now, his other half is in a different world.

He was left to grieve all alone, and his agony was strong enough to keep him from ever telling someone what happened. I find myself reaching for his arm, holding it, and rubbing soothing patterns over his skin.

I can't imagine losing my mom and dad, let alone if I had a sibling. But enduring that as a child, when he had only a thin understanding of the world—I can't fathom his pain. We learn from our experiences, and I can only imagine the awful things he believes about the world.

"Did you ever talk to anyone about all of this?"

He shakes his head. "After everything happened, I had no interest in making friends."

I frown. I hadn't realized the depth of his isolation until now. "What about a guidance counselor?"

"Nope."

I frown. "You had no one to talk to for so long, but I know you had much to say. You can tell me," I whisper. "If you wish."

He looks at me then. I mean *really* looks at me. "The woman you are..."

I tilt my head.

"You're compassionate, kind, beautiful...smart, of course. I could name thousands of adjectives if you'd like."

"That won't be necessary, and if I didn't know any better, I'd think you were stalling."

"I am."

"You don't need to say anything."

"I want to. God, I want to, but I don't even know where to start."

"Close your eyes," I say. He glances at me warily but does as I instructed. "You must have so many words trapped. Let them out, Grayson. Let someone else carry them for a while." I squeeze his hand encouragingly.

"Okay," he whispers. "Are you sure you want to hear it all? I don't want to bothe—"

"Yes. I want to listen."

"Macy. I really, *really* like you."

I grin. "You're stalling..."

"No. That's one of the things I wanted to say as a kid." He opens one eye to peek at me. I'm smiling. His left dimple appears, then he closes his eyes again. I'm patient, waiting for him to speak, tracing his features.

"Sometimes... I think tragedy follows me. I can't seem to escape its cruel way of popping out and scaring me when I least expect it to." *Oh, Grayson...* "Ever since I was a kid, I lay in bed at night and picture what it would be like to see them again. How it would look for a family to reunite after spending a lifetime apart." He opens his pained eyes to meet mine, inhales a breath, then continues. "I moved into my uncle's house in Fort Meyers. He took care of me in all the necessary ways, but he never spoke about my family. The more time that separated them and I, the more I wondered if they existed at all, or if I made them up in my head. Delilah especially seemed too good to have ever been true. She was a built-in best friend. We were together nearly every second of the day. When I discovered loneliness, I couldn't fathom ever having a different companion."

I frame his face with my hands and kiss both his temples. "I wish I could take all your pain."

He shakes his head. "If me enduring it keeps it from ever touching you, then I'll withstand it for eternity."

If I had the chance to carry the weight of his grief, I would do so in a heartbeat. Maybe that's what it means to truly love somebody. I place a soft kiss to his lips. "Keep going."

"Okay," he says. "As the years went on, I thought I'd burn alive in the silence. Or drown. Whichever is worse." He pulls me so I'm in his lap, then hugs me to his chest. "I just really need to hold on to you. Is that okay?"

"Yes," I breathe.

"Good." He continues. "It was so quiet, Mace. My uncle was there, but we didn't really interact with one another. He was always working. I didn't talk to anyone at school either. Sometimes my teacher would pair me up with other kids, and they would make it a game of who could get me to talk first. My raging silence was their entertainment. But at home, when it was just me and the quiet… It was *loud*. Does that make sense?"

"Yes."

"It was like static filling my head. Sometimes I wondered if my brain would explode." He sighs. "I've always wanted to tell someone that. To just, I don't know, complain."

"You're not complaining, Grayson." I wrap my arms around the back of his neck and tuck my face in his chest. "What else?"

He squeezes me a little. "I felt like a ghost the day I moved here and went into town. I even went to The BARnacle, but no one recognized me. I didn't think I wanted anyone to, but it still hurt, Mace. It *really* hurt."

How is he still standing? How could anyone survive what he did and still smile? How could he have it in his heart to be kind when the world has been so cruel?

"I made it through the school years because I knew I'd see you in the summer. When the pain felt strangling, I told myself 'Just a little longer until I see her again.' When you came, everything seemed to be all right, because there was a person right out my window who was always happy, and somehow, that made my grief smaller. It was like looking down from an airplane and realizing how small your life is compared to everything else out there. You saved me, Mace. Without even trying, you saved me."

I pull back to look at his face. "Don't give me credit for your survival. *You* did that, and I'm so in awe of you and your strength." I understand grief. Not to the extent of his, but I know how heavy it is. How it's hard to pull yourself out of bed. What it's like to not to let tears fall because once they do, they'll never end. "After all your heart went through, you still have it in you to—" *Love?* I point between us. "This. You still have it in your heart for *this*."

"This," he breathes. "Is the only good thing I've experienced since I was six, and I keep waiting for something to steal it away. I don't want you to feel pressured to continue this, and I certainly don't want your pity. I don't even know what *this* is, I just know it feels like—"

"Destiny," I answer for him. "It feels like destiny."

He kisses me then. My eyes fall shut and stars burst behind my eyelids. We get lost in each other, both of us breathless. "You make it better," he says into the next kiss. "You make me feel like I'm alive."

He makes *me* feel like I'm alive.

My body moves naturally against his, and I can *feel* just how alive he is. Veiled beneath the midnight sky, tucked under the lifeguard tower, it feels like our own separate world. I pull back to observe him in the dark. He always looks sharp around the edges when he's adorned in shadows. As if he can't stand the absence of my lips any longer, his face angles up to mine and he kisses me like he's starved. He tightens his grip on my hips, pushing and pulling me forward to create wonderful friction.

His hands slide toward my backside, squeezing me as he lets out a long groan. I pull down the waistband of his underwear and joggers, springing him free. His wide eyes meet mine with a mixture of shocked amusement. My shorts are loose enough for me to pull my underwear aside, and when I do, Grayson stills me. "I don't have a condom on me."

"I have an IUD."

He blows out a steady breath as I lower myself onto him. I move my hips with every ounce of love I have for him and with every year that has tried to separate us. My mind always returned to the memory of him, winning the test of time. And then I kiss him with every promise I have to make the future a place so beautiful that his mind doesn't want to return to the past. At least not the sad parts.

When it's over, I don't slide off him yet. We cling to each other for a while, with the wind's whisper against our skin. The nighttime sky hanging over us like a secret. He kisses my shoulder, then rubs his chin over the skin. I hiss from the scrape of his stubble. He kisses it again and whispers an apology.

A month ago, I was living in a place I longed to leave, engaged to a man I despised. I picture being stuck in a cave, with fallen boulders blocking the way I came. Trying to move the dozens of rocks with bloodied fingernails and shouted pleas. I envision dust coating my lungs and every ounce of strength being wasted on attempting to escape. That was my life, and then, I turned around and found a sliver of light, and it grew the more I followed it. It led me out. It led me *here*. To Daniel. To Grayson. To the dreams I never dared to hope for.

Sometimes the way out isn't the obvious path. Sometimes it's a faint sliver of light that you need to follow. Sometimes, that light leads you right where fate wants you to be.

Chapter 31
Grayson

My mom's car is in a million pieces. Delilah is somewhere in the mess, bloodied and sleeping. I scream her name while I rush to her, but the moment my grown-up hand touches her small one, her face morphs into someone else.

Long brunette hair and unseeing brown eyes. *Macy.*

The world shrinks around me, and I realize it's the hole in my chest, vacuuming every corner of pain that crowds the planet. It drowns my lungs until I'm screaming from the pit of my chest.

"Grayson," a sad voice whispers. "It's just a dream. Open your eyes." I do, and staring down at me are brown eyes with flecks of gold. Very *alive* ones, on a very *alive* girl. My throat burns like I've been screaming, my skin slick with sweat. I pull Macy to my chest and hug her tight to me. After what we did beneath the lifeguard tower, I insisted she spend the night with me, not expecting it to go this way.

I haven't had the nightmare since I was a teenager. It was always the same dream. An endless torment from my own mind, showing me what happened that day. But now it's changed. Now, Macy takes Delilah's place.

"Do you want to talk about it?" she whispers. My heart races beneath her ear, and she grabs my hand and interlocks our fingers. She places a gentle kiss to my sternum. I like when she peppers soft kisses on my skin.

"No." I sigh. "I'm sorry."

"Don't apologize."

"You're right. Sorry."

She shoots me a pointed look.

I chuckle. "I really do love when you look at me like that."

"Go to sleep."

"Yes, ma'am."

I shoot up the moment my hand reaches for her body and meets the unoccupied side of my bed.

"Macy!" My voice trembles with fright.

"Yes?" she walks through my open bedroom door with damp hair and a towel wrapped around her.

My entire body seems to sigh with relief. My heart races, and my hands shake but I set them down so she can't see. "Nothing. I thought you…" *Died.* "Went home."

She grins. "You would miss me if I did?"

I roll my eyes. "If I hadn't made it clear already, let me elaborate. My mind has a hard time focusing on anything other than the thought of you. So yes, Mace, I'd miss you."

She squints her eyes at me like my statement was sarcasm. I'm utterly serious.

"Oh," I say, holding up a finger. I pull open the drawer to

my nightstand and carefully grab the sand dollar. "This is yours."

She eyes the round thing in my hand, tilting her head. Then, her eyes turn to glass. "You saved it for me? After all these years?"

"I promised you I would, didn't I?"

She runs and jumps on me, tightly hugging me around the neck and nearly killing me with her strength. I rub circles into her back for several minutes.

"Pancakes for breakfast?" she eventually asks in a sweet voice that she uncommonly uses with me.

"Sure. Pancake mix is in the cabinet by the fridge."

She tilts her head and narrows her eyes.

"You want *me* to make the pancakes?" I surmise.

"You make them *really* good." She shrugs.

It's cute that she thinks she needs to persuade me. I'd do anything this woman asked me to. But I like her kissing up to me, so I drag this out. "I don't know. You look pretty cute in that apron of yours. I can go get it from next do—"

"Grayson," she interrupts. "You do *not* want to see me when I'm hangry."

Is it strange that I do? I want to see Macy in every facet of her day, including when she's miserable with hunger. I'm unafraid of the bad days. I want to be someone she can rely on. I'll always be patient with her, and I'll scour to the ends of this Earth to give her everything she wants and needs. I want to make her as happy as she makes me. So, I climb out of bed in nothing but my boxer briefs. I pull on sweatpants and squeeze her delicate hand on my way past her, and then I whip up breakfast for the woman I've known since I was a little boy.

Now I'm a man who wants to glue myself back together

to be everything she needs. Everything she wants. But more importantly, everything she *deserves*. And Macy Brookes, the angel that she is, deserves it all. From the tops of the stars to the burning core of this world, she deserves every bit of it.

I'm a grinning, lovesick fool, flipping pancakes and using chocolate chips to form a heart in the ones that come out perfectly round.

I'm hers. I always have been. Now I long to call her mine.

Chapter 32
Macy

"You are a brilliant woman," Grayson says, and when I turn to him, he has the brightest grin on his face.

I wrap my arms around myself, my toes buried in the sand. A gentle wave curls over my feet. The sun beams down on my head and shoulders, but the delicate breeze chases away the burning heat. "It's not a big deal," I say.

"Not a big deal?" He says, shocked. "You just announced the release date of your fourth book! You're only twenty-three. That's pretty fucking impressive."

I've never had another person to celebrate these milestones with. "I—yeah. You're right. It *is* impressive, and I worked really hard." I turn to him, clad in golden sunlight. "Thank you."

"Wear something pretty tonight. I'm taking you out." A dream. Grayson is my dream.

"Okay," I whisper. Then, he picks me up and twirls me in his arms, my laugh picked up by the breeze and my stomach in wonderful knots.

Sometimes I wish I could fold myself into a paper story with the promise of a happy ending. From an onlooker's perspective, we are a love story coming to the last chapter in a novel. If we were, I would proclaim my love, he would love me too, and we'd live happily ever after. But we aren't words strung together on a page, orchestrated by a woman's desire to fall in love a million times over through her own words.

The night begins with me curling my hair and trying on ten different outfits until I decide on an olive-green tank top with a deep neckline that shows off the little bit of cleavage I have. I pair it with black jeans and my Converse.

I nearly scream from the sight of Grayson sitting on my sofa when I come out of my bathroom. "What the hell?" I glare at him.

"You left the back door unlocked. You might want to be better about that if you don't want uninvited visitors sitting on your couch." His eyes rake over my body. They seem to darken when he says, "You are radiant."

I lift my chin and act nonchalant about his compliment. "I just threw on the first thing I saw hanging in the closet." I shrug and turn to grab my purse hanging on the wall. With my back to him, I smile.

He leads me to his car, and I take in his attire. He wears loafers, dark jeans paired with a button-down shirt, the cuffs rolled up to reveal the veins in his muscled forearms.

He holds the door open for me, and the space smells of leather, sandalwood, and a hint of strawberry lingering on his clothes. With tourists coming and going, a drive can sometimes take longer than a bike ride. "Where are we going?" I ask.

"Don't get too excited," he says, placing his palm on my knee.

"Don't be ridiculous. A night out with you? I would never."

His hand moves up my thigh by a hair. "The last night you spent with me, you seemed…rather enlivened."

I glare at him, and with his eyes on the road, they crinkle at the sides. "What will you write next?" he asks.

"I have something brewing in my mind."

"Will you ever run out of love stories?" he asks curiously.

"Never," I say. "A woman can never grow tired of romance, and I will never stop imagining fictional relationships."

"Can I ask you a question?" he asks after a few moments.

"If I can ask you one."

"Fair enough." He clears his throat. "I've read your books. All of them, might I add. The way you write about falling in love…it always feels so real. Like I'm falling in love alongside the characters."

"That wasn't a question."

"Right," he says. "Did you love Walter?"

"In the beginning I thought so. I felt all the things I write in my books, but it wasn't long until the euphoria of a new relationship vanished. Sobered, I was left with a man who didn't love or respect me, yet I stayed with him for years to get those feelings back. I wasn't in love with *him*. I was in love with love itself, and I confused the two. I tried to ignite a wet match, but it was never going to catch fire, because Walter wasn't a man I *could* love."

"So, if you've never been in love, how do you know what you're writing is real?"

"What makes you think I've never been in love?"

He's silent for a minute, his hand stiff on my thigh. "Oh. I guess I just assumed Walter was your first relationship."

Even when I was too young to understand the emotion, that string around my heart was tied to Daniel's. It's *always* been him. And here he is, sitting in the driver's seat, holding my thigh. The man who introduced me to love, the one who disappeared and left me with nothing but my words and the stories in my head. He's the foundation of every love story I've ever written. "He was," I whisper. I love him down to my bones, to the very atoms making up my existence.

He doesn't prod any further. "Your turn. Ask away."

Out of the millions of questions I could ask, I settle on one of insignificance. "Have you ever had a girlfriend?" I'm not sure I'd like to know.

"Oh," he says, appearing thoughtful for a moment when he says, "I actually *have* a girlfriend. She won't be happy when she finds out about you though."

I glare at him.

"No," he says, dropping the act. "I've never had one."

"But you've…" I let that part of my sentence trail off, hoping he'll pick up what was implied.

"Yes, Macy," he says in a bored tone. "I've had sex before." I'm not surprised. He definitely knows what he's doing in that department. "I've slept with girls I met at work conventions. I've never had sex with the same person more than once."

"Is that supposed to make me feel special or something?"

"No. Sorry, that came out wrong." He sighs. "Sex was a refuge for me. It was an escape from my own thoughts, similar to running. But it was never about feeling connected to another person. It was…I don't know—" he says with frustration. "It's never been how it is with you."

He spent nearly his entire life in isolation, to the point

where even his sex life was spent in solitary. My heart aches for him. But maybe this is a turning point for him. Hope inflates within the walls of my chest and if I could extend some to him, I'd do so in a heartbeat. I squeeze his hand resting on my leg.

"We're here," he says.

I look out the window and see the familiar parking lot of The BARnacle. I grin when he slides out of the car and comes to open my door. "Such a gentleman."

"You wouldn't be saying that if you knew the things I'm thinking every time I look at you. I *really* like that shirt by the way."

I tilt my head back and laugh. A breeze blows my hair into my face, so I turn the opposite way, so it blows behind me. I gather the strands in my hand and rush inside.

Dozens of voices yell at once. "Surprise!" Instinctively I flinch and ram backward into Grayson's chest. His arms twist around me, he whispers against my ear, "Congratulations on your fourth book, Minerva Day." I can hear the grin in his voice.

In the dim lit bar, all my friends laugh and record me with their phones. Sarah is standing on the bar holding a huge sign that reads *"Minerva Day is my favorite author!"* Tammy crosses the room and pinches my cheek. "Four books." She shakes her head in wonder. "I know you're making your grandma and grandpa very proud."

"Thank you," I say with emotion heavy in my voice.

Her eyes lift to the man whose arms are wrapped around me. "You've got a keeper, hun." *He did all of this for me.*

"Hey, man. Good to see you," Elliot says to Grayson, who releases me to embrace our friend.

Suddenly, a thin arm is draped across my shoulders, the

person whose appendage it belongs to leads me further into the restaurant. She has a head of long blond hair. I smile at Sarah's sister, Julia. "I have a bone to pick with you and my sister for not telling me you've been in town for an entire month, but for now, I'm going to need you to sit in this lovely chair."

I glance at the bar stool in front of me and then eye her. She raises her eyebrows and gestures to the seat. I sigh while plopping onto it, and suddenly I'm swarmed by four or five people, the only one I'm focused on is Elliot who yells, "Three…two…one!" I'm lifted into the air on the stool, my eyes wide and mouth agape. I let out a screech and find Grayson a few feet away laughing at me. I point my index finger at him, hoping it conveys brutal threats, provoking his heavy laughter. I beg them to set me down, which they eventually do.

"All right, let's give her a minute to breathe," Sarah says, pulling Elliot to a nearby booth. Everyone begins to fill the tables. I lock eyes with Grayson who sits at the bar with a gentle smile in his eyes. The bartender hands him a drink, and then he crosses the room to hand it to me. I take the cold cup and drag a sip through the straw, letting a sound free when I swallow the strawberry beverage. I gaze up at him and smile. I got this drink in New York with him. So much has changed, it's hard to believe it was only a month ago. I lean up on the tips of my toes and press a kiss to his lips. It's not as discrete as I'd hoped because my friends start applauding.

"Minerva and Dracula!" Sarah calls. I shoot her a look which she shrugs off. Grayson and I join the table she occupies, along with Elliot, Tammy, and Julia. A few other people I know from town are here, but they sit on their own and talk among themselves. Once we're seated, Grayson stretches his arm over the back of the booth, and I lean into him.

"I'm Julia." She reaches across the table to shake Grayson's hand. "You must be the fiancé." She lifts her brows up and down, but quickly stops when she sees Sarah shaking her head. Julia looks between us.

"We should probably get this out in the open," Grayson says wryly. "Macy had a fiancé who turned out to be a pig, and I happened to be at the right place when she realized it." He smiles down at me.

"To breaking off engagements to pigs!" Julia says, lifting her glass for everyone to clink. I laugh at how quickly everyone moves past it.

"So, what's this new book about?" Tammy asks with hopeful eyes.

I shrug. "I guess you'll have to read it to find out."

"Boo!" Julia says. "We don't get any exclusive perks by knowing the author?"

"I bet Grayson knows," Sarah says. "Maybe we should sleep with Macy too."

Grayson clears his throat as though open discussion of our sex life puts him in discomfort, understandably so. "I'm dying to read it too, but apparently being…closely intertwined with her doesn't include those perks."

"So, Julia, how is nursing school going?" I ask to change the subject. The six of us fall into a comfortable rhythm. The sisters and I order several cocktails since Grayson and Elliot are our designated drivers. The boys eventually decide to play foosball, which Sarah and Julia decide is the perfect time to get away to catch up. Tammy declines our invite and goes home, claiming its past her bedtime. Now, I walk between my two girl friends, our arms linked, giggling as we make our way toward the beach. The three of us plop down in the sand, forming a small circle.

"I hate to be the person who immediately asks you about the boy in your life after not seeing each other for so long… but I'm slightly too drunk to be polite. Spill," Julia says.

I laugh at her straightforwardness and then share the story of how we met. Well, the second time we met.

"How do you go from hating the man to falling in love with him a month later?" Julia asks, slightly slurring her words.

"He must have mind boggling skills in the bedroom," Sarah answers.

I shoot her a look, and then the three of us break out into a fit of laughter. "Oh, I should probably mention the good news," I say. I wait a few seconds to add to the suspense, and then say, "I'm moving here!"

"Finally!" Sarah says with the brightest smile I've ever seen.

Julia reaches over and hugs me. "Okay, you're forgiven for not telling me you were in town sooner, but only if we can do weekly dinners again like when we were kids."

I laugh. "But with alcohol." I wiggle my eyebrows.

"I'm making a group chat so we can plan it," Julia says.

I give her Grayson's number and when I see the group chat pop up on my phone, my hope becomes bigger than my body. A boy who spent his life in isolation will never know loneliness again if I have anything to do with it.

"Let's go for a drive," Sarah says. She stands and wipes the sand off the backs of her legs.

Julia follows suit and holds out her hand for me to grab. I only saw Sarah with a couple of drinks tonight. I hesitate, but

I think Sarah seems coherent enough to drive, so I take her sister's hand.

Chapter 33
Grayson

"That's another win." I smirk at my opponent. Some blond-haired guy whose name I didn't catch. He hands me a ten-dollar bill, which I pocket with the rest of my winnings for tonight.

I beat Elliot five times in foosball. Shortly, we developed a crowd around the small table, and people started making bets if they could beat me or not. I've never played the game before, but I'm pretty good. That, or everyone else is too drunk to possess any skill. I haven't had anything to drink since I'm Macy's designated driver.

I look back at our table and see it's still empty. Maybe the girls went to the bathroom. I have no idea what they do in there for so long, but I know they like to take care of their business in packs, which I'll never understand. I pull out my phone to check the time when I see a text from Macy and feel myself grin before I even read it.

Crash Detected SOS: This phone detected a crash. You are receiving this message because the owner has you listed as their emergency contact.

Blood rushes to my face and pounds in my ears. Suddenly

I'm out of the crowd and standing at our table, as if Macy will return to it at any moment.

My whole body shakes, and I can't hear a single thing besides my blood pumping loudly in my ears. Someone claps me on the shoulder. I recognize the man, he wanted to play me next. Words are coming out of his mouth but it's all gibberish to me at the moment. Then, his hands are on my shoulder and he's trying to pull me back to the game. Away from helping Macy—

Oh God, Macy.

"You scared you're gonna lose, big guy?" he gets in my face and the next thing I know he's knocked back and touching his bloodied nose. "What the fuck, man?" he seethes.

Suddenly Elliot's beside me, snapping his fingers in my face and telling me to slow down. Slow down? "Not Macy. Please don't take Macy," someone pleads over and over.

The voice follows Elliot and I as he drags me out of The BARnacle. The voice stops when I clear my throat. *My voice.*

It feels like every particle of my soul is carried away by a breeze, like dust in the wind. Like I'm nothing if not for Macy. I won't survive my world being ripped away from me a second time.

I gasp when my cheek stings. I blink at Elliot, who's voice finally registers in my head. "Talk to me, man. What's going on? Where is Macy?" As I bring my hand to my burning cheek, I realize he slapped me.

Words. Right. "S-she crashed."

"What?"

I show him the text with shaking hands. His eyes widen and he inhales a deep breath. He pulls his phone out of his front pocket and messes with it for a moment. "Come on," he says.

"I need to get to Macy." My voice is choppy with hysteria.

"I'll get you to her, man. She's probably with Sarah. I have their location," he explains, walking briskly to his car.

"I'll drive," I say, needing a semblance of control.

"You're in no state to drive," he says, opening the driver's door and climbing in.

No state to drive? I haven't even had a sip of alcohol.

"Everything's going to be okay. I'm sure it's nothing."

I hold my hand up in a desperate plea. I don't need a false sense of security. I refuse to hold onto hope until I can physically see her for myself. I'm numb to the external world, completely blind to whatever is in front of my eyes. I don't hear Elliot's voice anymore or see the inside of his car. I only see the vivid details in my nightmare, where Macy is in Delilah's place. Scarlet pooling on the road and anguish tearing through me when I see how much of it is a puddle on the ground instead of inside her veins.

My throat feels as if I've swallowed fire. My knuckles ache while something thuds repeatedly until delicate hands still my wrists. I blink back into reality, my fist aching, realizing I was punching the dashboard. I hear Elliot telling someone not to touch me because I'll hurt them.

And then the only thing that exists to me is her voice. I close my eyes against it, welcoming oblivion. "Grayson," Macy whispers. *My angel.* I must be in heaven. "It's okay," she coos. "Look at me. I'm right here." Her hand touches my cheek and the delightful weight of her rests in my lap. I feel her breath against my face and open my eyes to see gold flecks swimming in her wet eyes.

"Don't cry," I say in a choppy voice.

"I'm so sorry," she whispers. "I dropped my phone and it shattered. I forgot that I put you as my emergency contact since I'm so far from my family."

"You dropped your phone?" I ask.

"Yes. I wasn't in a crash. I was walking to my house with the girls, and I was dancing a little. I accidentally flung my phone and it shattered. I am okay. See? Completely unharmed."

"You were dancing?"

"Yeah."

I hug her to my chest and inhale the sweet scent of her hair. She's alive and she was dancing. I recall the summers she danced outside my window.

"Come on," she whispers after some time. My pulse has finally slowed, and I can think a bit more clearly. I open my eyes and see that Elliot, Julia, and Sarah are standing outside, a look of horror on each of their faces.

We climb out of the car, and I nod to Macy's friends before crossing the distance to my house with Macy as a much tinier shadow on my heels. "I'll talk to you guys later," she says, with no further explanation of my behavior.

Once we're inside, I rest my back against the door. I slowly sink to the ground.

"It's okay," Macy whispers, kneeling before me.

"It's not."

"It is, Grayson."

"Look at my hands!" I raise my voice, causing her to flinch away from me. My chest squeezes from the sight of it. Of the frown lines on her face. "I punched someone at the bar because he was unknowingly keeping me from getting to you. I didn't even realize I was beating the shit out of Elliot's dashboard. I'm a nutcase, Macy."

"This is completely normal for what you've gone through."

"What I've gone through…" I laugh without humor. "Let's just call it what it is. Everyone I loved died and left me here. You're the only person I have left." I clench my jaw. "How does that make you feel? To have just met me a month ago and to become the only thing I have to live for. I mean, shit, no pressure or anything."

"We didn't meet a month ago," she says.

"Regardless of when we met, it's too much for anyone. It's unfair for you to be relied on so heavily by me."

"We'll figure this out—"

"Stop," I say. "Your heart is bigger than this world and I know that you'd stay with me even if it made you miserable. You'd drown to keep me afloat."

"If you care about me, then you wouldn't be trying to breakup with me right now," she says, her voice cracking and tears filling her eyes. "After everything I learned from the breakup with Walter, I've promised myself to never do something unless I want to, including continuing our relationship. Give me some credit here. I want this, Grayson. I want *you*."

"I care about you too much to see you stay with someone like me." I inhale a deep breath and look at her pretty face. I've already memorized every freckle, every eyelash, and every expression she makes. "Move here, Mace. Be happy. I'll leave."

"Stop," she says with the fire she only has with me.

I lift myself off the ground and reach down to lift her up. She claws at me when I open the door and bring her outside, her friends are long gone by now. I tell myself it's like ripping off a bandage when her heartbroken eyes meet mine, and I slam the door in her face. I lock it before she can try to come back inside.

She bangs on the door, and her voice is muffled by the wood. "Let me in!"

"Go home," I say.

"Don't do this, Daniel Grayson Wright! Don't you dare break my heart."

I'm saving you from that, Mace.

I will my feet to drag me away from her, and then I lock myself in my bedroom to drown her out. I stare at nothing for a while. Hours—probably. I finally decide it's best not to see her for a while, so I pack a bag with the little clothes I have and plan to stay at the Inn off the island.

It's well past midnight when I open my front door but freeze in place when I find Macy reading a book on the hood of my car.

Chapter 34
Macy

I blink away from the pages of my book when I hear Grayson's voice. "Please don't make this harder than it needs to be."

I sit up and cross my legs. I never went home. I waited on the hood of his car, assuming he'd come to his senses, but hours ticked by, so I went inside to grab my current read to pass the time.

He's standing above me with a suitcase at his feet and a duffle bag in his hand.

"Do you want to know why I was in your bedroom the morning you found me holding the picture of your family?"

He doesn't respond.

"Because I needed to see you," I say. "I spent a month on this island trying to mend something within myself, so I could remember how to love my fiancé." I look at the stars and the moon, and then at him. "Instead, I found you, and you showed me that there was nothing about me that needed mending in the first place."

His eyebrows pull together, and his gaze doesn't waver from mine.

I slide off his car and stand before him. "My heart calls to yours. Don't you feel it?" I ask, pressing the palm of my hand to his chest, which beats in perfect sync to my own. Fast like we've been running. As though he's chasing me. *But now he's trying to run from me.* "I felt it since we were kids, and again the moment I ran into you at the airport."

"Please—" He looks down at his suitcase like he might make a run for it before he can hear another word from my lips.

"I hated you for it. I didn't *want* to feel for you. I wanted to fall for the person who gave me a ring in an ugly parking lot. I wanted it to be simple, because loving you wouldn't be." I drag my hand up his chest and around the back of his neck. "I got a sand dollar tattooed on my skin because the memories I had with you are one of the only ones I felt alive for. I've hardly felt the blood in my veins for eighteen years, but now, every day is thrilling because you're in my life." I close my eyes for a moment, and then whisper, "It means something that against all odds, I found you again. Everything I've ever wanted, every dream I've dreamed is *you*. How can you explain that every love story I've written feels like ours? Even the men I've created from my own thoughts are passionate, kind, and respectful like you." I think for a moment, then whisper, "If you can explain all of this with reason, then I'll let you leave." I look into his eyes and say, "But you want to know what I've concluded?"

His gaze pours into mine, but he doesn't move.

"I am yours, and you are mine."

His duffle bag slams against the pebbled driveway and then I am wrapped in arms of steel. His warm breath touches my lips and something electric flashes down my spine. His grip slides up my back and around the base of my head. "I thought heaven was a place that couldn't exist on Earth," he says. A tear slides down my cheek and falls to the places we touch. "I despised heaven and hated how there wasn't a staircase that could lead me there," he breathes. "I know heaven is a place, but it can also be a person." He steps closer until the backs of my legs are pressed against his car, and he holds me like he'll never let go. "You are my heaven, Mace." I lean on the tips of my toes and kiss the words on his lips. "A day never passes where I don't think of them. I can't tell you how many times I've wished to be up there too, but I don't anymore, because I'm happy where I am. Right here beside you." He pulls away to say, "But I don't deserve you."

"You do."

"I don't." He looks away and his jaw ticks. "I'm a wreckage and it's only a matter of time before I take you down with me. I'm broken and you can't fix me."

"You aren't broken," I say in a sad voice.

"I am."

"You were traumatized," I say. "You lost *everything* in a single day. You learned the very worst of this world, but I promise you, Grayson, I will show you the beauty. But you have to let me. You have to trust that I can lead you there."

"I'm scared," he whispers in a gravelly voice. "I can't lose you too."

"I'm not going anywhere."

"What if something happens to you too?" He sniffs and says with eyebrows pulled together "I. Won't. Survive."

I don't know my fate, and I certainly can't promise it. "Be scared, Grayson, but live your life alongside it. Wouldn't you rather have a lifetime of memories instead of wondering what your life could have been?" I take a moment to think, and then say, "Make memories with me. Be happy."

"God, I love you," he whispers in a sincere voice. His eyes widen and he tenses like he realizes what he's just said. "You don't have to say anythi—"

I kiss him with a smile on my lips. "I've fallen in love twice during this lifetime, and both times it was with you, Daniel Grayson." I pull back so he can see the words curling on my tongue. "I love you."

With parted lips and glistening eyes, I know this is the real him. Without his protective mask. He's purely himself when he says, "I loved you before you ran into me at the airport. Before I even saw your head in the crowd. I've fallen in love with you over and over for eighteen summers."

The light from his front porch goes out at this very second, flooding us in darkness. I can't see him when his lips press into mine. I let out a sound which he takes as an opportunity to deepen the kiss. I gasp at the feel of his hands on the back of my thighs lifting me on the hood of his car. He lays me against the hard surface and kisses me in all the right places. I gasp when he lifts my shirt and squeezes my breasts until I'm writhing beneath him. "I love the sounds you make," he rasps.

It's the middle of the night. No one is out here, and if they were, they couldn't see us. It's nearly pitch black. "Can I take these off?" he whispers, thumbing the hem of my jeans.

"Yes please."

He pulls them down hastily, and I hear the ruffle of him removing his own. "I need you," I say desperately. My back tries to arch to get closer to him, and he quickly lays his weight on top of me, which I fear will dent his car. Before I can give it anymore thought, he thrusts into me in one quick motion and presses his lips against my mouth to stifle the sound I release.

"Grayson." I say his name like it's a prayer. With his lips touching mine, we share the same breath. It's like we're one.

His car squeaks beneath us. My hands find their way beneath his shirt, fingernails digging into his back when my breath becomes sporadic. I feel myself tighten around him while he spills inside of me. His soft lips press firmly against mine to quiet the sounds of us coming undone together. Silence falls over us while we catch our breaths, the sound of crickets in the distance.

"I am so in love with you," he whispers.

Sometime later, when laying on the hood of his car becomes uncomfortable, we pull our clothes up and Grayson carries me inside his house. He drops me onto the sofa, peppering my face with dozens of kisses. He pulls away from me to grab his bags from out front.

Once he's back, I say, "Were you really going to leave?"

He runs his fingers through his hair, then joins me on the couch, making the cushion dip beneath his weight. "It seemed like the right thing to do."

"It would've broken my heart," I whisper.

"I thought I was protecting you from that. That's all I want for you. Is to be safe and happy."

I lift my chin. "I can handle myself."

"I know you can. I just like to pretend I'm useful in that department." He jokes.

"Everything that happened tonight really put into perspective how much you've been hurting." I crawl toward him and rest my head on his chest.

We are both quiet for a while, as if we've been pulled into our own thoughts. "Macy," he says. "Everyone is going to think I'm a nutjob."

I lean my head up and meet his gaze. "No one is going to think that."

He tilts his head and glances up at me with a look that says *bullshit.*

"Our friends won't think that." *Our friends.* "They will understand when you're ready to tell them. And anyone else who might think that isn't important enough to know what really happened tonight. They don't matter."

"Macy."

"Yes?"

He inhales a deep breath, and slowly releases it. "Will you tell them for me?"

"If that's what you want."

"I do," he says. "If there's one thing I've learned, it's that you shouldn't begin any relationship telling lies. Including friendships."

"It's not a lie, Grayson. And we can wai—"

"I already met them," he says. "Delilah and I came to dinner one night at Elliot's grandma's house."

I dig through my memory, and then I see it. The six of us went swimming after the sunset and got in trouble with our parents. Despite the lecture about sharks feeding at dusk, we had the time of our lives. "I remember that night." My lips split into a smile. After a few moments, I say, "Whatever you decide, I'll support you," I say.

"Actually," he says. "I'll tell them myself."

My brave man. I press a kiss to his lips. He rubs circles on my back, and we slowly drift to sleep from the exhaustion of everything that occurred.

∾

The sharp sound of shattering glass pierces my ears. I look around in a daze, still on Grayson's couch. I spot him standing perfectly still in the kitchen. He wears workout shorts and nothing else, staring at the wall instead of the tiny pieces of glass scattered across the floor.

I clear my throat. "Is everything…okay?"

He nods his head slightly.

I make my way to him. I step over the shards of what once was a plate, and stand directly before him, pressing my palm against his cheek. A bead of sweat drips from his temple onto my hand. *Did he just go for a run?* I glance at the time on the microwave and see it's just past seven in the morning.

As if he just recognized I am standing before him, his eyes widen, and his hands reach for my waist. I'm lifted in the air and set on the kitchen counter. "There's glass!" he all but shouts the words at me.

"I know," I whisper. "I stepped over it."

He doesn't seem to hear, because he crouches before me, not bothering to look on the ground for glass before kneeling. He lifts my left foot, inspects it thoroughly, then the right. When he stands, there are small shards of glass in his knee. "Grayson!" I point to the blood that's beginning to well. He looks around the room for a threat, his eyes alert.

"Look *down*."

Once he sees the scarlet running down his shins, he shrugs. "Oh," he says. "I'll be fine."

I move carefully around the glass and then step into his sneakers by the front door. They are about seven sizes too big for my feet, but they serve their purpose as I clean the shards with a dustpan and broom.

I lead him to the couch, he willingly obliges. I kneel in front of him with a paper plate, carefully pulling out the small pieces. I press a paper towel to the blood. His eyes are unseeing, as though he's someplace else entirely. Like he's stumbled into a thought he can't escape.

My stomach sinks. "Grayson?"

Nothing.

"You're scaring me," I whisper.

Then his gaze slowly drags down to me. "What's wrong? Why are you scared?" His eyes seem to inspect my body, as though he's searching for injuries.

"I'm fine. What are you thinking?" I ask. His eyes pour into mine, yet they don't truly see me. "Are you drunk?" The sun has hardly risen.

He flinches and shakes his head no. He blinks a few times at me, his eyebrows pulling together at the sight of me on the floor, like he's just noticed. He grabs me beneath my arms and pulls me onto the couch.

"Please talk to me," I say, curling into myself on the other end of the sofa.

He sighs and clenches his jaw. "I think I'm having an anxiety attack."

I tilt my head and take him in. He's very still. Not even shaking. I've had few anxiety attacks in my life, the most recent was when my grandparents passed away. They tend to make me feel as though I'm a second from death, like my lungs will stop accepting oxygen or my heart will explode.

"I keep having these thoughts…" he says. "God, it's so morbid, but I picture you dying, Mace. Over and over. It feels as though it's truly happening. I'm grieving you, yet you're sitting right beside me." His voice stumbles and breaks over the words. "I had nightmares all night, so I went for a run to clear my head but this feeling in my stomach keeps gnawing at me." He takes a deep breath. "It feels like I *finally* have you after years of pining for you from the window, yet I'll never be able to grasp onto you. Like one moment you'll be in my arms, and the next you'll slip away. Like if I allow myself to fully surrender to happiness, everything will be taken from me once again. Losing you is my biggest fear, and my mind likes to constantly remind me."

I digest every word and imagine a world where every good thing is tainted by the fear of losing it. "That sounds awful."

He lets out a huff of air. "That night at the inn," he says. "When we stopped pretending for the first time, that's when it began. When I finally allowed myself to indulge in every-thing I feel for you, it felt like the world around me was speeding up and I needed to grab every second spent with you. I told myself I needed to memorize every expression flickering across your face. The sound of your laugh and the words you spoke. I needed to remember because—" he slowly gathers himself to say, "If you left this world before me, I would want to have every moment memorized, down the fallen eyelash on your cheek. I think of a world absent of you and try to survive the idea by capturing enough memories to supply me the rest of my days."

The only thing I know is it makes perfect sense for him to feel this way after what he went through, but I have no idea how to help him. I move closer, the couch cushions dip beneath my weight. I squeeze his hand three times. *I love you.*

"I don't want to be *this* for you." He gestures to himself. "I want to be a man you feel safe with. A man who can give you everything you deserve."

"You're everything I want and need, Daniel Grayson."

"Maybe you'd be better off withou—"

"No." I interrupt. "I'm better *with* you."

"Mace—"

"Quit trying to end this because you think you're undeserving of someone who can love you when times are hard or something. Because I'm staying, Grayson. You're not getting rid of me, so stop."

"Okay," he says in a quiet voice. "Just so you know, if times ever get tough for you, I'll be everything you need too."

"I know."

Chapter 35
Grayson

I clench the steering wheel and watch a brunette head disappear behind the automatic doors at the airport. Something primal in me tells me I need to chase after her. To put her back in my car and not let her go. I inhale a deep breath like every website about post-traumatic stress disorder says to do. Macy "diagnosed" me with it. Apparently, she's done plenty of book research to know about the disorder, however, she's not a professional, so I take what she says with a grain of salt and read the articles she sends me because I love her. I check my phone at each traffic light on the drive home. I get several texts from her, per my request.

I'm through security.

At my gate.

Once I park my car in the driveway my phone dings again.

Just boarded the plane.

I have no idea how long she's going to be gone since she bought a one-way ticket to Idaho so she can sell her house and move her belongings across the country. She might rent a moving truck, which makes it feel as though my airway is being restricted every time the thought crosses my mind.

I've made it less than a foot through my front door when I see a blue hair tie on my kitchen counter. The one Macy always has on her wrist. She puts it in her hair when she writes or when the wind is relentless. Sometimes she mindlessly plays with it in her hands, tying it in knots or wrapping it around her fingers. I pick it up and slide it onto my left wrist. *This is all I'd have left if something happened to her, driving all the way from Idaho to Florida.* This flimsy blue band might outlast her. I bring my wrist to my nose and inhale the scent of her shampoo, which will fade overtime. If she doesn't return, I'll never smell it again.

It's not even noon and my morbid thoughts have already begun. To get my mind off such tragic possibilities, I grab my laptop and bring it out onto my porch and perch it on my lap. I work for an hour, numbing my mind with numbers. No matter what happens, two plus two will always equal four. Math will never be taken from me, so I cling to my numbers until something in my peripheral moves and gains my attention.

Standing on the railing of my porch is a pelican with an injured leg. The one Macy refuses to feed. My mind is back on her, and my worry is amplified to the point where I can't even add two plus two. I shut my laptop and go inside, where I see white dusty shoeprints covering the floor.

I pull out a mop and wipe away the tracks. Once I'm done, I feel slightly better, until I see new shoeprints. I slowly look down at my feet and realize I never removed my shoes.

My mom was vigilant when it came to reminding Delilah to remove her shoes when we walked through the door. My dad always seemed to have a million thoughts swirling through his head and never remembered to take his off. I can recall my mom's irritation and the look of confusion on his face when she'd cross her arms over her chest and glare at him. He'd look down and laugh at his forgetfulness, remove his sneakers, and mop up the chalky floor.

My dad and I are not the same. He was creative like Macy. I'm more analytical like my uncle. I've never forgotten to remove my shoes. In fact, I understand why it's necessary. The white pebbles in the driveway leave the soles white and chalky. I can't function in anything less than pristine.

I put my dirty sneakers by the front door and mop again, remembering my mom's glare, my dad's easygoing laughter, and Delilah's sigh as she sat and untied her shoelaces. I always think the pain will kill me, but it never does. My heart continues to beat, keeping me from them.

I want to drown in a bottle of bourbon or whatever will burn the most as it goes down to distract me from the grief, but if I did that every time it hurt, I'd never be sober, and that's not the life they'd want for me, so I put my shoes back on and run until my thoughts have cleared.

Chest heaving and sweat dripping down my back, I chug a glass of water from the sink and recall the last conversation I had with Macy.

"Please come with me," she begged from my passenger seat.

I wanted to. It'd be so easy to get a plane ticket and follow her. To ensure she was safe. But Macy deserves more than I could give her if I left and avoided my problems. I need this. I need to let her go across the country. I need to let myself be terrified. I need to see her return home in one piece. Maybe then, once she's back in my arms, I'll learn that my fear is irrational. Maybe it will finally loosen its grip on me.

"You know how much I want to see all those farms," I joked. "But I think staying will be... I don't know, good for me."

At night when I'm in bed, I get a text from her.

MACY

> Landed in Idaho. My dad just picked me up. Long flight. How was your day?

I roll over, squinting at the bright screen and text back.

ME

> I bet you look super sexy with plane hair. Day was great, have so much more time on my hands when I'm not distracted by your presence.

An image comes through, and I laugh. It's a selfie of her with wild hair.

MACY

> If my presence stumps your productivity that much, perhaps I should stay here.

ME

> Macy Elizabeth Brookes, you're coming home to me and I'm going to be the happiest, most unproductive bastard this island has ever seen.

MACY

> Elizabeth?

ME

> An estimated guess. What is your middle name?

MACY

> It's May for my birth month.

I google her zodiac sign.

ME

If I had known you were a Taurus, it would've saved us so much trouble. Our signs aren't compatible.

MACY

Well, they're the most sexually compatible.

ME

No surprise there.

MACY

I'm kidding. I don't know anything about astrology.

ME

Macy May Brookes.

MACY

Yes?

ME

Nothing. I just like the sound of it.

MACY

My dad doesn't play music when he drives. I should probably stop texting you so we can fill the awkward silence.

I frown.

ME

Text me when you get to your parent's house.

MACY

Will do. Talk later.

I set my phone beside me and wait for her text, which never comes. Two hours have passed, so I call her twice before she picks up. She sounds half asleep when she answers. "Hey."

"You never texted," I say. "I've been waiting for your message."

"I'm sorry," she says, sounding like she's mid-yawn. "I fell asleep in the car and hardly remember walking to the guest room. I fell back asleep the second my head hit the pillow."

I let out a breath of relief. "It's okay. I'm glad you're safe."

"Do you want to stay on the phone while we sleep?" she asks.

"Yeah." I curl onto my side and rest the phone on the pillow. "Goodnight, Macy May."

"Goodnight, Daniel Grayson."

She hardly texts me the next day. I know she's busy, but I imagine the worst.

A week goes by, and nightmares chase me awake every night. With little sleep, my thoughts become paralyzing. I hardly eat. I only leave my bed to use the bathroom. When I catch a glimpse of my reflection in the mirror, I curse myself. Macy can't return home to *this*.

After several Google searches, I call a therapist by the second week. Her name is Linda, and she says she'd be happy to help me. I'm seeing her Friday.

When Friday comes, I pace the living room and clench my phone, considering calling and canceling. I assume therapy is like ripping open the stitches that are hardly keeping me in one piece. Like rebreaking a bone so it heals properly.

Macy deserves someone who's brave.

I grab my keys and drive off the island to meet Linda at her office. My hands shake and I sweat through my clothes, not bothering to play the radio. I was too anxious to eat my omelet this morning, despite how hungry I was. Every time I tried to take a bite, I felt like I might gag.

I glance at the small office building; the outside is a beige color that begins to fade in some areas. I wipe my sweaty palms on my shorts.

I locate her office, and when I open the door to the small waiting room, cool air and the scent of strawberries greets me. I nearly freeze in place, my eyes automatically going to the candle on the receptionist's desk.

"How can I help you?" the lady asks.

I clear my throat, hoping my emotions don't break up my voice. "I have an appointment with Linda. My name's Grayson."

"Perfect, just have a seat and she'll be right with you."

There are only four chairs, so I take the one closest to the door in case I decide to make a run for it. I inhale the comforting scent of strawberries. I tell myself that Delilah pulled some strings to make the room smell of her favorite fruit, knowing that once I smelled it, I'd have no choice but to stay.

My knee bounces and I press my palms into my thighs, trying to calm myself. I stare at a painting on the wall, trying to decipher what it is. The spiky circles look like bacteria under a microscope, though, that's certainly not what the painting is supposed to be. The door to the hallway opens, stealing me from my thoughts.

"Grayson," a dark-haired woman with kind eyes says.

I stand and follow her through the short hallway to a

small office. A white noise machine is placed by the door to drown out any noise.

"First time seeing a therapist?" she asks as I stare at the blue couch, not making a move to sit on it.

I nod. "Am I supposed to lay down?"

She chuckles. "I've never actually had a patient lay down, but you certainly can if you would like."

I clear my throat and sit on the sofa. "That won't be necessary."

She sits across from me on a plush green chair. "So, Grayson, what brings you here?"

I blink several times trying to find the words. The white noise hums, and it is the only sound in the room. "My girlfriend says I have PTSD."

She raises her brows. "Does she now?"

I smile at the discussion of my favorite topic. Macy. "She's not a therapist, but apparently the 'signs' I'm showing are textbook. So, here I am."

"Can you tell me a little bit more about these signs?" She leans back, crossing her legs at the ankle.

"Nightmares. Anxiety. Um, a lot of…unwanted thoughts."

"Sounds like a lot to deal with. Why don't you tell me a little more about these unwanted thoughts."

"Right," I say. I glance out her window, tree branches blow in the wind. "I keep picturing my girlfriend…dying."

She writes something down. "Why do you think that is?"

"Well, I know why, but I've actually only said the words once." She waits patiently while I clench my jaw and try to steel myself enough to speak. My eyes sting when I say, "My entire family died in a car accident when I was six." A tear slides down my cheek when I blink. "I've been isolated since then, until recently. I haven't had much to lose, but now I love this girl and—" My voice breaks. "I can't lose her too."

Linda is kind and sensitive. I tell her about the anxiety and the reoccurring nightmare. She suggests an approach called EMDR. She explains that it stands for Eye Movement Desensitization and Reprocessing, and that it helps people heal from trauma. Linda says she can direct my eye movements by moving her hand from side to side, or I can choose to tap my thighs bilaterally while I recall the memory of that day. Apparently, this process will help me overcome the PTSD.

We schedule for twice a week. I leave through the waiting room, smiling when I inhale the scent.

The hot sun greets me when I step outside, and I glance at the beige building, not as intimidated by it as I was an hour ago.

I've already had four therapy sessions by the time I get Macy's text.

> I'm going to rent a moving van and drive my stuff down. I'll be home in a week or so.

The week she's on the road, Linda tells me it might be good to spend time with a friend. When I call Elliot, I hold Macy's hair tie in my hand, hoping the blue thing will give me the courage to say the words again. He answers on the second ring. "Hey, I know you probably don't want to hear from me, man. I-I wanted to apologize for the other night and explain."

It's silent for three heart beats. "Okay."

I tell him that we already met when we were kids and that my family passed away, not able to get into much detail. I explain my PTSD diagnosis, which Linda officially gave me. "That night when I got the alert that Macy was in a crash, it was like I was reliving it. I just wanted to let you know. I'm sorry that I scared you and the girls."

"Shit," he says. "I've heard bits and pieces about what happened to your family while I was growing up, but I had no idea it was *you*. I'm so sorry for your loss."

"How would you know? And hey, do you mind telling Julia and Sarah? I don't want them to think I'm some nutjob dating their friend."

"Of course, man. I'm not doing anything tomorrow; you want to do something?"

I release a relieved breath. "Yeah, that'd be great."

The next day, Julia and Sarah lay on chairs and bathe in sunlight. They don't treat me any differently than they do each other, and I'm grateful for it. Elliot and I sit on a sandy sheet beneath the navy-blue umbrella he brought. He hands me a slice of watermelon, and when I take the first bite, sticky juice drips down my chin.

"Hey, by the way, I need to spend the night at your house," Julia says to her sister.

Sarah lowers her sunglasses and raises a brow.

"There was a cockroach in my bathroom," she says as way of explanation.

"I'm not following," Elliot says.

Julia sighs. "I screamed and shut the door. I have no clue where it went! It could be *anywhere* now."

For the first time in weeks, I laugh.

"I'd eat a cockroach for the right amount of money," Elliot says.

"That's disgusting," Julia says.

"You would too for the right price."

"No, I wouldn't!"

"Ten thousand dollars?" I ask.

She looks at me like she's considering it, then Elliot claps his hands together and says, "Told you!" He leans back on his elbows. "You just have to get past that initial pop."

Sarah snorts and Julia looks like she might retch.

Later that day, Elliot and I search Julia's house for the insect. After an hour, Elliot sighs and says, "I guess Julia is sleeping on our pullout couch."

I'm so exhausted from being in the sun for the majority of the day that I fall asleep the second my head touches my pillow. No nightmares.

"How would you say your anxiety has been on a scale from one to ten since our last session?" Linda asks, crossing her legs at the ankle and tilting her head, awaiting my reply.

"Well, I spent time with my friends like you suggested," I say.

"And?"

"And I didn't have a nightmare that night. But the next day I couldn't focus on my work, so I requested Macy's location, which she sent. I watched a little blue dot slowly move across the map for several hours. So, I'd say nine."

She smiles and writes something down. "All of our sessions, you answered ten. What brought you from a ten to a nine?"

"A nine isn't good," I say.

"It's an improvement."

"Hardly," I mumble. "It's not a ten because after looking at her location for most of the day to make sure it was still moving, I made myself stop. And at first it felt like I had lost whatever semblance of control I had. I reminded myself that Macy is smart and she's a good driver. I realized checking her location wasn't going to change anything. It made me feel like I was in control, but I wasn't, and staring at a blue dot all day is pathetic, so I went for a run and then met my friend Elliot at the restaurant he works at."

Linda smiles the entire time I tell my story. "What did you do differently that day?"

"I accepted that I don't have control over everything."

"And how does that make you feel?"

"Horrible…but also a little relieved. Worrying was my way of feeling in control, but it doesn't change anything and just makes me feel sick to my stomach."

"Your anxiety might be at a nine, but your progress is substantial. This is really brave work."

I give her a tight-lipped nod.

"I think we can pick up where we left off last session with our EMDR. Are you okay with that?"

I inhale a deep breath. "Yes."

"Okay, I want you to bring up that memory we started with last time. Let me know when you have it."

I remember it. The look on that police officer's face when she struggled to tell me what happened. I nod.

"What thoughts come up when you think of this image. Tell me with an 'I am' statement."

I think of that moment when the officer told me my family went to heaven. And then my disbelief, so I say, "I am shocked."

"Okay, and how much do you believe this statement on a scale from one to seven."

"Um, I guess seven." I shrug.

"Think of that memory and the words 'I am shocked.' How disturbing is this to you on a scale from one to seven."

My heart races. "Six."

"Where do you feel it in your body?"

"My chest."

"Okay, let's get started Grayson, and if at any point it gets too much, I want you to say the word 'Stop.' Okay?"

I nod.

"Go to that memory and tap your legs bilaterally, and let's see what comes up."

I do so, closing my eyes and letting my mind take over. Fragments of that night come to mind. I feel every emotion I did when I was six, and then Linda tells me to open my eyes after about a minute and asks what came up. I explain it to her briefly, and she tells me to keep going with it. I let my mind lead me where it needs to go, to the memories that need to be reprocessed, so I can heal. By the time it's over, my eyes feel swollen from all the tears I shed.

We talk for the last five minutes of session. "I think what stuck with me after all these years is how *happy* I was that day. Obviously, I was upset that Macy was going home, but for the most part, it was a good day. There was no…*warning*. One second, I was a little kid playing with my best friend, and the next, I was an orphan who lost not only my parents, but my twin sister. I think my mind tries to protect me by constantly being ready for it to happen again, reminding me that tragedy can break out at any moment."

"And that part of you, the one that's trying to protect you, how old does it think you are?"

I feel my teeth grind, my chest skipping a beat when I realize the answer to her question. "It thinks I'm a child."

"That's what I thought. I want you to close your eyes and show that part of you how old you are now, and everything you've accomplished as a twenty-three-year-old."

I think of the job I have, and how hard I worked to buy my house. I think of Macy and how lucky I am to have found her again. I feel myself tear up.

"I want you to thank that part. It served to protect you when you needed it, but now let's ask it if it's willing to let up now. Is it?"

"Yes," I say after a moment.

"Good," she smiles. "How does that feel?"

Like the weight of the world has been lifted off my shoulders. "It feels pretty relieving," I say. Something sprouts in my chest. It feels like the beginning of hope, and I think if I continue to water it, it will grow into something beautiful. I vow to always put in the work, even when it's hard, because I want to see it flower.

So, when Linda asks if I want her to block me in for every Monday and Thursday at nine a.m., I say yes.

Chapter 36
Macy

I brush the baby hairs off my sweaty forehead, looking around the space that's cluttered with boxes. I open my old closet and tackle the last bit of packing I have left. I grab shirts off their hangers and fill my suitcases when I notice a small jewelry box in the back of my closet. I kneel down, forgetting the countless items of clothes I still need to handle. I run my finger over the rhinestones and gently lift the lid. There's a purple and teal beaded bracelet, and my hand lifts to my mouth in recognition. Delilah made this for me.

I slide it on my wrist, along with the one Grayson made. I stare at the beads she once touched, that she crafted just for me. And then something snags my attention. A photo I hadn't noticed lies in the box. Young Grayson has his arm wrapped around a much smaller version of me. We have matching grins on our faces. I flip it over and see my grandma's cursive handwriting.

Macy and Daniel

2006

I find another photo beneath it. The both of us are a blur on the beach as he chases me. On the back, my grandma wrote:

> It's only a matter of years until these two start dating. Young love is so precious. I'm rooting for them.

I tuck the pictures back in the jewelry box, imagining her cheeky smile and the scent of her perfume that accompanied all her hugs.

The dreadful feeling I've grown familiar with fills my chest when I think about the day my grandpa died. She was all alone, and then she passed away the next day from the heartbreak, with no one there to hold her hand.

Chapter 37
Grayson
Three Years Ago

Red and blue color my walls, bringing me back to the worst day of my life. I slowly set my burger in the Styrofoam takeout box, my heart beating loudly in my ears as I make my way to the window.

There's a police car parked in the driveway of Macy's grandparent's house. I swallow bile and step into my shoes, moments from retching at the sight outside. Macy's grandma repeatedly shakes her head. Her face is the perfect image of horrific as she digests whatever it is that the police say to her. Before I can think twice, my feet carry me to the old woman. She doesn't seem to notice me at first, standing only three feet from her and the man in uniform.

"Are you a family member?" he asks. The woman who used to greet me with warm hugs finally meets my gaze. Her face has fifteen years of new wrinkles, but the most prominent are the ones bracketing her mouth, and the crows' feet surrounding her distressed eyes.

I don't take my eyes off her when I answer. "I'm a family friend. What's going on?"

The officer pulls me a distance away from her. "Mr.

Brookes was killed in a car accident," he says stoically, a total contrast to the woman who handed me the news of my tragedy fifteen years ago.

"What do you mean? Is he at the hospital?"

He clears his throat. "I don't mean to be insensitive, but there wasn't much left of him for the EMTs to bring to the hospital."

It happens. I throw up all over the man's shoes at the image he so graphically describes. "Shit. I'm so sorr—"

He holds up a hand, the hard lines in his face setting with disgust. "Comfort the widow. There's not much else I can do here." He gets in his cruiser and speeds off. *Fucking asshole.*

Mrs. Brookes watches me. Her face is absent of despair, and I know it's only because she's in shock. Denial tends to come before the more gruesome emotions. It's the calm before an Earth-shattering storm.

"Do you want to come inside?" she asks from several feet away.

I nod and wipe my mouth with the back of my hand. I follow her as she slowly walks to her house. I don't miss the way her hands shake as she opens the door.

The familiar scent of flowery perfume makes it feel as though I've stumbled into a memory. The home hasn't changed a bit since the last time I saw it. It's hot despite the windows being open. The Brookes clearly still don't believe in air conditioning.

"Coffee?" she asks in a daze.

"Uh, No thank you." I stand in the doorway, unable to will myself to go further inside the house that embodies the happiness I experienced before my life changed. It feels like I'm taking a ginormous leap into the past. Macy's grandma floats around the kitchen, making a pot of coffee. "Mrs. Brookes," I say.

"Yes, dear?"

"Do you know who I am?"

She stills with her back toward me, a mug in her hand. She slowly turns around with the warmest smile spread across her face. "Of course," she says. "You're my new neighbor. We never got the chance to formally meet." She squints, her eyes moving over my face. "You look familiar."

"I'm Daniel," I admit, forgoing the new identity I've given myself. "Daniel Wright."

She smiles warmly. "No kidding! Wow, you look just like your father." Looking off into the distance with joy, she asks, "How have you been, hon? How is your family?"

I look down, squeezing my fists together. *After all these years, I still can't say it.* But the look on my face must reflect everything that was on hers before denial swept it all away, because her fingertips fly up to cover her mouth.

"They're…gone," I whisper brokenly. I look up only to see tears filling her eyes.

"No…" she says, shaking her head.

I nod.

"How?"

I clench my jaw. "They were in a car accident." *Same as her husband.*

She shakes her head. "When?"

"Fifteen years ago."

Her frail hand presses against her stomach. "Daniel…"

"It was a long time ago."

"What about Delilah?"

It feels as though I've been gutted at the reminder. "She's gone too."

She reaches for the kitchen counter, as though she can't hold herself up. I quickly move to her and grab her arm, leading her to the couch. "I'm so sorry. I had no idea. Macy told me you guys moved away," she says painfully.

"There was a cop car in my driveway the night it happened. The lights lit up my walls…didn't you guys see it?" I've always wondered.

Her misty eyes squint off into the distance and she shakes her head. "I don't remember seeing a police car, dear." She sighs. "My husband and I were always sleeping in bed by seven, sometimes seven thirty if we wanted to stay up a little later."

"Oh," I say. "And I did move. To Fort Meyers with my uncle. He took custody of me, but my house was in his name, so he'd bring me back here for a week or two in the summers. It was my uncle who told Macy my family moved away. I don't know why he did, maybe he didn't have it in himself to tell her the truth."

"Dear God…" she says dreadfully. "Why didn't you stop by when you were in town? Macy would've loved to see you. Oh, she's going to be so heartbroken."

"I couldn't bring myself to tell her what happened… Don't tell her," I plead.

Her thin lips part. "You think I can keep this from her? She spent weeks crying herself to sleep that summer. She frowns whenever she looks in the direction of your house. I don't even think she realizes she does it. It's like muscle memory at this point."

"Okay," I say, holding my hands up. Now is not the time to talk about this, and later I can convince her not to say anything to her granddaughter.

"When my husband gets home, he's going to be just as

upset as—" She stills. The denial seems to slip away when her face pinches into something akin to torture. She lets out a blood curdling cry and I feel myself tense. I have no idea how to comfort her. She shakes her head repeatedly and cries so hard that sound no longer comes out. I know better than anyone that I can't take her pain, so I stay with her while she drowns in grief.

I'm numb to it after an hour. She cries herself to sleep and I drape a knitted blanket over her. I drift off until the sun rises.

Daylight spills through the windows and birds squeak the way they do every morning. Time is relentless when you grieve, because when your entire world seems to have been cut in half, everyone around you moves forward. I slowly make my way off the couch and grab a glass from the cabinet. I fill it with water and chug the entire thing when I hear her stir awake.

There's a brief moment upon waking where tragedy can't touch you. When you open your eyes, assuming it's an ordinary morning. The peace you're granted in those initial seconds is another kind of torture, because after a few seconds of serenity, you remember everything.

I watch it happen before my very eyes. "I'm so sorry," I say. She cries for several minutes. I notice the sweat coating her skin right when she groans and touches her jaw, eyes shut tight in pain.

"Mrs. Brookes, are you okay?" I set down my water glass and make my way to her, but before I can even reach her, she vomits all over the floor. She inhales air like she's deprived of it. "It's going to be okay," I say, pulling my phone out of my pocket and dialing 911.

It all happens so fast. The EMTs strap her to a backboard

and lift her into a rescue truck. I hop in my car and follow them to the hospital. The nurse informs me that she was able to contact her family. *Macy.* Will I see her?

Hours tick by with machines and wires hooked up to a sleeping Mrs. Brookes. There's a breathing tube shoved down her throat. Nurses come in and out of the room, and a doctor tells me there were complications from the heart attack. He says they are doing everything they can.

I'm completely helpless, and the only thing I can do for Macy's grandma is hold her hand while the numbers on the monitor slowly drop. The steady rhythm of her heart changes from what it was moments ago, and then the line goes flat.

A bunch of medical people rush in, one of them pressing on her chest to do CPR. I squeeze her hand through all of it, the crunch of her bones breaking with each compression. I wince with each one, clenching my jaw when bile rises to my throat. It's too much, too painful. I suddenly shout, "Stop! Please, just let her go."

A bead of sweat drips off the person giving CPR. She keeps going for a few moments, when someone else says, "I'm calling it. Time of death—"

I don't listen to another word. I gently release her hand and amble out of the room. She doesn't need me anymore. She's with her husband, and somewhere among the stars, I hope my family is there to greet her too.

I think of Macy, and how she's about to find out from a stranger that she lost her grandma in less than twenty-four hours of losing her grandpa. I convince a nurse to give me her phone number from Mrs. Brookes emergency contacts. I call Macy from a payphone, and she answers on the first ring.

"Hello?" she asks, her voice pitched with concern.

"Macy," I breathe. *It's so good to hear your voice.* "I'm so sorry, but your grandma didn't make it..." I squeeze the phone. "She's gone."

The line goes silent for several heartbeats. "Was it painful?" she asks in a soft, sad voice.

"She went in her sleep," I say, squeezing my eyes shut. That's all she needs to know because she ends the call with a click.

Chapter 38
Grayson
Now

Somewhere at the cusp of waking up, I have the sensation of something cold and wet touching my face. I blink a few times to clear my vision. Is that...*gray fur?* I sit up quickly, pulling the comforter up to my shoulders.

There is a dog in my bed.

"Sorry! Come here, girl!"

My eyes set on the most beautiful woman I've ever seen. I'm up in an instant, eating the distance between us. I place my hands on Macy's delicate shoulders, my eyes take her in, and my mind tries to convince me that I'm dreaming.

I pull her to me and twist my arms around her lower back. "Mace," I breathe. She lets out a little huff like the embrace is too tight. I think it's perfect, but I don't want to hurt her, so I loosen my arms a bit, which she must think is the end of our hug because she steps back.

"Hi, Daniel Grayson." Her soft hands rest on my jaw, and she grins up at me.

I turn my head to kiss her wrist and I inhale the vanilla scent of her skin. "Hi, Macy May." I hook a finger beneath her chin, so her face is angled toward mine. "I missed you so much, baby." Her cheekbones pinken. "I'm so happy you're home."

"Home," she whispers. "I can't believe I finally get to call this place home." She lets out a gentle laugh which makes my heart jolt. "I still miss you somehow."

I step closer to her, so we are flush together. "I'm right here, Mace." Her body jolts against me when a loud howl pierces through the air.

I turn my head and look at the animal responsible for the sound. It wags its tail so hard; the momentum makes its butt wiggle. "I have a stupid question," I say. "Who is that?"

She pulls away and walks over to the dog. It wears a lavender collar and sheds all over my bed. Macy scratches behind its ears and the husky licks her arm. She turns to me with the brightest smile that makes my heart throb. "This is Daisy." The dog howls at her name and then hops off my bed to sit in front of me. "Remember when we saw her at the fall festival?"

I nod.

"Well." She brings her thumb to her mouth and bites the nail. "I couldn't stop thinking about her. She needs a stable home, which I couldn't give to her since I wasn't sure what I was even doing with my life. But since I'm living here now, and I don't plan on going anywhere...well, I figured we could help her, and she could help you." She gazes down at Daisy and her eyebrows bunch together. "She reminds me of you."

I felt a pull toward the dog the moment I saw her at the festival, but I never imagined adopting her.

"I don't know much about dogs," she says. "I never had one growing up. But I do know that husky's howl a lot, and well...I figured it would never be quiet again."

"I thought I'd burn alive in the silence. Or drown. Which-
ever is worse," I said to Macy once.

"You got me a dog?"

"Yes. Well, she can stay at my house if you don't want her
to be at yours. But I figured she'd be *our* dog."

Expressionless, I bend down. Daisy wags her tail and
opens her mouth to pant. It looks like she's smiling. I feel my
face shift to reflect hers. I smile so wide it probably looks
unnatural on someone like me. But then I realize Daisy *is*
someone like me, and her smile is fitting. "I love you," I say.
When Macy doesn't answer, I realize she thinks I'm talking to
Daisy. "I love *you*," I clarify. But I feel my heart expanding.
The love I thought I could only extend to Macy and my
family grows when Daisy licks my cheek. I laugh.

"I love you too."

I stand, grab Macy's hand, and lead her to the bathroom.
She tilts her head and eyes me with confusion, but I lift her
up and set her on the counter with no explanation. I brush
my teeth and swish around minty mouthwash, and then I kiss
Macy the way I've dreamed of every night for the past month.

She moans into my mouth and tastes exactly as I remember, and when her sweet scent wraps around me, I think that
this can't be real, because the girl who grew up alongside me,
who I've loved my entire life, just moved next door.
Permanently.

I make love to her right there on the bathroom counter,
and then I take her into my shower and rub soap on her skin.
I can't stop grinning.

To be loved is to be known, and Macy *knows* me. She got
me a dog to fill the quiet. So that I'll never drown in it again.
I don't deserve this woman.

"I'm so proud of you," she says, tilting her head back and

rinsing the shampoo from her hair. My eyes follow the suds trailing down her body. *God, she's heavenly.*

I've had countless sessions with Linda, ripping open the wound I once survived. I'm here, standing before the woman I love, feeling the water pelting onto us.

I'm alive.

I have a session in a couple of days, and I'm going to continue putting in the work for *me*. I'm learning to find happiness within myself, so I can be whole on my own. Because I won't be a burden to the woman I love. I won't draw my happiness from her and dim the light she finally got back. I refuse to see my girl anything other than glowing.

This is exactly what Delilah would want. She never liked to see me upset, and she'd make a fool of herself just so I'd laugh. I know that wherever she is, she's proud of me too. Along with mom and dad.

A muffled howl sounds from outside the bathroom door which causes Macy to laugh. "I think someone wants us to hurry."

We towel off and put our clothes on. Daisy greets us with the same level of excitement. She spins in circles and bounces between Macy and me. Then, Macy gives me a strange look, biting back a smile. She eyes me for a moment, then takes off sprinting down the hallway. I get to my feet and chase her. Daisy follows us out the front door, her nails clicking against the wood. Without shoes, Macy runs over the tiny pebbles in my driveway, but I step into my sneakers which gives her a head start. She runs toward the shoreline and breathlessly laughs when she sees how far I am.

Once I make it to her, she eyes my shoes. "Can you carry me inside?" she asks. "The rocks hurt."

I would carry her through fire if she asked. I lift her up and bring her into our new life.

It's been a week since Macy moved into her grandparents' house, and we're still unpacking. She sold that ridiculous treadmill yesterday, thank God.

I went out and bought an AC unit the first day of moving boxes since her and I were drenched in sweat. I'm standing in front of it now after putting together Macy's dream bookshelf with a sliding ladder to reach the top. The cool air blows against my skin.

"Look what I found in the back of my closet when I was packing," Macy says, walking over to me with her hair in disarray, wearing one of my T-shirts. She holds a glittering jewelry box and hands it to me. I open it and find a picture of us when we were younger, and when I turn it over and see loopy handwriting, I hear Macy sniffle.

When I meet her glassy eyes, I frown. "What's wrong?"

"I wasn't there," she whispers. "When my grandma died, she was all alone."

I slowly set the box down and pull her against me. "She wasn't alone," I admit. "I never got the chance to tell you, and I'm so sorry that you're just now learning this, but I was with her that day. I was the one who called 911."

She lifts her face, lips parted in surprise. Her crying eyes dance between mine, tears clinging to dark lashes. "She knew you moved back next door?"

"She found out who I was the night before she passed away. She was going to tell you." *But she never got the chance.*

"I stayed with her the entire night, trying to comfort her as best I could when she found out about your grandpa."

"Were you with her at the hospital?" she asks, her voice breaking over the words.

I remember that day so vividly. "Yes," I whisper. "I held her hand as she passed."

She tucks her face into my chest. "Thank you," she cries.

"I was the one who called you," I whisper. "I didn't want you to hear it from a stranger." Even though I practically was one.

She reels back, her face red. "That was you?"

I nod.

"I love you," she says. She wipes her eyes with the backs of her hands, and then picks up the two pictures and looks at them for several moments. "Let's frame these."

I pick up the one of us running. "Can I have this one? I'll hang it in my house."

She looks up at me, her gold eyes shimmering when she says, "Move in with me." She smiles widely from her words. "We'll hang both the photos in *our* home."

Chapter 39
Macy

"Write me a story," Grayson said once before.

Sitting before a bright screen, I clutch the locket resting above my heart. The one Grayson gave to me that once belonged to his mother. I'm honored to wear her jewelry, and the bracelet his twin made for me. I glance at the purple and teal beads adorning my wrist.

My fingers hover above the keyboard, and then, like magic, words spring to life on the page. I write a story of a young boy who lost everything, who survived by watching the sun through his bedroom window. Whose heart extended beyond the walls of his room and reached toward a girl he would find again as a man.

The Universe, or God, or destiny, whatever you want to call it, pushed in on them from all sides, leaving them no choice but to physically run into the other. That bubbly girl, whose life was a mess of tangled knots, would mistake the burning beneath her skin for hatred toward him the second time they met, assuming he was a mere stranger and not the person she once loved. But the broken boy inspired the angry girl to dance again, and without knowing it, every time he earned the sound of her laughter, a piece of his heart mended together.

A year later, seconds until midnight, the healed man turns to her, his stomach in knots. Fireworks explode in her eyes, reflecting off the midnight sky.

"Happy New Year!" she exclaims, finally meeting his tear-stained gaze.

Her eyes drop to the velvet jewelry box in his hand. With the sand beneath her bottom and his warm breath trickling against her ear, she clings on to every word he whispers.

Weeks later, beneath the stars, they speak their vows, with only their closest friends and a husky to witness. After sharing their first kiss as husband and wife, he says to no one in particular, "I'll have her pretty words filling the silence for the rest of our lives."

As if there's an audience among the constellations, five shooting stars flash across the midnight sky, but one burns bolder than the rest, as though the bright and fiery thing is the most eager for this union.

Epilogue

Grayson

10 Years Later

I slowly peel open my eyes to find two sets of blue ones staring back at me. Macy's side of the bed is empty when I reach for her. I groan and sit up, causing the little girl in front of me to giggle.

"Where's your mother?" I ask.

"She went running without you," Dominic says in his sweet, seven-year-old voice. He jumps on my legs hidden beneath the comforter.

"Can you make us chocolate chip pancakes? Pretty please?" Delilah, his twin sister says, dragging out the last word. She jumps on my other shin.

I quickly reach out and grab both of their ankles, causing them to fall on the soft mattress and let out their childish laughter—my second favorite song.

"Tickle him!" Delilah yells. My children tackle me on the bed and shove their tiny fingers into my sides. My laughter fills the room, summoning our elderly husky, who has just as much energy as she did when we adopted her.

She hops on the bed, bathing the three of us in kisses, and then the most beautiful woman I've ever set my eyes on walks through the bedroom door. Her tan skin glistens with sweat.

She freezes, taking in the scene. A bright smile spreads across her face, and she runs and joins the kids in tickling me. I grab her waist and pin her down, making her eyes widen. "Tickle Mommy!" I say.

I hold her wrists while they tickle beneath her armpits. Her laughter touches my ear, and even to this day, it's the most beautiful sound I've ever heard. She squirms beneath me, and then I release my hold on her and climb out of bed.

"The last one to the kitchen gets mommy's pancakes!" I call, sprinting down the hallway. Even with the head start, Macy whizzes past me, our twins on my heels. I slow down, letting them win. I feign shock. "How did you two get to be so fast?"

"We got Mom's genes," they say in unison, repeating the sentence Macy loves to throw around whenever they beat me in a race.

"Is that my grandchildren in there?" Macy's dad walks through the sliding glass door with his wife following close behind. Macy's mom gives her a hug, which is quickly interrupted by Delilah, who pries herself in between them, squeezing her grandma's legs, who is visiting for the summer, like they've done every year since Macy moved here. My mother-in-law smiles at me over my wife's shoulder. I return it warmly.

I lift Dominic up, causing him to gasp from the unexpectedness. He giggles when I put him on my shoulders. I bring us to the pantry to grab everything I need to make breakfast, and when I spot a frilly apron in the corner, I laugh to myself and put it on. "Why do you wear that every time you make breakfast?" my son asks, but as soon as we step out of the pantry, Macy's hysterical laughter fills the room and my stomach warms.

"That's why," I say. I feel his gaze on me from above. He starts to squirm, but I can't see what he's doing. Macy doubles over in laughter, and I catch sight of us in the reflection of the sliding glass doors. Dominic dances wildly to make his mother laugh. *That's my son.*

Delilah rushes over to us, dancing similar to her brother, and then Macy joins us, grabbing our daughter's hands and twirling her around. Everyone's laughter cascades around us, and Daisy's high-pitched howl pierces through the air.

I pull Macy to me, pressing my lips against her smile, embracing the loud room. Joy fills every corner of our home, and to this day, my theory proves true.

It's bigger than the grief.

The End.

A Note from the Author

If you or someone you know is struggling emotionally, or has concerns about their mental health, please call the National Institute of Mental Health:

1-866-615-6464

Or visit:

https://www.nimh.nih.gov/health/find-help

Acknowledgments

Writing *Her Pretty Words* has been an emotional rollercoaster, to say the least. Bringing Grayson to life was both thrilling and heartbreaking. His dialogue often surprised me, and I've blushed over him more times than I'd like to admit. I'm inspired by his character, because despite his circumstances, he clung to hope.

This is only my second book, but with both stories, I find myself returning to the theme that even in life's darkest moments, the story isn't over. We're all on this journey together, and my deepest wish is that we keep allowing our stories to unfold, especially when times feel impossible.

Okay, wiping my tears and taking a deep breath. I want to show my appreciation to some special people, in no particular order.

You, the reader, thank you for picking up *Her Pretty Words*. I sincerely hope you've enjoyed Macy and Grayson's story.

To my boyfriend, Michael—my muse and the foundation of every respectful, kind, and compassionate fictional man I write. You've been my biggest support throughout my journey as an author, and I am so grateful to have you by my side.

To my grandpa, who tells any stranger that looks like they might be into romance novels about my books, and who comes over every day to ship the signed copies that I sell on my TikTok shop, thank you for believing in me.

To my sister, who read books long before I dared to, and who I saw cry over words on a page—which I once thought was so silly—thank you for being my biggest fan.

To my mom, who has always encouraged me to follow my dreams and shaped me into the woman I am today, thank you. I hope to have even an ounce of your strength one day.

To my editors, Heather and Amy, thank you for your invaluable feedback, and for polishing this story into everything it needed to be.

And to my aunt, a best-selling author, who cheers me on from the stars. You always seem to show up for me in mysterious ways when I need encouragement. Thank you for every sign you've sent me to keep writing. I love you. I miss you.

About the Author

Amber Evergreen is the author of *The Moment Promised* and *Her Pretty Words*. When she isn't writing heartfelt romances that tug at her own heartstrings, you can find her near a body of water or tucked beneath a soft blanket with a good book. She lives and writes in the American Southeast. Find her on TikTok @Amberevergreenwrites and Instagram @Amberever-green.author

www.ingramcontent.com/pod-product-compliance
Lightning Source LLC
Chambersburg PA
CBHW032010310726

48972CB00002B/353